SAN LOMAH
SHOOTOUT

CALIBER
BOOKS

Also from DOYLE TRENT

Claim Jumper
Gambler's Gold
Squaw Mountain Massacre
San Lomah Shootout
Tombstone Lode
Treachery Town
Shadow of the Gallows
Winchester Law
Cheyenne Brother
Rustler's Trail
Colorado Desperadoes
The Rawhider
Gunsmoke Justice
Dodge City Trail
Shotgun Canyon
Apache Creek Ambush
Dead Man's Badge
Night Rider
Texas Trackers
Rawhide Ransom
Gambler's Gun
Fire and Gunsmoke
Devil's Disciple
Gunpowder Legacy
Fear Town
Outlaw Justice
Mountain Marauders

SAN LOMAH SHOOTOUT: Tales of the Old Wild West
Book Four

For further information visit the Caliber Comics website:
www.calibercomics.com

Cover image by: Dubya2x

CHAPTER 1

All Jim Kinslow wanted when he rode into San Lomah that day in July was pleasure. He had earned it, he had the money to pay for it, and he knew it was here for the buying.

The last thing he wanted was a fistfight, especially with a man who outweighed him by sixty-five pounds, and he sure didn't want to get into a gun battle. Hell, he didn't even own a gun.

But the town seemed peaceful when Jim dismounted at the livery barn, off-saddled his horse, and turned him into a feed lot. And the attractive young woman who approached him as he walked stiff-legged away from the barn looked harmless.

"Excuse me, sir," she said. "Are you by any chance Mr. Kinslow?"

At first, Jim couldn't believe she was speaking to him, and he merely touched his hat brim and nodded.

"Are you Mr. Kinslow?" she repeated.

He stopped, looked around, and saw nobody else within hearing distance. "Why yes, ma'am," he answered, puzzled.

She was a proper young lady, wearing a long dark dress with a lacy white collar and cuffs. Her light brown hair was pulled back in a bun. She wore no makeup, but with her naturally healthy color she didn't need any. At first glance she was handsome. But when she smiled, as she did now, she was very pretty.

She held out her hand to shake, man-fashion. Jim looked at his dirty, callused hand and at her small white hand, then finally shook with her, reluctantly and briefly.

"I was told you would be coming into town today," she smiled. "I was hoping I could find you."

Jim didn't know what to say, so he said nothing. She read the puzzled look on his face and said, "Let me introduce myself. I'm Priscilla Newhouse. My father James C. Newhouse, is president of the Valley State Bank. I'm vice president."

"Pleased to meet you," Jim said. He was afraid he had mumbled the words.

He looked down at himself. He was filthy. His denim pants were covered with dried blood from the knees to his boots, the result of holding calves down while they were branded, castrated, and earmarked, and the seat of his pants was covered with manure from sitting in it while he wrestled calves.

He hadn't had a haircut in over three months and he hadn't shaved in four days.

He looked past Priscilla Newhouse and saw the barbershop sign hanging over the plank sidewalk, and the saloon sign beyond that. Those were his destinations. He hadn't decided which would be first. He couldn't believe a well-dressed, well-groomed lady like Priscilla Newhouse had any business with him, and his interest in the conversation reflected that.

Her smile turned businesslike. "Let me explain, Mr. Kinslow. The bank holds a mortgage on a ranch owned by Mr. and Mrs. John Holcomb. The Holcombs raise horses. They have some very good four-year-olds ready for breaking, and they have a buyer for them when they are broken.

"You see, Mr. Kinslow, Mr. Holcomb had an accident with a horse six weeks ago and suffered a fracture of the right leg. Now he can't do the work and the Holcombs want to hire someone. I'm told that you are one of the finest horse breakers in the business." She paused to allow Jim to comment if he cared to.

"Well, I don't know, ma'am. I get along with colts pretty good, but..." He didn't know what else to say so he merely shrugged.

"It was Mr. Carter Ziegler who told me about you. When he came into the bank yesterday, I asked him if he knew someone the Holcombs might hire. He spoke very well of you."

Jim glanced again at the saloon sign. He decided he would stop there first. Across the street was another sign that said clothing and hardware were sold there. That would be another important stop.

"Mr. Kinslow, I have a business interest in the Holcombs' ranch, and they are also personal friends. I'm trying to help them."

He glanced back at her. She had sensed his lack of interest and her eyes had taken on an almost-pleading look. "They will pay you well. I—I will guarantee it."

"Well, ma'am, uh..." Jim felt awkward standing there talking to a lady, and he had to grope for words.

"I, uh, just got to town, and, uh..."

"Of course. Mr. Ziegler told me you worked with the Rafter H crew, who just pulled the roundup wagons into ranch headquarters. He told me the rest of the crew came into town yesterday, but that you had stayed an extra day to turn the remuda out. Of course, I—we can't expect you to go right back to work but I was hoping that after you have had a, uh, rest, and when you are ready to go back to work, you will consider working for the Holcombs?"

It made Jim feel better to see that she was groping for words too. It made him feel not quite so inferior. "Sure, Miss, uh Mrs...?"

"Miss."

"Miss Newhouse. I'll think about it. Where can I find Mr. Holcomb?"

"Their ranch house is only five miles east of town. Come to the bank and I'll show you how to get there."

"I'll do that, Miss Newhouse."

"Thank you very much, Mr. Kinslow. You won't regret it. The Holcombs are very nice people."

She held out her hand again, and again Jim took hold of it gingerly. She turned and walked away, back straight, every inch a proper lady.

Jim Kinslow watched her for a long moment, then shook his head and grinned wryly. "Well, I'll be damned."

"*Slim Jim.*"

Jim recognized the voice as soon as he stepped inside the St.

Louis Emporium, better known as the saloon. The room was similar to a hundred other barrooms Jim had seen, with wooden tables and chairs on one side and a long mahogany bar with a long mirror behind it on the other. The light was bad and Jim didn't see Skeeter Jones until his name was yelled again.

"Slim, c'mere."

Jim grinned when he saw his friend. Wouldn't you know it, Skeeter was standing up to the bar and he had his arm around a girl. "C'mere, you hungry lookin', long-headed, bottle-assed hunk of jerky."

Still grinning, Jim stepped up to the bar.

"Let me buy you the first drink you've had in three months," Skeeter said, digging into his pants pockets. "You ain't drank nothin' but water for so long you're spittin' rust."

"I'll take a beer," Jim said.

Skeeter spoke with a southwestern drawl, "Beer, hail. It's gonna take some strong whiskey to cut all that rust." He yelled at the barman, "Pour 'im a shot of that good stuff."

The whiskey was poured by a barman in a striped shirt with garters on the sleeves, and Skeeter pushed it toward him. "He-yer, this'll start you quicker and run you slicker."

Jim put the shot glass to his lips, threw his head back, and drank the whiskey in one gulp. He nearly strangled. Tears came to his eyes. "Aaagh," he gasped as the liquid burned its way down his throat.

Skeeter laughed. "It gits better as you go along. Pour 'im another."

"No," Jim croaked. "Not now." Tears were still visible in his eyes.

"Hail, Slim, the second one tastes *good.*"

"Another one of them and I'll be chasin' rabbits where there ain't any." Jim's voice was back to normal now. He noticed that Skeeter was clean-shaven and had obviously just had a haircut. White skin showed above his ears and on the back of his neck. He also wore a clean shirt and brand-new denim pants. Jim knew the pants were new because they were cut full to allow for shrinkage and they obviously had not been shrunk. About four inches of the cuffs were turned up.

As the two men stood at the bar, they looked enough alike to be brothers, although they were not related. Jim was an inch or two taller—almost six feet—and weighed only about one hundred and fifty pounds, while Skeeter Jones was huskier. But they both had the slim hips of the cowboy. Some would say they were built like inverted bottles. They both had light-colored hair and sun-reddened complexions, and they both talked with a Texas twang.

They had met after each had hired on with the Rafter H. They were attracted to each other immediately because they were both in their middle twenties. And when they learned that they were both from Texas and knew some of the same people on Exchange Avenue in Fort Worth their friendship became even stronger.

Jim had acquired his nickname because of his leanness. Skeeter's handle was hung on him because of what he called the mosquitos that plagued the Rafter H cowboys as they camped out with the chuckwagon in southwestern Colorado.

The girl had been forgotten, but she tugged at Skeeter's shirtsleeve and smiled at Jim.

"Say, Slim"—Skeeter had practiced pronouncing the two words so that the S's came out with a whistle—"Meet Maria. Ain't she the purtiest little thang you ever saw?"

"Happy to meet you." She continued smiling.

"My pleasure," Jim said.

Skeeter grinned wickedly. "They tell me she's got more gears in her ass than a cotton gin, but she ain't let me touch 'er yet."

The girl's smile dropped for a moment and she shot a scowl at Skeeter. "It's not so. I don't care what they said." The smile came back when she turned to Jim.

She was pretty in an over-painted way. She had dark hair piled on top of her head, and large brown eyes, and was dressed in a satin dress that ended just below her knees. She wore an artificial rose in the deep V at the top of her dress. The portion of her breasts that showed in the V were fascinating to a man who had been out on a calf roundup for three months.

She touched Jim's arm. "Jimmee," she spoke with a slight Mexican accent, "you're nice, but"—she wrinkled her nose prettily—"you need a bath."

9

Jim chuckled. "Can't argue with that." He turned to go. "I'm gonna get some clean clothes and a haircut, then I'm goin' over to that hotel and get me a room and a bath with hot water in a real bathtub."

"Hail, Slim"—Skeeter looked stricken—"you cain't do that. You warsh off all that dirt and there won't be enough left of you to make a shadder."

Still chuckling Jim allowed, "My clothes won't fit me no more, but I'm so dirty I can't hardly pack it around." He turned away from the bar and almost ran into a man who stood three inches taller.

"Whup." Jim said. "Sorry, mister."

"Sorry, hell," the man growled. He stood over Jim and looked down at him the way he would look at an insect. He was wide-shouldered and solid. Suddenly his face brightened. "Say, ain't you Jim Kinslow?"

Jim stepped back a step so he could see the man's face without having to look up. "Yeah."

"Well, you're just the man I'm lookin' for." The big man held out his right hand. "I'm Jake Tooley. I own the Hash Knife outfit and I've got a job for you."

"A job?" Jim was puzzled again.

"Yeah. I heard you're a good hand with young horses. We got some that need breakin'."

Jim shook hands with him. His hand looked small in the big man's hand. He turned to Skeeter, still puzzled.

"It was ol' Ziegler that told 'im." Skeeter said. "Seems like ever'body around here is lookin' to hire a bronc stomper."

"Yeah," the big man talked affably, "I bought 'im a drink and ast 'im if any of his crew was any good at snappin' out broncs, and he said you broke some for the Rafter H. I pay top wages. Get your saddle and outfit and I'll take you out tonight."

"Well, uh," Jim said, "I already got a job."

"You what?" The affable expression left the big man's face. "Where?"

"I already promised I'd work for some people named Holcomb."

"The hell you beller." Jake Tooley was scowling now. "The Hash Knife hires the best men." Then the scowl left and he tried to

10

force himself to smile. "You don't know what you're gettin' into, cowboy. What're they payin' you?"

"I don't know," Jim shrugged. "I ain't talked to 'em yet."

"Ain't talked to 'em?" The big man threw his head back and laughed. "I'll bet it was that woman at the bank that talked you into it. That woman that tries to take the place of a businessman. Hell, cowboy, you don't know what you're gettin' into." He laughed a loud "Haw-haw!"

Jim was uneasy. He wished he could get away from Jake Tooley and go on with his plan to get cleaned up. He started to step around him.

But the big man stepped in front of him again. "Listen, whatever they offer, I'll make it a dollar a head more. Hell, if you're as good as they say you are, I'll make it two dollars more. Hell, if you work for them people you won't get anything. They ain't got a pot to pee in." The loud "Haw-haw" came out of him again.

Jim scratched the stubble on his jaw. "Well, I don't know who I'm gonna work for. Maybe nobody. I ain't even sure I'm gonna stay around here."

The big man stopped laughing. "That's a smart attitude, that not stayin' around here. Get it? You work for the Hash Knife or you don't stay around here. Get it?"

Jim got the message. He looked over at Skeeter. Skeeter stepped back from the bar and stood with his hands on his hips. He nodded at Jim to let him know that if it came to a fight and Jim needed help, he would help.

Jake Tooley stood spraddle-legged, hands on his hips, blocking Jim's way to the door. Jim didn't want to fight with anyone—much less with a man that big—but it looked as if he might have to. He knew he wouldn't have much of a chance, but he had been knocked around by livestock all his life, and a few more bruises wouldn't matter. And he decided right then that he wasn't going to let anyone, no matter how big, keep him from going where he wanted to go. He decided he would try once more to step around the big man, and if the man continued to block his way, he would take aim at the end of his nose and swing at it with all his might. All he could do after that was try.

11

He stepped to his left, expecting Jake Tooley to move with him. He was surprised when the big man didn't. Jim stepped around him and walked to the door, slowly, deliberately, without looking back. He squinted and pulled his hat down lower to shade his eyes as he stepped into the sunlight.

CHAPTER 2

San Lomah was not a railroad town—the railroad hadn't reached that part of Colorado yet—nor a mining town nor a trade town. It was strictly a cow town. It sat on the northern edge of a wide sagebrush and grama-grass valley, a valley where in a normal year cattle could be wintered without being fed. The high mountain ranges to the north provided good grazing in the summer.

A half-dozen creeks poured down out of the mountains, sometimes swiftly as the high-country snow melted, and sometimes with only a trickle. But with hand-dug wells and windmills providing more water, the valley was one of the best cattle-growing regions in the southwest. It was also good horse country, and with the U.S. Army's sometimes-insatiable demand for horses, the horse-raising business was sometimes a profitable one.

The town itself was home to fewer than a thousand people, but the ranchfolk and their hired help furnished enough business to support a barbershop, two saloons, a two-story hotel, two mercantile stores, and, among other things, a saddle-and-harness shop. The most modern building in San Lomah was the two story stone courthouse. Nearby were a lawyer's office and the white-frame residence of a young doctor. The doctor maintained two beds for the ill at his residence, and his home was often referred to as the hospital.

The shops and houses were all built with rough lumber and most of the shops had false fronts.

There were also several two-room cabins on the western edge of town where feminine favors could be bought. Hitchrails had been built in front of the cabins, and on almost any evening a half-dozen or more saddle horses were tied there.

Main Street was almost deserted before sunup, and Jim Kinslow's boots went *thump-thump-thump* on the plank sidewalk as he made his way to the town's livery barn and corrals. He had to see for himself that his horse was being fed.

The high-altitude air smelled good and Jim was feeling good. His black, curl-brim hat didn't fit exactly right now that he had a fresh haircut, and the new brown duck pants felt a little stiff. But he was clean-shaven, and he wore clean underwear and socks, and he was clean, and that alone was enough to make a man feel good.

"Mornin'," he said to the stableman, a short man with a paunch and a floppy black hat.

"Mornin'."

"How's that brown horse of mine this mornin'? He didn't eat the barn down, did he?"

"Naw. He's in the big feedlot with some other geldings. They done a little squealin' and pawin', but they're gettin' along all right now."

Jim chuckled. "You can't fatten him up. He always looks like a gutted jaybird. But I keep pourin' the feed to him, tryin'."

The stableman chucked too. "He eats as much as two hosses. I ought to charge you double for feedin' 'im, but I won't."

The two of them walked over to the feedlot and looked through the pole fence. Jim's awkward-looking tall brown horse had his nose in a hay rack, and was busy eating. "With them long legs of his, a cow can run right under him," Jim chuckled, "but I want to tell you, when he gets them long legs a-goin' there ain't a cowpony in the country can keep up with him."

"He looks like he could run, all right," the stableman agreed. "That is," he chuckled, "if he don't trip over hisself."

"I've won a few bets on him," Jim said as he turned to go.

Out of the corner of his eye, Jim saw a small figure duck around a corner of the barn, and he turned to stare, curiously.

"Oh, that's that breed kid," the stableman said. "I let 'im sleep in the barn and I pay 'im a couple of nickels sometimes when I need some help cleanin' corrals."

"A couple of nickels?"

"Yeah. That's all I can afford to pay 'im. I got a big family of my own to feed."

They walked out to the front of the barn together, and Jim saw the boy again. He was pushing a wooden-wheeled cart piled high with manure, and he was so small that he had to strain to get the cart moving.

"Hey, kid," the stableman yelled, "don't do that. I can't afford to pay you anything today."

The boy looked to be about ten years old, dark-skinned, with black hair that hung straight to his shoulders. His clothes were ragged and he was barefoot.

"Who is he?" Jim asked.

"Oh, he's a half-breed that used to live with his grandpa in a shack out east of town a ways. His pappy was a Mex and his momma was a full-blooded Ute. After his folks drunk theirselves to death he lived with his grandpa, another Ute. A couple of months ago his grandpa died."

"Where does he live now?"

"He ain't got no place to live. He sleeps here in the hayloft when he's here. He's got an old bay mare he rides, and he goes off up in the mountains ever' once in a while and he's gone for two, three days. When he comes back he's half-starved, and I sometimes pay 'im a nickel or two for workin'. But I can't pay 'im today."

"Hey, kid," Jim said. The boy paid no attention to him.

"He can't speak much English. His grandpa didn't know nothin' but Ute. He savvies a little Mex, though."

"*Muchacho.*" Jim, a southwesterner all his life, knew a few words of Spanish, but only a few. The boy looked his way.

"Are you hungry?" The boy only stared. "Food? You know, *¿comida?*"

The boy's eyes grew larger.

"That's it. Come with me." When the boy didn't move, Jim went to him and took him gently by the shoulder. "Come. To the *restaurante. Extento.*"

"Are you gonna feed 'im?" the stableman asked.

15

"Yup. I can't stand to see kids go hungry."

"He's only a breed."

"He's human, ain't he? And even if he was only an animal, I'd feed him."

The stableman shrugged.

With the cowboy leading the way, the two of them walked down the boardwalk to the New Kansas City Steakhouse. Inside, the cowboy steered the child to the counter and motioned for him to occupy one of the stools. They sat side by side.

Only two of the half-dozen wooden tables were occupied and only one other man sat at the counter. It was still early morning. The man at the counter gave the boy a long hard look, and when the waitress, a middle-aged overweight woman, came in from the kitchen he remarked:

"I didn't know you fed barn rats in here."

She stood in front of the cowboy and the child and asked, "Yeah?"

Jim ignored the man, read the menu on the wall, and said, "I ain't had any eggs for a long time. Give us some fried eggs. And some ham. And coffee. Lots of coffee."

"Him too?" She looked hard at the boy a moment, then turned to Jim.

He gave her the same hard look. "That's exactly right."

She shrugged finally. "Okay. But I hope he knows how to use a knife and fork." She went to the kitchen.

"If he don't I'll teach him," Jim said to her back. The man at the counter was still scowling at the boy. Jim turned toward him and matched his scowl. The man looked away.

Two steaming cups of coffee in china mugs were placed before them. Jim picked his up immediately, blew on it, and sipped. The boy didn't move.

"Say, that's good," Jim said. "Go ahead, try it." The boy only looked at him. "Go ahead." Jim nodded toward the boy's cup, then took another sip from his cup. "Go ahead."

The boy had to reach up to get his arms on top of the counter, and finally he took the hot cup carefully in both hands and put it to his lips. One quick sip was all he took before he put the cup down again.

"Too hot? Or maybe you never drank coffee before. Oh well, maybe you're too young to drink coffee anyhow." The boy only looked at him.

Breakfast was delivered with a clatter in two china platters. Knives and forks were dropped carelessly beside the platters. The overweight woman stood before them, hands on hips. "That'll be one dollar."

"A dollar?" Jim asked, surprised at the high price.

"Yeah, and you pay now."

The cowboy dug two coins out of his pocket and handed them to her. Then he picked up his fork and started eating. The eggs were delicious, and the ham, something he was not used to, was mighty good also. The boy just sat there.

"Go ahead." Jim picked up the boy's fork, placed it in his right hand, and motioned for him to dig in.

The boy held the fork awkwardly, but managed to reach up and get some egg on it and to his mouth. Jim smiled and nodded to let him know he was doing the right thing, then went back to his own breakfast.

Every bite tasted delicious to the cowboy, and he quickly cleaned his plate. When he looked back at the boy, he was surprised. The boy's plate was clean too.

"Good, huh?" The boy smiled, his white teeth gleaming against the dark mahogany of his face.

"You must've been one hungry kid. How long since you et?" All Jim got in answer was the gleaming smile. Jim drained his coffee cup and stood up. "Time to go."

The boy climbed down from the stool and stood beside the cowboy. Together they went out onto the sidewalk. The sun was just coming up over a range of low hills far to the east. Jim stretched and allowed it was going to be a "purty day." The town was alive again, and there was horseback and wagon traffic on Main Street, and foot traffic on the plank sidewalk.

The cowboy couldn't help staring when he saw a strange-looking little man coming toward them. The man had a white goatee and thick white eyebrows. He wore khaki clothes with lace-up boots and a flat-brim campaign hat. He looked like an easterner who was trying to look like a westerner outdoorsman. He was marching right along on the sidewalk in a near-military fashion, carrying a walking stick and a light pack on his back.

"Mornin'," Jim said as the man passed them.

"Good morning, sir," he said cheerfully, glancing their way. He went on, walking briskly toward the livery barn.

"I thought I'd seen all kinds," the cowboy said to himself, "but that's a breed I never saw before."

He watched the man's back a moment, then dug two more coins from his pants pocket and handed them to the boy. "In case I don't see you again, that'll keep you eatin' for awhile."

The boy took the coins, but he wasn't smiling anymore. He was studying the cowboy's face.

"Well, I got to go now," Jim said. "See you later." He walked off toward the hotel. The boy stood motionless, watching him go.

In his room on the second floor of the Eldorado Hotel, Jim counted his money again and decided he wouldn't have to go back to work for a few days. But he didn't know what to do next. He felt restless. For a long time, while he had gathered and wrestled calves on the Rafter H, he had been thinking about town: about how good it would be to sleep in a bed on springs and eat the kind of food that couldn't be prepared on the drop board of a chuckwagon, and how good it would be to wear clean clothes. And he had thought about girls.

Strangely, women and sex were seldom mentioned on a working ranch. Cowboys were accustomed to being away from women, and they seldom talked about them. Once in town, however, the first place most cowboys went was to the saloon and the second was to the cabins on the west side.

Jim considered the cabins. But, aw hell, it was too early. Those gals probably stayed up, or up and down, all night and slept all day. Then there was Maria at the St. Louis Emporium and the way she had smiled at Jim... But, aw hell, she probably smiled at anybody who had money in his pockets, and it was too early for her too.

The young cowboy went down onto the street again, stood on

the boardwalk and watched the traffic go by. Wonder what ol' Skeeter's doin? He wondered if Skeeter was in bed with a girl. He's a better talker than I am, Jim thought. He can get girls where I can't. But that Maria seemed to have taken to Jim. Wonder where she lives. Wonder if she hangs around the St. Louis Emporium all the time.

Idly watching the traffic, Jim saw Priscilla Newhouse walk past him on the opposite side of the street and turn into the bank. She knocked on the door and waited for someone to open it from the inside, then went in out of sight.

Now there's a gal a man could build to, Jim thought. She's got all her fixtures in the right places, and if she tried, I'll bet she could have any man she wanted beggin' like a baby. But, aw hell, she ain't interested in no dumb cowpunchers. Not a lady like that.

Just the same, Jim wished he could meet her again now that he was cleaned up and presentable.

He stood on the sidewalk and watched people until his back ached from standing too long in high-heeled roots. He wondered if the saloons were open yet, and decided to stroll over to the St. Louis Emporium.

As soon as he stepped in the door, Jim saw two men he immediately recognized—his former boss, Carter Ziegler, and standing beside him and four inches over him, the boss of the Hash Knife outfit, Jake Tooley.

CHAPTER 3

"Mornin', Slim" Ziegler said as Jim approached them. "Get them old ponies up to that rock pasture?" Ziegler was a portly man in his fifties. He wore wool pants and generally a better cut of clothes than most cowhands, and he had a white mustache to match his white hair.

"Yeah, I shoved 'em up on to where the creek comes out of that canyon and left 'em."

Ziegler, foreman of the Rafter H, looked up at the bartender. "Pour him one on me." Turning back to Jim, he allowed, "That's where they ought to be, where they want to be. Make it easy to run them in again next fall when we go to gatherin' beef. Say," he said as an afterthought, "meet Jake Tooley, owner of the Hash Knife over east of town."

"We've met," Jim said without much enthusiasm.

Tooley nodded. "Make up your mind yet?"

"About what?" Jim asked, although he knew.

"About who you're gonna work for, that's what"

"I'm thinkin' about it."

"Well, you better not think too long. We got enough drifters in this town already."

"He's got a job at the Rafter H if he wants it," Ziegle put in. "I've got to keep a few men on horseback prowlin' pastures and all that open range to the west."

"Hell, I thought he was a bronc stomper." Tooley had what

almost amounted to a sneer in his voice.

"He is if that's what he wants to do," Ziegler said. "He broke the few colts we had at the Rafter H and he did a damn good job. If we hadn't got out of the horse business I'd be offerin' him top wages right now."

"I offered 'im top wages," Tooley said, "and he said he was thinkin' about hiring out to John Holcomb."

"Is that right, Slim? That good-lookin' young woman at the bank, that Priscilla Newhouse, ask me if I knew someone the Holcombs could hire and I told her about you. I guess she found you, all right."

Jim grinned. "I no more'n got off my horse than she nailed me."

Ziegler grinned too. "She's a go-getter. If she ever sets her cap for a man, Lord help him. But I'll tell you, if I was a few years younger, I wouldn't mind bein' that man."

"She'd do." Jim drank his whiskey. It burned, but he managed to keep his face straight.

Tooley tossed his drink down in one gulp, wiped his mouth with the back of a big hand, then stepped around behind Ziegler and put his hand on Jim's shoulder. "You think some more about who you're gonna work for, and you think about what I said. Get it?"

Jim didn't look at the man. "I heard you." Tooley left.

"What was that all about?" Ziegler wanted to know.

"Aw, he told me I either break horses for him or I don't work for anybody around here. Trouble is," Jim frowned, "he's big enough to mean what he says and do what he means."

Ziegler signaled the bartender for a refill. "He's got a reputation for beatin' up men he don't like. The only help he can keep is a bunch of toughs like himself. Keep away from him, Slim. He's mean."

"Don't worry," Jim grinned. "If anybody wants to know how tough I am, all they have to do is ask me."

The sound of cards being shuffled came from behind them, and a man's voice asked, "How about a game of cards, fellers?" They looked back at a slender middle-aged man sitting at a felt-covered table, shuffling a deck of cards. The man had a white hat pulled low and wore a dark hip-length coat over a fancy vest. "Name the game," he said.

"Nope," Ziegler said, turning back to the bar. In a low voice, he said to Jim, "Don't play with him. There ain't an honest workin' man alive that can beat him at cards."

"I learned that lesson the expensive way long ago," Jim said. "What kind of outfit has this John Holcomb got, anyway?"

"He's a good hand. Use to work for the Rafter H. He didn't drink and carouse like most cowhands. A few years ago his pappy died somewhere up north and left him a little money, then he married that schoolteacher, that Margaret Johnson, and she had a little money, and they bought title to some good grassland just under that high ridge northeast of here. They ran a few cows at first, then the horse market picked up and they bought a bunch of mares off a rancher over by Durango and got a pretty good stud and planned on raisin' colts. Old John was always a good hand with horses, and he liked havin' mares and colts around.

"Trouble is, they run their mares sometimes on the free range south of them—and the Hash Knife runs cows in the same part of the country. They've had some unpleasant words with Jake Tooley, and one day they found their stud horse dead. Shot. John thinks Tooley or one of his men did it, but he can't prove it."

"I guess that put 'im out of the horse business for awhile," Jim mused.

"No. John got lucky. He moved his mares off the flats and threw them up in the hills to the north. The grass is stirrup-high up there in the summer, and them mares got fat. But the best break he got was when Colonel James' prize stud got loose and went wild. You heard about that horse, ain't you?"

"Yeah, I heard about 'im. Too bad they can't catch 'im."

"Well, the colonel told me the other day he don't want to raise any more colts on the Rafter H and he don't care about that stud anymore. He's so disgusted he said he'll sell the horse for ten dollars to anybody that can catch him."

"That'll be a bargain. Way I heard it, the colonel paid enough for that horse to buy a whole herd of cows, and had him brought as far as Durango in a special boxcar."

"He did. For awhile he planned on raisin' the finest horses in the territory, but when the stud got loose and ran wild, the colonel got disgusted and said he'd buy his horses from now on."

"So," Jim said, staring into his whiskey glass, "I guess John Holcomb is gettin' the benefit of that horse without ownin' him."

"That's right. That Kentucky thoroughbred took up with John's mares, and now John's got the best four-year-olds in tire west."

Jim chuckled. "That's one time a poor man took advantage of a rich man. I'll bet the colonel's havin' a hemorrhage of the bowels over that."

"Naw. He don't care. He hated losin' that horse and he sure wanted him back, but too many men have rode too many horses down tryin' to catch him." Ziegler chuckled. "The colonel wanted speed when he bought that horse and he sure got it. More'n he wanted."

The second shot of whiskey went down easier and Jim barely blinked. He continued chuckling at Ziegler's story. "This John Holcomb must be countin' his chips."

"Naw. He's got financial problems. Trouble with raisin' horses is it takes too long to realize any profit. When you raise calves, you can sell them as soon as they're weaned, if you want to. But colts ain't worth a nickel till they're old enough to put to work."

"So," Jim finished for him, "you have to feed 'em for four years before you can sell 'em."

"That's right. And then you have to have them broke. The Army's a good customer sometimes, but the Army won't buy them unless they're broke gentle. Old John has been borrowin' to keep goin', but he was figurin' on gettin' well this fall after he broke them four-year-olds. But now he got himself busted up and can't do the work."

"That's what that Priscilla Newhouse said. That's tough."

"Yep, and the Army only buys so many, and Jake Tooley's got some to sell too. You going to work for the Holcombs, Slim?"

"I don't know. Their business is none of my business. And ol' Tooley said I wouldn't get paid if I worked for *them*."

Ziegler's voice turned sour. "You'd probably have to wait till they sold the colts to get your money. Last time I saw John, he was buyin' groceries on credit, and his credit was about to run out."

"I never did like workin' for nothin'. But say," Jim's face brightened, "come to think of it, that lady banker said she'd guarantee it. Said she'd guarantee I'd be well paid."

"She said that? Well, if that's what she said, you'd get your money. And you wouldn't have to wait for it, either. The Newhouses don't lied."

"Yeah"—Jim's shoulders sagged again—"but the Holcombs and ol' Tooley probly hate each other, and I don't much want to get mixed up in somebody else's fight."

"That's never a good idea," Ziegler agreed. "I wouldn't blame you if you just drifted on."

After they'd talked a while longer, Ziegler said he had to go. Said he'd "layed" around town long enough, and that he had to get back to the Rafter H before Colonel James came looking for him. "If you need a job after you spend all your wages, come on back," he said to Jim. "I think your pal, Skeeter Jones, is comin' back. He's a good hand when he behaves himself."

"That's a good offer," Jim said. "The colonel's a good man to work for, but I don't know. I don't know what I want to do."

"I was kind of restless, too, when I was a young buck," the ranch foreman said. "But a man's got to stay in one place if he wants any kind of a future. This is good country here."

Jim grinned. "Way I heard it, the snow gets ass deep to a tall Indian around here in the winter. I don't think I want to spend the winter tailin' calves out of the snow."

"Don't blame you," Ziegler said, turning to leave. "See you around."

Jim looked about him. A dozen men had entered the saloon since he had, and the gambler had finally attracted two men to his card table. He recognized two of the men at the bar as former employees of the Rafter H, and they exchanged greetings.

"Seen ol' Skeeter this mornin'?" Jim asked.

"Seen 'im down at that cafe ten, fifteen minutes ago," one of them answered. "He was stuffin' his face. Where you goin' from here, Slim?"

"I don't know. Ain't decided yet."

"A man that can break broncs the way you can don't have to look for a job. I hear the Hash Knife is combin' the country for a bronc stomper."

"Yeah, I heard that too," Jim said. He picked up his empty whiskey glass, thought about ordering a refill, then decided he didn't really want another drink.

He left the saloon, squinted at the sun, raised his hat and ran his fingers through his newly-cropped hair, liked the feel of it, and reset his hat. He looked at his boots, decided to look at some new ones, and walked off toward the saddle-and-harness shop.

The smell of new leather was always pleasant, and the shop had four new saddles on display. Jim ran his fingers over one of them, squatted on his heels and looked under the skirting to see what kind of rigging the saddle had. He saw it was a three-quarter rigging, and lost interest. A short bald man with a green eyeshade came out of a back room and offered to sell him the saddle "for a good price."

"No." Jim smiled a friendly smile. "I'm a southerner. I can't use anything but a full double rig, a rim fire."

"That saddle won't crawl back on a horse," the shop owner argued pleasantly.

"No," Jim said, still smiling, "but you get a cow on the end of a rope and she'll pull that riggin' right up on the horse's neck."

They argued pleasantly, more to pass the time of day than for any other reason. Jim asked to see some boots, and he bought a pair for eight dollars. He walked out of the shop wearing the new boots and carrying the old ones. He walked the length of the boardwalk, crossed the street, and walked down the other side.

He soon wished he had a creek to stand in and soak the new boots, so they would stretch in the right places and shape themselves to his feet. He decided to go to the livery barn and soak them in a stock tank.

The stableman was raking manure when Jim got there. "New boots, huh?"

"Yeah. They ain't got used to my feet yet." Jim sat on the edge of a wooden water trough, pulled the boots off, and held the lower half of them under water.

The stableman continued raking manure into a pile near the wooden-wheeled cart. He stopped finally, took a red bandanna from a hip pocket, mopped sweat from his forehead and leaned on the rake handle. "You made that breed kid happy."

"How's that?"

"You must've gave him some money, 'cause he bought himself a few groceries, put 'em in an empty gunnysack, and got on his old bay mare and went off to the mountains."

"Where'd he go in the mountains?"

The stableman shrugged. "I don't know. He does that all the time. Goes off by himself. Stays two, three, maybe four days. I asked 'im once where he went and he didn't understand me. Or maybe he didn't want to understand me. Anyway, nobody knows where he goes."

Jim took the boots from the water and pulled them on. "Maybe he just likes the mountains. The Utes came from the mountains, didn't they?"

"Yeah, they're mountain Injuns?"

The cowboy stood up. "Guess I'll have to walk these things dry." He looked around. "Ain't much else to do anyhow."

"Nothin' but work," the stableman said, going back to his task.

It was late afternoon when Jim went back to the St. Louis Emporium. As soon as he stepped inside he heard his name called again. But this time the voice calling him was feminine and had a slight Spanish accent.

"Jimmee."

The cowboy smiled a wide smile when Maria hurried to him and took him by the arm "Jimmee, I'm glad to see you still here. Come."

She pulled him by the arm to a table in the corner, got him seated, and sat beside him. She smelled good. Her dark hair was combed down to her shoulders. Her teeth were small and even and white.

Jim couldn't help but stare at the two cream-colored mounds that were only half hidden by the low-cut dress. She took his left hand in both of hers and smiled, her brown eyes a-twinkle. "Jimmee, I'm glad you don't go back to the ranch yet. You look handsome today." Her nose wrinkled, "Not like yesterday." She smiled again.

Grinning, Jim drawled, "I was pretty rank, all right. I hate

26

washin' clothes in a creek, and they don't stay clean long anyhow."

She moved one hand up his arm to his shoulder. Her touch made his skin tingle deliciously. Jim didn't know what else to say, so he said, "Let's have a drink."

"Okay, Jimmee."

He started to rise to get it, but she pushed at him and said no, she would get the drinks. As she walked to the bar, the cowboy watched the way her hips moved inside the sheath dress, and a small groan came out of him. "Oh lord."

"He wants fifty cents, the bartender," she said when she got back to the table, carrying two shot glasses of liquid. He placed two quarters on the table and picked up the glass in front of him. It looked and smelled like whiskey. But her glass contained a pale brown liquid that had no odor. He started to reach for the glass out of curiosity, but she grabbed it and drank hurriedly.

"What was that?"

"Whiskee."

"You sure?"

She didn't answer, but took his hand in both of hers again and smiled at him. Jim drank half the whiskey in his glass, liked the feel of it going down his throat and into his stomach, and relaxed. This was what he had longed for during all those nights he had slept on the ground beside a chuckwagon. This was living.

They had two more drinks—she was downing hers immediately—and Jim was beginning to lose his shyness. Maria was easy to talk to and she laughed at every joke he made. Sure, she was drinking sweetened water that he paid a whiskey price for, but a girl had to live and there probably were no jobs for a girl like Maria.

After the third drink he fell silent, thinking. He was trying to find the words. She broke the silence. "Something wrong. Jimmee?"

"Listen," he said, not at all sure of himself, "listen do you"—he cleared his throat—"have a room out back somewhere?"

She frowned. "No, Jimmee."

"You don't?"

'Well yes, but I...not for money."

He thought that over. "If not for money, for what?"

She playfully slapped his shoulder. "I'm not going tell you."

"Well, what do you live on?"

She put her head close to his and spoke in a whisper. "I'll tell you, Jimmee, but no one else. You know, Jimmee, I don't drink."

"Oh, I figured that. You mean you make enough that way to live on?"

"Yes. Please don't tell."

"Well, I'll be damned. And you don't, uh, uh, go to bed with anybody?"

"Only when I want to." She squeezed his arm.

"Well, I'll be damned." He sent for more drinks, even though he knew he was being used. Somehow, he didn't mind. She was pleasant company, and he knew no other girls. And maybe, he thought, if he was good to her and treated her with respect, maybe he would be one of the lucky ones.

Jim's stomach was telling him it was suppertime when Skeeter Jones came in.

Skeeter joined them at the table, and they had another round. Jim allowed it was time to eat and suggested all three go to the New Kansas City Steakhouse. She was hesitant.

"Oh, I can't go there."

"Well, why can't you?" Jim wanted to know.

"They don't like me there."

"They didn't like that Indian kid I took in there this mornin' but they liked my money. Come on."

The two cowboys took her by the arms and pulled her to her feet. She protested a moment, then, laughing, gave in. The three of them were in a laughing mood and were headed for the door when take Tooley came in and blocked their way.

CHAPTER 4

Jim knew there was going to be trouble when he saw the look on Tooley's face. Skeeter knew it too, and he stepped up beside Jim. Tooley was scowling, not at the younger men, but at the girl.

"Where you goin'?" he demanded.

She shrank back, fearful.

Tooley took a step toward her but the two young cowboys stood in his way.

"Step aside, saddle bums."

"Don't talk like that, Mr. Tooley," Jim said. "She's goin' with us."

Skeeter spoke up, "Yeah, they tell me you've been tryin' to get in her pants and she cain't stand the smell of you."

Rage built up in the big man's face. He doubled his fists and turned to Jim. "You made up your mind who you're gonna work for?"

Perhaps it was the whiskey that made Jim reckless. He knew he was being foolish, but he couldn't help it. "I'll work for whoever I damn well want to, and it sure as hell ain't gonna be you."

The rage exploded. "Why you piss-headed pile of Texas horseshit. If I see you one more time I'm gonna tear your goddamn Texas head off and poke it up your dyin' ass."

Skeeter nudged Jim without taking his eyes off Tooley. "Let me try 'im. If he whups me you can have 'im."

"No," Jim said through clenched teeth. "I've got to fight 'im or get out of town."

"Then he'll have to whup both of us."

"No. Not as long as he fights fair."

A cruel smile came to Tooley's face. "One or both of you. Or are you too yellow?" He stood with his feet apart, large hands clenched. There was a pause, and he added with contempt, "You're yellow."

Jim hit him.

The young cowboy side-stepped to his right so he was squarely in front of the big man, and at the same time he took aim at the cruel mouth and swung his right fist as hard as he could.

The blow landed solidly, and Jim felt the shock clear up to his shoulder. Tooley had to stagger back to keep from falling, and Jim had no intention of letting him recover his balance. He bored in, with a left to the jaw and another right to the nose. Tooley had to cover his face with his arms.

Jim punched at the stomach, landing solid blows, and the big man grunted.

Skeeter yelled encouragement. "Keep it up, Slim. Give 'im hell."

Chairs fell over as men stood up hurriedly from the tables to get out of the way.

The blows to the stomach brought Tooley's arms down and Jim threw two good punches to the head. The big man staggered against the bar, and turned facing it, covering himself.

Jim stood back, panting from the exertion.

"Don't let 'im rest, Slim," Skeeter yelled. "Keep at 'im."

Jim wanted to hit the big man again, but Tooley had his back to him and was facing the bar. He stayed that way for a moment, and Jim partially relaxed. Suddenly, the big man spun around and swung a big fist at the same time.

Jim got his guard up and the blow hit him on the arm. But it rocked the slender cowboy back and almost caused him to lose his balance. Moving fast for a big man, Tooley followed up with a left-hand blow that caught Jim on the side of the head. It hurt, and Jim was rocked again. He managed to punch straight put and felt his left fist connect with Tooley's face, but he knew it was not a solid punch.

Tooley had Jim backing up now, trying to ward off the blows.

The big man swung wildly, believing that sooner or later one of his big fists would connect solidly, and the young cowboy would be hurt again. It only took a couple of hard punches to knock the fight out of any man, Tooley believed. Experience had taught him that.

Jim tried to counterpunch, but the blows coming his way had too much power behind them, and he had to back pedal. He tripped over a chair and fell. A boot caught him in the ribs as he struggled to his feet, and he fell again.

Skeeter grabbed a bottle off the bar and held it at his side for a club. "None of that," he yelled. "You do that again and I'll warp your goddam skull."

Tooley ignored him, but waited this time until Jim got to his feet, then started swinging wildly again. Jim managed to duck under the first onslaught and get in a couple of punches. The young cowboy was slender but strong, and his punches hurt.

The big man had to turn his back again and shake his head to clear his vision.

Skeeter screamed, "Hit 'im again, Slim. Don't let 'im do that."

Jim dragged a shirt-sleeve across his eyes and waded in. His next punch caught the big man in the right side and staggered him. He followed up with a left to the jaw. Tooley, staggered, tripped and went down.

Skeeter was jumping with joy. "Atta boy, atta boy, atta boy."

The big man stayed down until he got his wind, then got to his feet, big fists doubled, looking for an opening in Jim's guard.

"Now, Slim," Skeeter yelled. "Hit 'im now. Don't let 'im rest."

But Jim was having a problem. His right eye was swelling fast, and his opponent was becoming only a blur. The blur moved, and Jim felt as if his head had exploded. The blow hurt him so badly that he was only vaguely aware of falling. He tried to get up, and he managed to rise to a half-crouch, then his head exploded again.

The floor felt good. It was cool. It kept the rest of the world away. Jim felt that if he could just lie there long enough everything would be fine. He wanted to just lie there.

Skeeter jumped between Tooley and Jim, gripping the whiskey bottle threateningly. "That's it, mister. Stay back."

Tooley swayed drunkenly. He was spent enough that he didn't

want to challenge Skeeter.

Jim knew there was something he had to do. What was it? Oh yeah, he was in a fight. He had to get up and fight. He pushed himself up to his knees. The floor was spinning. He forced himself to stand. He heard himself mumble. "I'll...take care of it, Skeeter."

"No, you cain't," Skeeter yelled. "He's just too goddam big for you."

"I'll take care of it," Jim mumbled.

"You sure, Slim?"

"Yeah."

Skeeter stepped back, and Tooley swung again. Jim blocked the blow and punched straight out. His punch connected, but it had little authority. He tried an uppercut to get inside Tooley's wild punches, and this time his fist came up under the big man's nose, shoving the nose upward.

Tooley was in pain. He grabbed his nose in both hands, tears in his eyes. Jim stood drunkenly, blinking, trying to see his opponent.

His opponent stood covered up for a long moment, then lashed out. The floor came up and hit Jim again.

The young cowboy was too numb to feel the pain now, but his mind kept telling him to get up. It was as if a horse had bucked him off and no matter how badly he felt, he had to catch the horse and get back on. Get up, his mind yelled to him. He got to his knees.

"Stay down, Slim," Skeeter yelled. "He'll kill you."

Jim got up. He didn't see the blow coming and he didn't feel it. He only knew he was on the floor again. The floor felt good. But he had to get up. A man can't just lie on the floor, he thought. He had to get up.

"Don't do it, Slim. Stay down"

Jim tried to push himself up.

Again, Skeeter jumped between him and Tooley, still gripping the whiskey bottle. "Git out of here," he yelled at Tooley. "I can't let you hit 'im again. Git to hell out of here."

Tooley glared at Skeeter a moment, then turned and walked, unsteadily, to the door.

Instantly, Maria was on the floor, lifting Jim's head and sliding her knees under him. "Poor Jimmee. Oh, you poor Jimmee." She stroked his hair and touched his face lightly.

Her hand was cool and soft, and it was the best medicine Jim could have had. He managed a lopsided grin and mumbled something. "What, Jimmee?" He mumbled again. She put her ear to his mouth. "What, Jimmee?"

"I done...I done got kilt...and went to heaven."

"Oh, Jimmee." She held Jim's head in her lap and rocked back and forth.

Skeeter knelt beside him. "Let's git 'im up." He took hold of Jim's arm. "Can you make it, podnah?"

Still grinning crookedly, Jim said, "I can...I can try like a steer."

With Skeeter's help he made it to the table that he, Skeeter, and Maria had vacated earlier. He sat with his elbows on the table and his head in his hands.

"Would whiskey help?" Skeeter asked.

"Naw. Water is what I need."

"I get it," Maria said, and went to the bar.

The bartender came over, pulling up his sleeve garters. He leaned down and said, "That was some fight, cowboy. I've seen Jake Tooley whip a half-dozen men, and that was the closest he ever came to being whipped."

"You hurt 'im, Slim," Skeeter added. "He didn't know where he was at when he left here."

"I hope he hurts half as bad as I do," Jim grinned.

Maria brought a glass of water, and Jim felt better after he drank it. His right eye was swollen shut, but the vision in his good eye was clearing. He'd taken hard knocks before.

He was surprised, though, and his head came up sharply, when he saw Tooley approaching.

Jim glanced around for a weapon in case the burly rancher wanted to continue the fight. But he relaxed when he saw that Tooley was following another man who was walking straight toward them.

The man in the lead was as slender as Jim and about the same height. But while Jim had the slender hips and strong shoulders of the cowboy, this man had narrow shoulders and wide hips. He wore a pearl-gray flat-brim Stetson and he had a silver-colored star pinned to his shirt pocket.

"You're under arrest," the man said as he approached the table. He was looking at Jim.

"How come?" It was Skeeter who asked.

"For fighting. We don't allow that in this town."

Jim saw the word "Marshal" engraved on the star. "Do you allow big bullies like him to run people out of town, or is that the law's job?"

The marshal reached for Jim's arm.

"How about him?" Skeeter asked, nodding toward Tooley.

"He said he didn't start the fight. He said this cowboy hit him first. Is that right?" He directed the question at Jim.

"Yeah, but he called me some purty bad names."

Skeeter's sun-reddened face was even redder. "You mean you ain't gonna arrest him too?"

"He said he was only defending himself." The marshal turned to the bartender. "Did you see who hit who first?"

"Well, I..." The bartender didn't want to answer.

"Well, did you?"

"Yeah."

"Well, *who*?"

The bartender nodded at Jim. "He did, but—"

"That's it." The marshal grabbed Jim by the arm. "We don't stand for that kind of hooliganism around here. Come on."

"Now just a damn minute," Skeeter exploded. "That ain't fair, arrestin' one man and lettin' the other go. Is it 'cause he owns property and Slim don't? Is that it?"

The marshal let go of Jim's arm and turned to face Skeeter, his hand on the butt of the six-gun he carried in a low holster. His narrow, lipless mouth was almost hidden by a long handlebar mustache. "You'd better shut up, cowboy, or I'll arrest you too. You're interfering with an officer of the law."

"I ain't touched you yet, but that don't mean I ain't a-goin' to. I never did like John Laws. All you John Laws do is go aroun' lookin' for an excuse to lock up the workin' men. You're afraid of people like him." Skeeter poked a thumb in the direction of Jake Tooley.

"Don't, Skeeter," Jim said, standing up. "If you whip 'im he'll have the whole Union Army after us. I'll go along."

"Aw hail, Slim," Skeeter's voice dropped an octave. "It just ain't fair."

"I know it ain't, Skeeter. But whoever said the goddam law was fair."

The marshal's office was in a stone building next door to the St. Louis Emporium. The building was partitioned three ways. One section was for the marshal and his staff. Another was a meeting room for the mayor and town trustees, and the other was a one-cell jail.

Jim had to empty his pockets and hand over his wallet, containing all his money, and his folding pocketknife. The marshal tossed them into a desk drawer. "The judge will be back in a couple of days," he said. "He's hard on brawlers. You're going to be here awhile."

"I've got enough money there to pay my bail," Jim said.

"Bail is high for you drifters, and I like to keep you locked up awhile. Makes you damn happy to pay up and get out of town."

Jim sat on the bare steel bunk in his cell and stared at the floor. He stood up and walked back and forth, then rolled a smoke. He was alone in the jail.

The cell contained two steel bunks, no blankets or mattresses, a galvanized steel bucket that he could use for a toilet, and a narrow window just under the ceiling.

The slender cowboy muttered to himself. He cursed. He paced the floor. He smoked. He sat.

At night he was handed a plate of pinto beans and fried potatoes, but he had worked himself up to such an angry mood by then that he told the marshal where he could put the meal.

"You're just making it hard on yourself," the marshal said.

"Take them beans and your goddam law and go choke yourself with 'em," Jim hissed at him.

"I don't have to take that kind of talk," the marshal warned.

Jim put his hands on his hips and stood straddle-legged. "Why don't you try to do somethin' about it. The biggest mistake I made was comin' here peacefully. I won't make that mistake again."

The two glared at each other for a long moment, and finally the

35

marshal left.

It was a long night. Jim slept very little. He tried to stretch out on the bunk, but it was too uncomfortable.

The cowboy, accustomed to sleeping on the ground with little under him, found the concrete floor a better place to rest. But he was too restless to stay still very long.

He wondered how his horse was being treated. The stableman seemed to take pretty good care of the horses there, but he wondered about it. He also wondered about the half-breed Ute boy he had befriended, and where the boy had gone. He hoped Skeeter wouldn't bad-mouth the "John Laws" too much and end up in jail with him. On second thought, it would make it easier if he had Skeeter to visit with in jail. But no, he wouldn't wish that on anyone.

The night passed, and breakfast, consisting of a cup of cool coffee and two pancakes, was brought to Jim. "You'd better eat it," the marshal said. "You only get two meals a day in here."

Jim tasted the coffee and spat it out. "Nothin' worse than cold coffee. Shove it up your *culo.*"

"All right, one more remark like that, by God, and I'll teach you some respect for the law."

Jim was so angry and so depressed that he didn't care much what happened anymore. "Why don't you go get your goddam army and come in here and try it. You ain't got guts enough to do anything by yourself."

"You just keep talkin', cowboy, and—"

"Aw shut your stupid lawman face." Jim turned his back to the marshal. The marshal left. Again, the young cowboy was alone in a jail cell.

Another meal was brought to him at dusk, this time by a deputy marshal, a small man with a big pistol at his side. He shoved the tin plate under the cell bars and left. Neither man said anything. Jim tasted the slice of meat and ate part of it. The best part of the meal was the homemade bread.

The second night went slower than the first one, and Jim thought daylight would never show itself in the narrow window above his head.

Breakfast was the same—cold coffee and pancakes. Jim ate the pancakes. "I knew you'd eat," the deputy sneered. "You cowpunchers ain't so tough."

Jim scowled at him. "If you didn't have that badge and pistol, you wouldn't be nothin' but a pile of shit." The short deputy's face grew so red and his rage became so severe that he almost strangled when he tried to talk back. His hand went to his pistol and he half-drew it out of the holster. He stood like that for a moment, hand on the gunbutt with strangling noises coming out of his throat.

Finally, he wheeled and left.

Jim sat on the bunk, paced the floor, cursed, sat, smoked, paced. He wondered if Skeeter had tried to visit him. Sure he had, he said to himself. That mean sonofabitch marshal probably wouldn't allow him any visitors. When did he say the judge would be back from where ever he went? In a few days, that's what he'd said. How long is a few days? And what's goin' to happen when His High-and-Mighty-Political-Hack Honor does get back? Is he going to give me a bawlin' out about how the law must be obeyed and violators must pay the penalty and all that horse manure? How long am I going to have to stay in this damn jail? Till the snow flies? Hell, I'd rather be dead.

Supper was barely edible, but Jim ate it. His temper had cooled somewhat, and now he was more worried than angry. He knew how caged animals felt, and he knew now why some animals, caught in a trap, would rather chew their own legs off than remain in a trap. He wished he could free himself that way. He was made to realize how important freedom is to an animal—and to a man. He knew now why his forefathers had fought a war against almost-impossible odds for freedom. And, he muttered to himself, the goddam laws just go around lookin' for an excuse to lock a man up.

Jim had smoked up all his tobacco but he had a few papers and matches left. He picked up a half-dozen cigarette butts he had dropped on the floor, tore them open, and pinched out the unburned tobacco. Eventually he had enough to roll another smoke. By saving the unhurried portion of the tobacco in each hand-rolled cigarette, he estimated he would have about three more smokes. What then? He'd go crazy, that's what.

He managed to sleep a little that night on the concrete floor. He used his hat for a pillow, and in the morning he pushed the crown of the hat out and managed to reshape it. He ate the pancakes that were brought to him—by the marshal himself this time—and again ignored the cold coffee. Lord, but a cup of hot coffee would have tasted good.

At midmorning, the marshal was back. This time he unlocked the cell door and swung it open.

"All right, you can go."

"What?" Jim couldn't believe it. "How? Is the judge here?"

"No. You were bonded out."

"Bonded out? How? Skeeter Jones?"

"No. It was a lady. A real lady. I don't know what she sees in a common saddle tramp like you, but she vouched for you. Maybe you'd better leave the country. You're a troublemaker. If you don't like jail, you'd better leave the country."

Jim stepped through the cell door. "What lady? Who?"

"Her name is Priscilla Newhouse. I don't know what she sees in the likes of you."

CHAPTER 5

The sunlight was blinding. Jim had to shut his eyes and open them a little at a time. He stood on the boardwalk, listening to the sounds of freedom. He heard trace chains rattle and the sound of a horse-drawn wagon go by. He heard the *clip-clop* of a saddle horse pass at a trot.

As soon as he was able to open his eyes enough to see where he was going, he went to the hotel, paid for the room his belongings had occupied, plus one more night, and went up to his room. He shaved, took a bath out of a washbasin, and put on the second change of new clothes he had bought. Then he packed his belongings into a canvas warbag, which he sat on the floor next to his tarp-covered bedroll.

He was headed for the livery barn to check on his horse when he heard his name called from behind him. He stopped and waited for Skeeter Jones to catch up.

"Slim Jim," Skeeter greeted him. "I heard they was lettin' you out. How come?"

"That lady banker paid my bail," Jim said.

"The hail she did. Well that's funny. I tried to pay your bail, and that stump-headed marshal wouldn't take my money."

"Well, that's the way the law works, Skeeter."

"Yeah, I know about the law. When the big boys—or the big ladies—holler, the John Laws listen. When us little fellers holler, nobody gives a good goddam."

"Well, I'm sure glad to be out."

"What're you gonna do now, Slim?"

"Guess I'd better get a job or leave the country."

"I'm goin' back to the Rafter H. It's a good outfit to work for. I done gave all my money to that gambler in the St. Louis Emporium. Ol' Ziegler'll hire you too."

Jim's gaze drifted up the street to where a light-spring wagon was parked in front of a grocery-and-general-store. He saw a woman in a shapeless dress climb down from the seat of the wagon while the driver, a man, kept his seat. He saw that the man had a cast on his right leg.

"I'm itchin' to handle some colts again," Jim said to Skeeter. "I know where I can get a job."

"Hail, Slim, you can git a job anywheres. You got a real talent for educatin' broncs."

Jim lifted his hat and ran his fingers through the close-cropped pale hair. "I'd better go see how my ol' brown horse is doin', then go hunt up that lady banker and thank her. I wish I didn't have to, but it's worth it."

At the livery. Ji looked through the corral poles and saw his tall brown horse standing head to tail with another gelding. They were switching flies off each other's heads. "Found a friend, huh?" Jim grinned. "Don't get too friendly, old feller, I'm goin' to have to move you purty soon."

He was about to leave when he saw the half-breed boy again. The boy was sitting cross-legged on the ground eating a piece of bread with nothing on it. "Hello, young man," Jim said. The boy smiled, but said nothing. "Ain't much of a meal you've got there," Jim added. The boy still said nothing.

"Tell you what, *mushacho*, soon's I take care of some business, we'll go back to that *restaurante* and put on the *morals*." The boy continued smiling, showing a good set of white teeth.

Back on the street, Jim was walking toward the bank when he saw the light wagon still standing—with two good-looking bay horses hitched to it—in front of the mercantile. He saw the woman come out of the store carrying a bag of groceries, followed by the proprietor, carrying a fifty-pound bag of flour. They placed their burdens carefully inside the wagon and the woman climbed up onto the seat beside the man. Jim walked faster, his boots chomping on the plank walk, to catch up to them before they left.

"Say." he said loudly. "Say, Mr. Holcomb."

The man and woman both looked back, curiosity on their faces, as Jim approached.

"Excuse me," Jim said, "but you must be John Holcomb."

"That's who I am, all right," the man said pleasantly. He was of average height and build, with a weather-lined face and a curl-brim hat pulled low.

"My name is Kinslow. Jim Kinslow. I heard you was lookin' for a man to break some colts."

John Holcomb's face split into a wide grin. "I sure am, Jim. I heard about you. I can sure use you."

Jim approached the man's side of the wagon. Holcomb held his right hand down to shake. They shook hands. "This is my wife, Margaret," Holcomb said. "You can call her Maggie."

Maggie Holcomb nodded to Jim. Her eyes took in the bruises on his face, and she said accusingly, "You've been fighting, haven't you."

"Well yes, ma'am," Jim said apologetically, "but I didn't start it. I had to."

"Who with?" Holcomb asked.

"A man named Jake Tooley. He told me I had to work for him or leave the country."

John Holcomb nodded as if he understood.

"I'll tell you somethin' else," Jim said. "I just got out of jail, if that makes a difference."

"What for?" asked Mrs. Holcomb.

"For fightin'. That marshall arrested me and didn't bother Jake Tooley."

"That's not unusual said Holcomb. He turned to his wife. "It's no disgrace. It happens to everyone sometime or other."

She pondered the statement and finally smiled weakly. Jim noticed that she had good features and was pretty in a plain sort of way. She said, "We'd be happy to have you help us, Mr. Kinslow."

"Call me Jim, ma'am. Or Slim. I heard you got the best bunch of colts in the territory."

41

"Sure have. And they're halter-broke too, Jim. I started leading them when they were two-year-olds."

"That's the smart way to do it," Jim allowed. "They're ready to ride now, huh?"

"They're ready. They've never had a saddle on their backs, and they're big stout colts"—Holcomb's eyes narrowed—"but all it takes is a man with two good legs who knows his business. You have to know your business, Jim."

"I've broke a few and ain't hurt one yet."

"We've heard good things about you," Mrs. Holcomb said. "Mr. Ziegler said you are the best he has ever known."

Jim looked down at his new boots.

"How much pay do you figure you have to have?" Holcomb asked.

"Well," Jim drawled, "the last time I was paid by the head was in Texas. I got six dollars a head, and I heard the pay is better around here."

"I'll pay you seven to lope them out in any direction and turn them around and lope them back. You have to be able to get on with a slack rein and without hobbles or cheeking. And I'll pay you eight and a half a head if you can turn running figure-eights on them and bring them to a sudden stop with their noses down."

Jim chuckled. "Nobody likes to ride a horse that's got his head back in your lap all the time. Have you got a place to work colts, Mr. Holcomb?"

"John. And yeah, I built my place for handling colts. It's what I like, anyhow. What do you like?"

Jim kicked a small rock aside with one of his new boots. "Well, I guess I don't just have to have a round corral, but it sure would help."

"We've got one, Jim."

"Then if you want to hire me, you got yourself a colt breaker."

They shook hands again. "When can you come out?" Holcomb asked.

"Soon's I take care of some business," Jim said. Upon Jim's suggestion, John Holcomb drove the team and wagon across the street to the hotel, and Jim brought out his bedroll and warbag and dropped them in the wagon. Holcomb gave him directions to the ranch, and said they would wait supper for him. Jim was about to turn away when he saw the half-breed boy standing in front of the livery stable, watching them.

"Oh say," Jim said. Holcomb had gathered the lines and was about to flip them at the team. He pulled up, a question on his face.

"I forgot to tell you somethin'," Jim said, uncertainty in his voice.

"What's that?" Holcomb was suspicious, wondering if the cowboy had to have an advance on his pay to bail his saddle out of hock.

Jim pushed dirt around with his right foot. "I've got a friend. He's just a kid. He needs a home. He won't eat much and he can prob'ly do some work. He's a good worker."

It was Mrs. Holcomb who spoke next. "Who's that, Jim?"

Jim pointed to the boy. "Him."

"Why, that's that breed kid," John Holcomb exclaimed. "How come you know him?"

"Me and him got acquainted," Jim said. "He's a good kid and he needs a home."

"Why, of course," Mrs. Holcomb said. She turned to her husband. "A cowboy who can be kind to a homeless child can't be hard on horses, John. You always said a good horseman must also be a good human being."

John Holcomb acted as if he wanted to say something, but didn't know what to say. He shrugged.

"John," Mrs. Holcomb continued, "I have always felt guilty about that boy. I have always prided myself in being a good member of society, and a good member of society can't let a child go hungry."

"Well," John Holcomb stammered, "well, maybe he doesn't want to go home with us. Maybe he's too wild."

"Nonsense."

"Well, all right, Maggie, if you think you can tame him."

"Call him over, Jim."

"Hey, *muchacho*," Jim yelled.

The boy stared.

Jim waved his right arm, motioning the boy to him. The boy

wasn't sure he understood the motion, but he did understand the wide smile on the cowboy's face. He took two hesitant steps.

"Come on," Jim waved again.

The boy looked from Jim to the couple in the wagon. The woman was smiling and trying herself to motion him forward. The boy walked forward slowly, carefully, as if he feared he might find it necessary to run. When he reached them, Jim put his hand on his shoulder.

"Home," Jim said. "*Casa. Tu casa.* No that's not right, *su casa.*" He looked up at the couple in the wagon. "He don't understand English, but he can learn." Looking down at the boy again, he said, "*Comida.*" Finally, the boy nodded. Jim motioned for him to get into the wagon, but the boy shook his head and pointed toward the livery barn.

"Oh, I forgot," Jim said. "He's got a horse somewhere. Tell you what, I'll get 'im on his horse and bring 'im out with me."

"All right, Jim," John Holcomb said.

"I'll set two more plates at the table," Maggie Holcomb added.

John Holcomb clucked to the team, and the wagon pulled away.

Jim squatted in the street in front of the boy, looked into his face, and tried to make him understand. "I got to go over to the bank, then you and me're gonna take a little ride." The boy's brown eyes were blank. But Jim grinned and slapped him gently on the shoulder.

"You know somethin', 'chacho? I think we've got a home."

Miss Priscilla Newhouse saw the slender cowboy come into the bank and look around with a lost expression on his face like a man in a foreign country. She called his name and waved him over to her desk. He stood before her, hat in hand, first on one foot then on the other.

"I just want to thank you, Miss Newhouse, for gettin' me out of, uh, jail. They wouldn't take my money, and I ought to have enough here to pay you back." He reached for the wallet in his hip pocket.

She smiled, and her smile was not altogether a business smile. "Oh no, you don't owe me any money, Mr. Kinslow. I heard about your arrest and the altercation, and I had to do what I could to help."

"I don't owe you any money?"

"No. I gave my word you would go to the marshal's office if the judge wants to see you. But the judge is obviously not interested in your case."

"Your word is all it took?"

"Yes. I have a hunch, however, that you will hear no more from the marshal. You have a right to a jury trial if you want one, but I don't think the marshal will want to press the point. He had an opportunity yesterday when the judge was here. The judge left again this morning to resume his circuit."

"The judge was here?"

"Yes, here and gone again."

"Well"—the cowboy had a crease between his eyes—"it's a cinch he don't want to see me, 'cause the marshal told me to get out of the country."

A scowl appeared on the lady banker's face. "He did? He has no right to do that."

"That's what he said."

Miss Newhouse was outraged. "He can't do that. As long as you stay out of trouble, stay out of fights, he can't do that." She was deep in thought a moment, then said, "Look, Mr. Kinslow, if he gives you any trouble, come to me. I have same influence in San Lomah. The marshal's jurisdiction ends at the town limits, and besides, Sheriff Walt Umbaugh is the top law officer in the county—and he's a fair man."

Jim had to grin at her concern. "I know you have some influence, ma'am. That's what it took to get me out of jail. Influence. Not justice or anything like that, but influence."

She shook her head affirmatively. "Sadly, that's true." She scowled at the floor a moment, then looked up. "I'm going to have a talk with the board of trustees about Marshal Chitlow. Sometimes I think he goes beyond the law himself."

"Is that his name, Chitlow?"

"Delmar Chitlow."

Jim wanted to get out of the bank, out of town, and into the country. He had seen enough of town life for awhile. He shuffled his feet, trying to find a way to leave. She spoke again.

"Where are you going from here, Mr. Kinslow?"

"Why, I just hired out to John Holcomb."

Her smile returned. "You did? I'm so glad. John and Margaret Holcomb need your talents and skills, and you will like them. Your work there will almost assure them of a highly competitive Army remount contract, and that is just what they need to make their ranching venture a success."

Jim grinned wryly. "I heard about that competition."

She stood up and shook hands with him again man-fashion. "If there is ever anything I can do for you, Mr. Kinslow, please don't hesitate to call on me."

"You already helped me, and I sure do thank you."

CHAPTER 6

Jim found the boy near the livery barn, and with combination of sign language and a few words of cowboy Spanish, he made the boy understand that he was to get his horse and they were to leave together. The boy picked up an old work-horse bridle with the blinders cut off and walked away toward some open country a block from the livery barn. Jim followed out of curiosity.

A bay mare was grazing alone on the grama-grass that grew among the sage bushes. The boy stopped and whistled. The mare's head came up and she nickered in a low gasp then ambled up to the boy. He fed her some oats he carried in his pants pocket, and slipped the bridle over her head.

"Well, I'll be damned," Jim mused. "You and that mare talk the same language."

Jim knew from the gray around the mare's ears and the deep hollows behind her eyes that she was no colt. But she was fat and well-groomed. He guessed that the boy allowed her to graze freely wherever he found grass and was able to catch her anytime and at any place.

The cowboy caught and saddled his tall brown gelding, and together they rode out of town, following a wagon road. Jim was seated in his Texas saddle with the full double rigging, low cantle, and narrow fork. The boy rode bareback.

It was good to be on horseback again and breathing country air, and Jim was enjoying the ride. He looked north to the mountains and wondered if they really were as blue as they seemed to be from down in the gentle hills, and he looked across the wide sagebrush-covered valley with the Sangre de Cristo mountains far to the south. The country was mostly rolling and sandy, and there were a few ravines washed out by snow runoff from the mountains, perhaps hundreds of years earlier.

Two miles out of town they came to a barbwire fence that followed the south side of the road for as far as the eye could see. After another mile they came to a gate in the fence. The gate was nothing more than four strands of barbwire stretched between two short, thin roles that were wired to two larger, taller poles on either side of the opening. A board had been nailed across the top of the tall poles, and a brand resembling a hash knife had been painted crudely on the board. A road consisting of two ruts with grass growing between them led from the gate over a hill and out of sight. Jim wondered where the Hash Knife headquarters was.

They rode another mile and came to the corner of a fence on the north side of the road. One side of the fence went north to the mountains and the other side ran along the road. Jim guessed that this fence belonged to the Holcombs. The two riders were now on a wagon road between two fences, and Jim allowed as how the free range "is sure comin' to an end."

The boy studied Jim's face, trying to understand what he was saying. Jim grinned and resumed studying the country.

The Holcombs' gate was easy to recognize. It was be same type of gate the riders had passed earlier, but this one had four sticks in the shape of an H Bar nailed on a board at the top of the gate posts.

Jim got down, opened the gate, and led his horse through. The boy followed on his bay mare. They rode another quarter of a mile, then topped a low hill and looked down at the Holcomb ranch buildings. Jim reined up and sat there, studying the layout.

The buildings were clustered perhaps a half-mile from the foot of the mountains where a stream came out of a canyon and gurgled its way across the flats behind the bunkhouse. The main house was easy to recognize because it was built with wide boards and painted white. Small trees grew in the yard, and had obviously been planted there. A strip of flowers of several varieties grew along the front of the house.

Jim grinned. A woman's touch. So were the lacy curtains in the windows.

The bunkhouse was a one-room log cabin, and Jim knew the logs had been hauled down from the mountains. There were a small barn, an open-sided shed, four corrals, and, Jim noted with a grin, a roosting house. White chickens scratched the dirt in the ranch yard. The cowboy recalled having to clean roosting houses when he was a boy working on a farm in Texas. That was not such a pleasant memory. But he also recalled the eggs for breakfast and the fried chicken for supper. That *was* pleasant.

But it was the corrals that interested the cowboy most. There were three square corrals and a round one. The round one had two gates. One opened onto a wide meadowland, what Jim and most southwesterners called a *vega*, and the other opened into a small square corral that had a stout snubbing post in the center.

"If a man can't handle colts down there," Jim grinned, "he'd better roll up his bed, sack his saddle, and go to town." The boy smiled because Jim was smiling.

John Holcomb was hobbling on one crutch from the barn to the house when Jim and the boy rode up. He was carrying a bucket, and Jim could see that the bucket contained milk. "I got a hunch you're gonna have to learn to milk a cow," he said to the boy.

"Get down and turn your horses into that corral over there," John Holcomb grinned. "I've already put some hay in the feed rack. And come on in the house."

When they got to the main house, Jim removed his hat and stepped across the threshold into the kitchen. But the boy stayed back. "Come on," Jim said. The boy stayed back, fear in his eyes. "Ain't you ever been in a house before? Come on. It can't hurt you." Jim took the boy by the shoulder and steered him inside. The boy's eyes took in everything and his lower lip trembled slightly. "It's all right," Jim said. "*Bueno, bueno.*"

The room was immaculate. A cast-iron wood-burning cookstove stood against one wall near a bank of handmade wooden cabinets. A wooden table sat in the center of the room surrounded by wooden chairs. A checkered oilcloth covered the table.

Maggie Holcomb came in from another room, smiled, and went

straight to the boy. "Don't be afraid," she said, stroking his head. The boy's lip stopped quivering. She steered him toward a chair at the table and got him to sit. "How about a cup of fresh milk? That's what little boys need."

John Holcomb cleared his throat and spoke to Jim. "Maggie likes milk and butter and I bought an old Jersey cow. I give half the milk to the cow's calf and we keep the other half. I'm glad we've got somebody to feed it to."

The boy had to be urged to drink the milk, but he drank it.

Supper was fried chicken, just what Jim had hoped for, with canned corn, buttermilk biscuits, and milk gravy. Jim was almost ashamed at the way he stuffed himself, and he noticed that the boy, though shy at first, was soon stuffing himself too. "That'll make you grow like a hogweed," Jim said. Then he said, "I sure hope I didn't work a problem on you folks, bringin' him here. I don't know why I did it. It's none of my business, but I can't stand to see kids go hungry."

"It's all right," Maggie Holcomb cut in. "We'll get along fine. Somehow I've got to get him cleaned up, though. He's filthy, and I don't quite know how to go about it. And we've got to get him some clothes."

"Maybe I can do it," Jim said. "Bein' a man, maybe I could take him to the creek and give him a bar of soap, and maybe he'll know what to do."

"I'll heat some water in the washtub. But I think I'll wait awhile. I don't want to force anything on him just yet. I'll wait until he gets completely over his fear of us."

The boy knew they were talking about him and he looked from one person to the other, trying to figure out what they were saying.

The cowboy pushed his chair back and stood up. "Think me and 'Chacho'll hit the blankets. We got to get to work first thing in the mornin' and pay for this good supper." He picked up his dirty dishes. "Where do I stack 'em?"

CHAPTER 7

John Holcomb kept only his light harness team and one saddle horse in the corrals. Hay was not plentiful. And he told Jim next morning that he would have to run the colts in by himself.

"I've got 'em in a six-section pasture under that mountain," he said, pointing to the northwest.

"How many gates do I have to bring 'em through?" Jim asked as he tightened the cinch on his tall brown gelding.

"Only one. We'll keep 'em in that trap just below the house while you're workin' with 'em. I kept stock out of that trap all summer so they'll have plenty of grass." It occurred to Jim that Holcomb, when he was away from his wife, talked like any other cowboy. Only when he was in the house did he use better grammar. That made Jim grin. Oh well, he thought, if I was married to an ex-schoolteacher, I'd do the same.

Jim looked over the corrals to where Holcomb was pointing. "Looks like a good place for 'em. I can ride colts over east, on that *vega*. I never did like to ride a colt through a bunch of loose horses."

"Me either. It gives 'em ideas I don't like. I'd help you, Jim, but I can't bend this knee and I have a hell of a time gettin' on a horse."

"It would help if I had someone to lead the way for 'em while I pop 'em from behind, but I'll get 'er done. This ol' horse I'm ridin' don't look like much, but he won't let them colts get away from him."

Holcomb chuckled. "Where'd you get 'im, Jim?"

"Bought 'im from a Mexican down south. I needed a horse, and

51

I only had a few dollars. But I'll tell you, this ol' pony'll fool you. His front legs look like they came out of the same hole, but when he gets them legs to pumpin' he can sure stack the scenery behind him..."

Jim turned the horse around once to let it get the feel of the saddle before he put his foot in the stirrup and swung aboard. He rode out of the yard, again admiring the layout of the ranch buildings and corrals. "Yessir, ol' John Holcomb knew what he was doin' when he built this placed," he said to the brown gelding.

When he saw the colts he was hired to break, the cowboy wasn't disappointed. He could see the thoroughbred in them, the handsome intelligent heads, the long springy pasterns, the strong rib cages. They were all bays and sorrels. He could also see the toughness and the good feet of the rocky hiller mares in them. He counted thirty-eight, and knew he was seeing them all.

"Hello, young fellers," he said, reining up. "The boss says you got to be broke to ride and that's my job, so let's get acquainted." He rode through them, looking at each one, then gathered them into a loose bunch.

"The gate's over that way. Let's go." He took down his catch rope, doubled it, and swung it over their rumps. He whooped and hollered, and got them going at a trot in the direction he wanted. A few of the four-year-olds broke into a gallop, kicked up their heels and bucked, just for the fun of it.

They followed the bottom edge of a high mountain ridge for a ways, and at one point they had to cross a creek that came down from the mountains. The creek poured out of a grassy pocket that narrowed into a shallow ravine which cut upward into the ridge.

And what Jim saw there caused him to bring his mount to a stop and whistle in disbelief.

"Lord. What in hell's goin' on here?"

What he saw was a dozen loose coils of barbwire spread over a half-acre in front of the opening to the pocket. The pocket would have been a natural place to chase horses into to catch them. But that barbwire made it a deadly trap.

The colts had gone on ahead, still bucking and kicking up their heels, while Jim looked at the barbwire and tried to figure out why it had been put there. Surely, John Holcomb hadn't put it there. No, it couldn't have been put there by the owner of the colts. It was new wire, and it could serve no purpose other than to trap horses and cut them to pieces.

Jim went on after the colts, his mind disturbed. He would have to ask Holcomb about that. There had to be a reason for that wire.

He and the colts had traveled two more miles when he heard a pistol shot, and suddenly he knew the reason.

Another pistol shot sounded and another. Riders were heading right at the bunch of colts. There were four of them. They were riding hard and firing pistols into the air as they rode.

"Oh no," Jim said, suddenly scared. "They can't do it. I can't let 'em do it."

He knew the riders intended to stampede the colts into the pocket and the barbwire, where they would become hopelessly entangled and where the barbs would cut them to ribbons.

The colts were running back his way now, terrified. They were in a full, uncontrollable stampede. Jim touched spurs to his brown gelding and raced alongside them. He caught the leaders and slapped at them with his catch rope, trying to head them into another direction. He hollered and screamed at them like a terrified woman. He *was* terrified. He knew what barbwire could do to a horse.

Three of the riders were on the other side of the herd now, yelling and firing, keeping the animals headed toward the spirals of wire.

"Get out of here, you crazy apes," Jim yelled. It was useless. The riders were determined. Jim wished he had a gun. But he didn't— and they did, and one of them, a man in a red shirt, was aiming a pistol at him. Jim ducked low in the saddle and heard the angry hornet sound of a bullet go over his head.

His mind raced. They'll kill me. They'll kill the colts. And I can't do nothin' to stop 'em. They've got guns and I ain't. He had never in his life felt so helpless.

Well, he had to at least try.

He spurred the brown gelding and raced to get ahead of the bunch. He yelled, screamed, and beat at the colts with his rope. Gradually, his mount pulled ahead, and Jim reined him over to the other side of the bunch, to the left side. He was ahead of the colts now, and on the same side as three of the riders.

He pulled his horse down to a slower gallop and let one of the riders get ahead of him. Then Jim built a loop in his rope and fell in behind the man. He whirled the loop twice over his head and pitched it. The man knew he had been roped and tried desperately to take the loop off his shoulders, but Jim brought the brown gelding to a stop and jerked him out of the saddle.

He had no time to retrieve the rope. Jim spurred his mount ahead again, trying again to catch the leaders. There was only one man on the other side of the herd. If Jim could get to the front again, perhaps he could turn the bunch. But the barbwire was not far ahead and the colts were headed right for it. Now it was a horse race.

"Get after 'em, 'ol feller," Jim pleaded. "Go get 'em." The man on the other side of the bunch was falling back. His horse, carrying over two hundred pounds, couldn't keep up with the stampeding four-year-olds. Jim's mount was holding its own, but not gaining much on the leaders.

"Sic 'em, feller. Get after 'em." Jim was riding recklessly, desperately. He was waving his hat at the colts, trying to turn them. He had to catch the leaders. "Do it for me, feller. Go get 'em."

He heard a gunshot behind him, felt the bullet pluck at the side of his shirt, knew he was being shot at. He couldn't stop now. The brown gelding was stretched out, long legs pumping, hooves pounding. He was gaining. "Atta boy. Keep after 'em."

The barbwire was closer. He had to turn them now.

The brown gelding, with a yelling, screaming cowboy on its back, caught up with the leaders and raced alongside. Jim beat at the leaders with his hat. He beat one of the terrified colts in the face. "Turn, you dumb brutes. *Turn, damn you.*"

Suddenly, one of the leaders put its head down, bounced twice on its front feet, and ducked sharply to the right. Another followed. The barbwire was just ahead. Then the whole herd turned, splashing across the creek and past the barbwire.

Jim brought his mount to a stop and watched them go. They could run another two miles without coming to a fence, and Jim knew they would have all the running they wanted before they went that far.

The three riders were far behind, and Jim watched them catch the fallen man's horse and lead it up to him.

As the brown gelding's sides heaved, Jim watched the man mount up and watched the four of them ride away. He wondered who they were. He remembered seeing a strange brand on the fallen man's horse. It was two B's joined together with one of them backward. A double-B brand. Was there a bar under it? Yes, he remembered seeing a Double B Bar on the horse's left hip.

"They ain't Hash Knife riders, then," Jim said to his badly winded horse, "but who in hell are they? Hell, they have to be Hash Knife. Who else would want to butcher John Holcomb's colts?"

He loosened the cinch on his saddle and waited until his mount got its wind, then tightened the cinch, gathered the colts, and completed the work he had started out to do. The four-year-olds had had all the running they wanted by then, and Jim had no trouble driving them where he wanted them to go.

CHAPTER 8

John Holcomb was furious when Jim told him what had happened. "They even shot at you? It isn't enough they want to ruin my colts and ruin us, now they want to kill my hired help."

"Who do you figure it was, John?" Jim asked.

"Jake Tooley. Who else could it be?"

"They wasn't ridin' Hash Knife horses."

"Of course not. Tooley hires nothing but thugs, and most of them have horses of their own. They were riding their own horses so they couldn't be identified if they were seen." John Holcomb let out an obscenity, then apologized to his wife.

"We were lucky, John," she said. "Today was the first time in over a month that anyone from this ranch even saw the colts. We were very lucky that they picked this day to try to stampede them."

The half-breed Indian boy sat in a chair, worried. He was worried because he could see that his friends were angry at something.

"You counted thirty-eight of them?" John Holcomb asked for the second time.

"Yeah."

"They're all there. But what kind of dirty trick is Jake Tooley going to try next? Maybe next time we won't be so lucky."

"The thing to do, John, is to report this to Sheriff Umbaugh; then, if anything happens, he'll know who to blame."

Holcomb snorted. "I know exactly what the sheriff will say.

He'll say he can't do anything because we have no proof. We can't prove those men came from the Hash Knife. Why bother reporting it to the law?"

Holcomb left the kitchen for a moment and came back carrying a rifle and a pistol in a holster. "I'm going to keep this Winchester handy wherever I go, Jim; maybe you'd better carry this .45."

The pistol and holster were hanging from a cartridge belt. Jim took the gun, weighed it in his hand, and handed it back. "I don't much like to carry a gun when I'm workin'."

"I know," Holcomb said. "I don't like to carry a six-shooter either. It's heavy and awkward and it gets in the way sometimes, especially when you're handling a rope. But I'm worried, Jim. You had a mighty close shave out there."

"I'll prob'ly be workin' colts pretty close to the house for awhile." He motioned to the boy. "Come on, Chacho. Let's see if you can learn how to milk a cow." He and the boy went to the door.

"Jim." Maggie Holcomb's voice was solemn. "You were shot at today because you work for us. You know you're in danger if you continue working for us. We wouldn't blame you if you left. But Jim"—the crease between her eyes deepened—"we hope you stay."

Jim had his hand on the door knob. He looked down at his boots. He remembered hearing a discussion among older cowboys once about land wars, water wars, rustlers, and gunfights. The consensus among the older hands had been that it was extremely foolish for a hired man to become involved. A hired man had nothing to gain and everything to lose. Let the big bosses do their own fighting. Jim could still hear the bullet going over his head and he could still feel the slug tearing through the side of his shirt. Breaking horses was dangerous enough. A man could easily get hurt that way. Breaking horses with someone shooting at him was almost impossible. Jim had thought about it while he was driving the colts to the smaller pasture, and he was worried. But he had already hired on. And he liked the Holcombs.

He looked back at Maggie Holcomb. "Yeah, I'll stay."

John Holcomb leaned on one crutch and looked over the

snorting four-year-olds in one of the big corrals. He pointed out the four that he wanted Jim to start on. The first one he pointed to was a bay that weighed about eleven hundred pounds and had a tail so long it almost dragged on the ground. Holcomb was apologetic.

"That's one I missed when I gathered these colts a couple of years ago, and he hasn't had a rope on 'em—except when he was branded and cut. The others are halter-broke and they ought to lead pretty good, but this one you'll have to start from the beginnin'."

Jim stood in the center of the corral while the colts milled around him. "Let's see if they remember what a rope is," he said. When Holcomb pointed out a sorrel with stocking legs and a snipe nose, Jim swung a loop overhand in one motion. The loop shot out, turned over in the air, and dropped over the sorrel's head. The young horse wheeled and tried to run, but Jim held the rope against his left hip and braced his feet. The colt turned toward him, head up, ears twitching.

"You're sure a pretty feller," Jim said, talking quietly. As the other horses drifted away from the captured one, Jim started walking toward it, slowly, carefully. The colt snorted, nostrils flaring. "Easy, son," Jim said. "You know what a rope is." The cowboy pulled his hat down low to keep the colt from seeing his eyes. It was his opinion that a man should not look a nervous horse in the eye. Keeping a close watch on the animal's forefeet, Jim reached out carefully and touched it on the neck. The colt relaxed a little, and Jim turned and led it through a gate into another corral.

"He leads pretty good," Jim drawled as he walked back into the corral, shaking out another loop.

Holcomb grinned. "You throw a good horse loop, Jim. Catch that sorrel over there next."

Jim caught and led two more of the animals into the next pen. Then came the chore of cutting out the wild one. Holcomb hobbled into the corral with the young horses. "I can work the gate, Jim. At least I can swing it shut. If you can get him cut out and headed this way, maybe I can help."

A worry frown appeared on Jim's face. "Now, don't you go and get yourself run over, John. You're not too quick on your feet, you know."

"They won't run over me."

Working on foot, Jim eased his way through the four-year-olds until he was on the other side of the wild one. He waved one hand and got the colt moving toward the gate. Quietly, but stepping quickly when necessary, the cowboy worked the colt out of the bunch. Holcomb had a short rope attached to the gate, and when the colt was looking in the right direction, he pulled the rope and swung it open. The wild one saw the other horses in the second pen, snorted once at Holcomb, and stepped through the gate. Holcomb gave the gate a push and it swung shut.

"We got 'em," Holcomb said. "You can turn these out, Jim."

It was midmorning when Jim got the wild colt separated and into the small square corral, the corral with the snubbing post in the center. He shook out a loop. The animal ran nervously back and forth along the pole fence, looking for a way out.

Holcomb hobbled away with his crutch, but stopped when he reached the wagons parked in the yard. He leaned against one of the wagons and watched him work.

The hired cowboy was a little resentful at being watched. He had always insisted on working colts alone. "You can't learn a colt anything with somebody breathin' down your neck," he had always said. But he could understand why his employer watched. After all, they were almost strangers, and Holcomb couldn't allow just anyone to handle his young horses.

"Just so he don't make a habit of it," Jim muttered to himself.

He faced the colt. "You're a big ol' boy, ain't you," he said quietly. "First thing I'm gonna do is trim that tail of yours. Make you look like a usin' horse anyway."

The animal ran past him. Jim pitched his loop out in front of the colt where it had to run into it. He jerked the slack out of the rope, and the colt put its head down, squealed and bucked, trying to shake the loop off its neck. Jim got the colt running past him in the other direction and took two quick wraps around the snubbing post. The colt hit the end of the rope and was jerked around hard.

And the work that Slim Jim Kinslow had hired out to do had begun...

After the young horse had been jerked around three times, it refused to run against the rope. It had to stand and face the man. Jim unwrapped the rope from around the snubbing post, pulled his hat down to his eyebrows, and began the most dangerous part of breaking wild horses his way.

He knew there were easier ways to get a halter on a wild one. He could run the colt into a chute and halter it there, or he could forefoot it, throw it on its side, and halter it while it was down. But Jim believed it worthwhile to put the halter on while the colt was standing on its four feet watching him. He believed it helped to teach the colt that man was nothing to fear.

He worked his way up the rope toward the animal slowly, watching the forefeet. He knew from painful experience that a horse could strike quickly. Twice the colt tried to turn away, but Jim immediately jerked it back. With the rope high on the animal's neck, Jim had the leverage, and the colt, having been jerked around hard before, knew it was best to stand still.

Talking softly, the cowboy eased his way closer. The animal stood spraddle-legged, head up, its ears pointed at him. Once, it put its head down, rolled it eyes and snorted, but then its head went up again.

"That's the way," Jim said quietly "just keep watchin' me. I can learn things to a colt that watches me." He was close enough that he could reach out and touch the animal on the nose, but he knew that was not the place to touch it. It would be inviting an attack from those hard forefeet.

Moving closer, slowly and carefully, Jim reached out with his right hand toward the left side of the animal's neck. The colt rolled its eyes and watched him. Carefully, ever so carefully, Jim touched the animal on the neck.

Immediately, the colt ducked its head and swum away, and just as quickly, Jim jerked it back around as hard as he could. The colt was facing him again, but running backward. Jim let the rope slip through his hands, knowing the horse would not run backward very far. Soon it was standing still again, head up snorting. Jim picked up the halter, stuffed enough of it into his back pocket so that it stayed there, and started the process all over.

He was able to reach the animal a little quicker this time, and when he touched its neck, the colt trembled but stayed still. "You're a smart one," Jim crooned. "You're a smart young horse. Just keep usin' your head. We'll get along." Making no sudden moves, the cowboy eased the halter out of his pocket, eased it toward the animal's nose. This was another tense part of the procedure, getting the halter over the colt's nose and over its head. Jim's jaws were clenched with the tension, but he stayed calm. It was not a job for a nervous, quick-moving person. A horseman had to be quiet and calm at all times. A nervous man made nervous horses.

The young horse's eyes rolled as Jim eased the halter toward its nose. He carefully touched the nose. With a loud snort, the animal spun away. Jim had to start over again.

"That's all right," he said. "We've got a lot of time." It took the cowboy another twenty minutes to get the halter buckled onto the colt's head, but when it was done he knew he had taken an important first step in turning the wild colt into a useful, dependable saddle horse.

The tension came out of Jim with a long sigh. He walked over to the side of the corral, leaned against it, pushed his hat back, and wiped the sweat from his forehead with a shirt-sleeve. He had haltered wild colts numerous times before, but it was always a relief when the halter was finally in place.

"What're you gonna do next, Jim?" Holcomb yelled.

"Oh, I think I'll lead him around a little and turn him out for the day. I'll sack him out tomorrow."

Holcomb looked up at the sun. "Soon be time for chuck. Why don't you wait till after we eat?"

"Won't take long."

The crippled rancher hobbled over to the corral and stood on the outside of it. "How long do you figure it'll take to get 'im leadin'?"

"Oh, I'll have him followin' me around in about fifteen minutes."

Holcomb grinned. "The hell you will. What kind of a come-along're you gonna use?"

"Nothin' but that halter and lead rope."

"Aw come on, Jim. Fifteen minutes?"

"Want to bet?"

Holcomb squinted at Jim, still grinning. "Sure, I'll bet with you." He pulled a pocketwatch from the small pocket at the right front of his Levi's.

"How about bettin' a drink of whiskey at the St. Louis Emporium?—that is, if we ever get to town."

"You've got a bet. Fifteen minutes."

"Startin' when I get him in that round corral." Jim opened the gate and the colt ran into the larger, round pen, dragging a twenty-foot, half-inch halter rope. Jim closed the gate and picked up the end of the rope. "Startin' now," he said.

CHAPTER 9

The hired cowboy pulled on the rope to get the colt facing him, then stepped to one side about twelve feet away, gave the rope a light pull, then a hard yank. The animal was jerked roughly toward him. Immediately, Jim stacked up on the rope. The young horse snorted and ran backward, and Jim just let it back up until it stopped. Then he stepped to the other side of the colt, gave the rope a light pull, then a yank. The animal was jerked roughly to that side, and again it ran backward. Jim walked back and forth in front of the colt, jerking it first to the left and then to the right. Always, he gave the rope a light pull first, and he always instantly blacked up on the rope when the colt was jerked toward him.

After only five minutes, when he stepped to the colt's right and gave the rope another light pull, the colt, to prevent being jerked around, took one step toward him.

"Atta boy," Jim said. "That's a smart horse. I said you was a smart one."

He didn't yank on the rope then, but instead walked to the other side and gave it a light pull. The colt took two steps toward him.

And all of a sudden, the animal was following Jim around the corral.

Jim led it around a few minutes, and when it balked, as it did several times, he merely stepped to one side and yanked. He led it to the gate and opened the gate. Seeing what it thought was freedom, the young horse stampeded to the outside. But with a halter on its head and twenty feet of lead rope tied to the halter, it was at a disadvantage. The man had the leverage. The colt was forced to a stop.

Jim got it facing him, stepped to one side, gave the rope a light pull and then a yank. He stepped to the other side and gave a light pull. The colt turned toward him, then followed him around like an old broke horse.

"How much time?" Jim yelled.

"Twelve minutes," Holcomb answered. "I'll be damned. His face split into a wide smile. "I owe you one, Jim. Where'd you learn to do that?"

"I knew an old man in Texas. He was so old and stove-up he couldn't ride, but he sure knew how to handle broncs on the ground. He learned me a lot."

Jim led the horse back through the corral and out to the small pasture. Carefully, he unbuckled the halter and let the colt run free. "I'll give him his next lesson tomorrow," he said, "and I'll work two more colts this afternoon."

They walked to the main house, Holcomb hobbling awkwardly on a crutch, and Jim slowing his steps to keep abreast of him.

Inside, Maggie Holcomb had a pot of chicken stew bubbling on the stove and homemade bread in the oven. She had just brought in a hunk of homemade butter from a wooden box through which cool creek water ran. Jim allowed the meal was going to be worth the work he had done that morning. He looked around for the boy.

"Where's Chacho?"

"He's playing with an old pocketknife of John's that I gave him this morning. Wait until you see him. You won't recognize him."

Jim went out looking for the boy and found him whittling on a stick with his latest and only possession. The boy was still barefoot, but he was wearing a pair of faded denim pants that had been cut off at the knees and pinched together at the waist with a narrow leather belt. He also wore a khaki shirt that had been cut off at the elbows and was held together at the collar with a safety pin. But even more noticeable was the boy's hair. Maggie Holcomb had given him a haircut. It was a ragged haircut, certainly, but the boy's hair no longer fell to his shoulders. Now it came only to his ears.

"Well for..." Jim exclaimed. "Danged if you don't look like a peeled onion." The boy looked up at him, solemn-faced. "You have to excuse these women, Chacho. They can't help tryin' to make a man over. She meant well. Come on, let's eat." He motioned, and the boy followed him.

"How'd you get 'im so clean?" Jim wanted to know.

"I heated some water in the washtub, put it on the kitchen floor, handed him some soap, and left the room and closed the door. He knew what to do. His parents no doubt gave him a bath once in a while. I had to wash his head for him, thought." She chuckled. "He didn't want to get his head wet."

Maggie Holcomb had placed a small wooden box on the seat of a chair, and she urged the boy to climb up on it. Now he could reach the table.

"He knows what to do with that good bread, too," Jim grinned. "He don't know what butter's for, though. Here, Chacho, let me show you."

The boy's face brightened when he tasted the fresh butter on the still-warm bread.

"I'm a little worried about him," Maggie Holcomb said. "He hasn't spoken one word since you brought him here. Have you ever heard him say anything?"

"No," Jim said. "I ain't. But that's because he can't speak English."

"He's no doubt self-conscious about that, but I'd feel better if he would speak."

"Hey, Chacho," Jim turned to the boy. "Can you, palaver? Uh, *¿habla usted 'Spanol?*" A puzzled expression was all he got from the boy. "Come on, *habla.*" Jim made a circular motion with his hand under the boy's chin. "*¿Habla 'Spanol?*"

"*¿Que?*" the boy said.

"Huh?" Jim asked.

"*¿Que?*"

A wide grin spread over the cowboy's face. "See there. He's a smart kid."

"What did he say?" Maggie Holcomb asked.

"He said 'what' That's what *¿qoe?* means."

"That's a beginning," she said. "Now I'm going to teach him

65

English."

"Can you teach him?"

"I taught school for seven years, Jim. I can teach him."

"This sure is good stew," Jim said, forking a piece of stewed chicken into his mouth. "There just ain't nothin' as good as a woman-cooked meal."

In twelve days Jim had four of the colts broken well enough that he could mount them with the reins hanging slack, gallop them off in any direction, turn them around, and gallop them back. If he had been breaking horses for a cattle ranch, the colts would have been ready to be put to work, and what they learned from then on they would have learned by doing.

But without cattle to train them on, Jim had to try something else. He picked out two clumps of sagebrush forty feet apart and turned the colts in figure-eights around them. He turned them first at a walk, then at a trot, then at a gallop. It was time-consuming, but Holcomb believed it profitable. "You can get more for a colt after you've put a rein on 'im," he said.

Jim broke and reined four more of the colts, and by then he had worked for the Holcombs a month. "I'd like to take the day off and go to town," he finally said one day. "I've got to see what the rest of the world is doin'."

"Sure, Jim," Holcomb said. They were standing in the yard and it was early morning. Holcomb suddenly looked away, reluctant to meet Jim's gaze. He looked at the top of the mountain range to the north. "Jim...I know you'd like to get paid, and you sure have earned it, but...would you mind waitin' till I sell some of these colts? We're a little hard up right now." He twisted around on his one good foot so he was facing the cowboy again. "I can pay you a couple of dollars, though."

"Aw, that's all right. I still got some of my wages from the Rafter H. I got put in jail before I got to spend it."

The brown gelding had had a month of rest and was feeling

snorty when Jim caught, saddled, and turned him toward San Lomah. Jim let him lope a few miles before he pulled him down to a trot. "A feller's got to get his dirty socks washed once in a while. I hope that Maria is still around."

As Jim rode into town he met a familiar figure riding out. It was the odd-looking old gent with the white goatee, white bushy eyebrows, and khaki clothes. The man sat hunched down in the saddle, and Jim could tell at a glance he was not used to riding.

"Mornin'," Jim said, reining up. Mindful that he was riding a gentle horse for a change, he hooked one leg over the saddle horn, rolled a smoke, and hoped to talk awhile. "Purty day."

The man appeared to be in a hurry. He was kicking the horse with spurless bootheels. But the horse, which Jim recognized as belonging to the livery barn, would not be hurried. Finally, the man gave up with an exasperated sigh and allowed the horse to stop. "Yes, sir," he said, "it's a beautiful day."

"Where you headin'?"

"Up there," the man waved toward the mountains. Jim didn't want to pry into someone else's business, but curiosity was about to burst from him. "Lookin' for somethin'?"

The man's face suddenly turned red and he refused to look at Jim. "I really don't know, sir. I must be going. Good day, sir." He kicked the horse and the horse moved on, taking its time.

Jim watched him go and chuckled. "He'd prob'ly make better time afoot. That old pony's been mauled around by so many people he knows better'n to hurt himself."

"I don't know anything about him," the stableman said in answer to Jim's question. "Sometimes he walks, and sometimes he rents a horse from me. He goes off in that same direction almost every day."

"He don't say where he's goin'?"

"Naw. He's a nice old fella, but he don't say nothin'."

"Did he give a name?"

"Said his name is Doctor George Sanderson." The stableman emphasized the "Doctor."

"A doctor?" Jim scratched his jaw. "What in hell is a doctor doin' climbin' around in those mountains?"

"He's a quare one." The stableman shrugged. "It's a mystery to me."

As before, it was too early in the day for anything interesting to develop in San Lomah, and Jim had time to kill. He walked down one side of Main Street and back up the other side, looking in store windows and staring at the townspeople.

He walked past the saddle-and-harness shop and decided to go in and see if the shop had a bosal that he liked; his old one was a little too small for some of those half-thoroughbred colts. A bell on a spring over the door tinkled when Jim entered and again the proprietor came out of the back room.

"Good morning, sir. What can I sell you today?"

"I need a new *bosal*," said Jim. "What've you got?"

"A what?"

"A *bosal*—you know?"

The proprietor pulled at his chin. "You're that Texas cowboy that was in here looking at saddles awhile back, aren't you?"

"Yeah, we talked saddles awhile."

"Well," the proprietor grinned good naturedly, "would you mind telling me in English was a *bosal* is?"

Grinning with him, Jim said, "I heard a Yankee call it a hackamore once."

Jim bought one of the heavy plaited-rawhide nose-bands he called a *bosal*, stuck the narrow end of it in his hip pocket, and went out on the street. There was horseback and wagon traffic on the street, and Jim looked each rider over to see if he recognized any of them. He smiled with anticipated pleasure when he saw Skeeter Jones riding toward him on a bay horse.

"Skeeter, you ol' Texas cow chip."

Skeeter reined up and grinned down at Jim. "Wha-t're you doin' in town, you poker-assed Fort Worth rounder?"

"Hell, a feller's got to come to town once in a while to keep the bartenders in business."

Skeeter dismounted and wrapped the reins around a hitchrail. "Well hail, let's go hoist one."

Inside the St. Louis Emporium, Jim looked around for Maria. She was not in sight. They bellied up to the bar and Jim allowed, "It's my turn. I got money I ain't spent yet."

They drank their whiskey in one gulp and Jim made a wry face. Skeeter's expression didn't change. "There's got to be a trick to that," Jim said.

"Hail, Slim, it's like anything else—if at first you don't succeed, try and try again. Hey, barkeep," he yelled, "hit us again."

The shot glasses were refilled, and Skeeter downed his immediately. Jim stared at his awhile.

"Say, Slim, how you gittin' along over there?" Skeeter made the S's whistle.

Jim told him about the attempt to stampede the H Bar colts into a tangle of barbwire. He showed Skeeter the hole in his shirt where a bullet had torn through.

Skeeter whistled through his teeth. "Hail, Slim, a man could get kilt workin' over there. It ain't never happened to me, but they tell me gittin' kilt is permanent."

"If I had any sense I'd tell the Holcombs to fight their own battles. I never worked for anyone yet that cared whether I lived or died as long as I got the work done. But, aw hell, they're nice folks and I ain't got any sensed."

"That Jake Tooley's a mean sombitch. You want to borrow that old .44 of mine?"

"Naw." Jim changed the subject. "How're you doin' nowadays?"

"Good enough. I'm stayin' horseback while some of them other fellers're shovelin' manure and diggin' post holes."

"When're you goin' to start gatherin' beef?"

"Won't be long. We're gettin' short of horses, though. The colonel ordered ol' Ziegler to pension eight of them old spooks. We're liable to be chousin' beefs on foot."

"John Holcomb's got some for sale. Good ones too."

"I heard he had some good colts. Heard they're out of that thoroughbred stud the colonel had shipped out from Kentucky a few years back."

"They've got some thoroughbred in 'em, all right. They're good big stout boogers."

"Ever see that stud, Slim?"

"No. You?"

"I got a glimpse of 'im a week ago. Jim and some of John Holcomb's H Bar mares was runnin' along the rim of one of them canyons. Soon's he saw us, he quit the mares and took off like a barrel-assed ape. I chased 'im aways, but he makes a cowpony look like a hobbled puissant."

"I'd sure like to see him."

"If you can hang a loop on 'im, Slim, he's yours. For ten dollars, that is. Colonel James said he'd sell 'im for ten bucks to anybody that can catch 'im."

Jim downed his whiskey, blinked, said, "Gaahh," and looked around. "Wonder if that Mex girl still comes in here."

"Maria? I seen her in here a couple of weeks ago. She asked about you. Bet you could park your boots under her bed if you wanted to, Slim."

"Yeah, me and everybody else."

"No, she ain't like that, Slim. Hail, I tried and had to end up goin' to the cabins."

A wolfish smile crossed Jim's face. "She might talk me into it if she talks long enough."

"Ain't no girl purtier than a purty Mexican girl," Skeeter commented.

They ordered another, and Jim sipped this one. Suddenly. Jim stiffened and the happy expression on his face turned sour. "Look who's here."

"Who?" Skeeter asked, looking in the direction Jim was looking. "Oh, him. He won't start nothin'. He whupped you, but it wasn't easy. He only picks on the easy ones."

Jake Tooley had come in with two men, one of them wearing a red shirt, and they were standing at the bar.

"Who's that jasper in the red shirt that's with him?"

"I don't know. I seen 'im in here before, but I don't know who he is."

"I think I've seen him before, too."

"Where?"

"Out there in John Holcomb's horse pasture. He might be the one that shot at me. That jasper was wearin' a red shirt."

"You think it's him, Slim?"

"It sure as hell could be. Who else but ol' Tooley would want to ruin john Holcomb's young horses." Jim was staring at the man.

"They're packin' iron," Skeeter said. "I seen ol' Tooley twice since the fight, and both times he was totin' that bit pistol."

"I saw the guns before I saw the men," Jim said. "I can't think of any reason a man would carry a shootin' iron around here. They ran the Indians off a couple of years ago."

"The only thang a pistol's good for is shootin' people," Skeeter said. "They ain't worth a damn for hunting'."

"That old .44 of yours still shoot, Skeeter?"

"As good as it ever did. Wanta borrow it? You was purty good at blastin' tin cans with it. You even got so you could fan the hammer back like a gunfighter."

"John Holcomb wants me to carry a gun. Right now I wish I had one."

"Mine's in the bunkhouse. I'll git it to you if you want it. What would you do if you had a gun?"

"I don't know. I guess the law-abidin' thing to do is go get the sheriff and point that feller out to him."

"Huh," Skeeter snorted. "The way the law works, he'd probly put you in jail for startin' trouble."

The man in the red shirt saw Jim staring at him. He stared back.

"Gun or no gun, that might be the son of a bitch that shot at me," Jim said. "I cain't let him get away with that." He turned from the bar and took a step toward the man. Skeeter turned with him and spoke earnestly.

"No. Listen, Slim, you know I ain't one to run from a fight, but you ain't sure, and those hooligans're armed. And there's three of 'em."

Jim paused and thought about what Skeeter had said. "You're right. I can't be plumb sure. There's a lot of red shirts. But I think I'll buckle on that .45 John wants to give me."

The man in the red shirt scowled at Jim and took a step toward him. Tooley took him by the arm, said something in a low voice, and gave him a gentle shove toward Jim.

"He wants you to fight," Skeeter said. "He wants you to git shot."

The bartender was looking from Jim to the man in the red shirt and back to Jim. He sighed audibly with relief when Marshal Delmar Chitlow came through the door. The man in the red shirt immediately turned back to the bar.

Jim's hands were trembling slightly and he was angry and frustrated. Then Maria came in.

CHAPTER 10

"Jimmee," Maria said, smiling happily as she approached. She put her arm around Jim's waist and hugged him. Slowly, the tension eased. Jim liked the smell and feel of Maria. He shot another glance at the man he had almost fought with, and put an arm around her shoulders.

"How've you been, Maria?"

"I'm fine, Jimmee." She ran her fingers lightly over his face. "You not hurt no more?"

"No. I got over that the next day." Not knowing what else to say, Jim said, "Let's have a drink."

Two drinks later it was past noon, and Jim suggested they go to one of the two cafes in San Lomah. Skeeter excused himself.

"I see ol' Tooley and them gunsels're gone," he said. "I got to git back. I'd like to stay and pitch one with you, Slim, but ol' Ziegler sent me in to pick up some fence staples, and I cain't stay too long." He pronounced staples as "steeples."

"All right, Skeeter. Look out for the streetcars." Jim turned back to Maria. "Let's you and me get somethin' to eat."

She said again she didn't want to go to a restaurant, and suggested they go to her cabin a block away from the saloon. "That is," she said, "if you like tacos." Jim was feeling the whiskey, and he quipped, "My favorite fruit."

The food was a little too spicy for Jim, but he ate it anyway and washed it down with two tin cups of cool water. He liked Maria's cabin, and he liked Maria.

The cabin was only one room, with a small wood-burning combination-heating-and-cooking stove in one corner and a narrow cot against the far wall. The bed was covered neatly with a bright hand-crocheted coverlet, and a large picture of Jesus looked kindly down on the bed. Maria had two thick handwoven Navajo blankets on the floor and a crucifix on another wall.

Her few articles of clothing hung on a hat rack in one corner and were covered by a white linen sheet. Her few dishes and cooking utensils were stacked neatly in a wooden box on a wooden table. Except for the two small Navajo blankets, the floor was bare and scrubbed clean. Maria was a neat housekeeper.

And Maria herself was clean and neat. She wore her hair piled high on her head today, fastened there with a turquoise-studded clip. Her dress was the same satiny one she had worn before, but it was clean. Jim liked the way her white teeth sparkled against her dark skin, and he liked her dark, expressive eyes.

The meal of tacos and refried beans finished, Jim leaned back in his chair and studied her. "You're a darn fine woman, Maria."

She was washing the dishes in a tin pan. "What, Jimmee?"

"I said you're a good-lookin' girl and a fine cook."

She wiped her hands on a linen towel and stood before him. "You're nice, Jimmee."

He reached for her and pulled her down on his lap.

Her arms went around his neck and she kissed him on the mouth. It was a sweet kiss, and Jim wanted more. A terrible need grew within him. He pulled her tighter and they kissed again. The young cowboy stroked her back, her waist, and then her hips. And then suddenly she stood up.

"No, Jimmee. I got to go."

"Go?" Jim said, frustrated and disappointed. "Where?"

"To work?"

"Work? You mean back to the saloon?"

She straightened her dress and looked at herself in a small cracked mirror hanging on a wall beside the crucifix. "It's what I do, Jimmee. They don't like me to stay away too long."

Jim stood up, his face flushed. He didn't know whether to be angry or not. He thought about it, then decided he couldn't blame her.

She had to make a living. "Maybe later, huh?"

"Yes, Jimmee. You not go back to the ranch tonight?"

"Yeah, I got to go back."

She was disappointed. "Oh, Jimmee."

"How late do you have to stay at the saloon?"

"Very late, Jimmee."

"Damn. And I got to get up early in the mornin' and start some more colts." He went to the door. "Oh well, there'll be other days." He grinned a wolfish grin. "And nights."

"Yes, Jimmee."

Jim thought about going to the cabins on the west side of town, but he had heard that the women there were mostly middle-aged and not very attractive. He knew that compared to Maria they would not be worthwhile. He couldn't get Maria off his mind—her soft lips, her body inside that sheath dress, and the cot in her cabin—and he muttered, "Damn."

Not wanting to drink any more that day, Jim stood on the boardwalk awhile and watched the people go by. He had often wondered how it would be to work in town and live the town life. If he worked in town he wouldn't have to get up so early in the morning, and he would have Sundays off, and he would have time to wait up for Maria. "Damn," he muttered again.

He remembered something else he wanted to buy in town. He kept his brown horse shod and the steel shoes were almost worn out. The horse, bigger than most ranch horses, took a number-one shoe while the cowponies took an aught or a double-aught. There was no "ones" at the Holcomb Ranch.

He hunted up the blacksmith shop. The smithy happened to have some shoes already made up that were the right size, and Jim bought four and some beveled nails to hold them in place. The smithy gave him a burlap bag to carry the shoes in.

The slender cowboy from Texas walked back to Main Street, swinging the weighted bag at his side. He walked past the bank and almost ran into Miss Priscilla Newhouse.

"Hello, Mr. Kinslow," she said cheerfully. "How are you? How are things at the ranch?"

Jim lifted his hat briefly. "Hello, Miss Newhouse. I'm fine." He considered telling her about the barbwire and the stampede, but decided it would serve no purpose.

"How are Margaret and John Holcomb?"

"They're fine too. John is still walkin' on a crutch, but he's feelin' good." Somehow Jim always felt shy and out of place before the lady banker even though she was certainly easy to talk to.

"I heard about your friendship with the orphaned Indian boy, and how you took the boy with you to the Holcomb ranch. I think that was just magnificent, Mr. Kinslow. I'm ashamed that I didn't do something for that child. How is he? Do Margaret and John like him? Does he like living there?" Sincere concern showed in her gray eyes. They were very pretty eyes.

"Why yes. Mrs. Holcomb is teachin' him English, and she cut down some of John's clothes for him. He's well-fed and happy."

"I'm so glad." Priscilla Newhouse smiled. Jim remembered the kiss he had gotten from Maria, and he wondered what it would be like with Priscilla Newhouse. He hoped she couldn't guess what he was thinking. It embarrassed him to think she might, and he looked away.

"Mr. Kinslow, I was wondering. Did they pay you? Do you need any money? I promised that you would be paid—remember?"

"No, I don't need any money right now, Miss Newhouse. I still got some of my wages from the Rafter H."

"If you do run short of funds, come to me, will you?"

"I sure will," he said, but he hoped he would never find that necessary.

She held out her hand to shake, man-fashion. He shook with her and again wondered what it would be like to take her in his arms. He couldn't help thinking about it, but to be sure his actions didn't give his thoughts away, he made his handshake too brief and his departure too hasty.

As he walked away, he mentally compared Priscilla Newhouse to Maria. The Mexican girl was pretty and very desirable. It would be wonderful to go to bed with her. But after that, what? The lady banker, now... Now there was a woman a man could build to.

But hell, she couldn't get serious about a hired cowpuncher with a third-grade education.

Jim met a former employee of the Rafter H on the street and

they spent a pleasant half-hour talking about the calf roundup and of cowboys and horses they knew. They drank coffee in one of the cafes, then went their separate ways. He decided he would have another, stronger drink, but since he didn't want to have to say good-bye to Maria again he went to the other saloon, the Buckhorn Bar.

The interior was almost exactly like the interior of the St. Louis Emporium, with a long bar on one side of the room, a long mirror behind the bar, and tables scattered around. Jim stood at the bar and ordered a beer from a short, bald bartender. He noticed a lanky ranch hand standing beside him, nursing a mug of beer. The ranch hand, a middle-aged man with gray hair around his ears and a ragged hat pulled low, looked Jim over.

"You work for John Holcomb, don't you?" the man said in a flat, dull voice.

"Yeah," Jim said. "How'd you know?"

"A feller pointed you out to me on the street. I used to work there."

"Hell, you did?" Jim said, conversationally.

"Yeah. I worked there four years. I built fence and I built most of them corrals."

"They're good corrals," Jim said.

"My name is Clebe. Clebe Howell. They ever mention me?"

Jim couldn't recall ever hearing the name before, but he didn't want to disappoint the man. "Come to think of it, I b'lieve they did talk about you. Said you done good work."

The man was pleased at that. "I worked purty hard. I like the Holcombs. But they had to let me go. Ol' John said he was sorry, but they fell on hard times and couldn't pay me anymore. They paid you yet?"

"No, but I'm not worried. They'll pay me."

"I ain't worked much lately. Jist doin' some buildin' around town when I can find work. This beer has to last me all afternoon."

"Well, have another on me," Jim said, reaching into his pocket.

"Thanks. I ain't et much lately either. Could you maybe spare a feller a buck?"

"Sure," Jim said, digging a silver dollar out of his pocket. He mentally added up the money he had left, and decided he had better get out of town before he went broke. He finished his beer and left.

Outside, it was growing dark. Jim knew they wouldn't wait supper for him at the ranch, so he went to the New Kansas City Steakhouse and ate one of their steaks. He had about one dollar left of his Rafter H wages. By the time he went to the livery barn and retrieved his horse, it was completely dark.

He was still carrying the horseshoes in the burlap bag when he mounted the brown gelding and rode out of town, following the wagon road. He came to the place where there were fences on both sides of the road, and met four riders coming toward him.

He could see in the moonlight that one of the riders wore a dark shirt, possibly a red one. They all carried six-guns on their hips, and they drew their weapons and pointed them at Jim.

"Reach," one of the men barked.

Too surprised at first to be scared, Jim placed the sack of horseshoes on the saddle in front of him and raised his right hand. He continued holding the bridle reins with his left hand. When they drew closer, Jim could see that one of the men did indeed have on a red shirt, and it was the same man he had seen twice before. That man stayed in front of him while the others got behind him—between him and San Lomah.

Jim's heart beat quickened as he realized that his life was in danger. Fear crept into his throat. Red Shirt's pistol was aimed right at his face and the bore looked to be as big as a barn door. "What—" Jim's voice came out strained and he tried again. "What do you want?"

"Your money," Red Shirt said. The man's face in the moonlight looked eerie and cruel. Jim looked around at the other riders. None of them wore a mask.

"I only got a dollar," he croaked. "That's all I got."

Someone behind him tittered nervously. "It don't matter, long's he's found with his pockets inside out."

Again, Jim studied the faces around him, hoping desperately to find a grin and then a laugh to show that they were joking. But each face was grim, like an executioner's. One man looked away, unable to meet his gaze.

Jim knew then that he was to die. He croaked, "What—whatta

you think you're doin'?"

One of the men behind Jim rode up alongside and struck a wooden match with a thumbnail. Holding the match near Jim's head, he said, "I just wanted to make sure it was him." He dropped the match as it burned his fingers. "Let me. I'm the one he roped off a horse."

"Better get around in front of him, then," Red Shirt said. "It'd look more like a robbery that way." His gun was lowered as the two men started to trade places.

There was no time to plan a defensive move. For a fleeting moment, while they were changing places, Jim had a fraction of a chance. But whatever he did, he had to do it *now*.

Fear forced a wild rebel yell out of the cowboy as he grabbed the sack of horseshoes and swung it at the man beside him as he spurred the brown gelding.

The sack connected, and the rider was knocked half off his horse. The brown gelding leaped forward and collided with Red Shirt's horse, and the man's shot went wild.

Red Shirt's horse was knocked down, and the brown gelding stumbled over it, going to its knees. Two shots were fired, but they went over Jim's head.

It took Jim a second to make up his mind whether to stay on his horse and try to outrun them, or to quit the horse and try to lose them in the dark. He believed his brown gelding could outrun their horses, but he knew it couldn't outrun bullets.

Dropping the sack and his reins, Jim rolled off the horse while it was still on its knees, fell to his hands and knees, then scrambled up and ran, bending low, for the barbwire fence.

"He's afoot," someone shouted. Bullets kicked up dirt around Jim as he hit the ground on his stomach and rolled under the fence. A barb caught his shirt and tore it, but he didn't notice. On the other side of the fence, he ran a zigzag pattern in the dark, bending low. A volley of gunshots sounded behind him.

"Get after him."..."I can't get through this goddam fence."..."Get off the horses and chase him on foot."..."Don't let him get away."..."I see him."..."Where?"..."Right over there."

Guns boomed. Bullets tore into the ground, tore through the

sagebrush, tore through the air over Jim's head. One slug nicked the heel of his boot.

Jim ran, and his mind raced too. There's got to be a low spot in this ground somewhere, he thought. There's got to be a spot where a man can take cover. He listened again to the words floating to him through the night air.

"Cut the goddam fence."..."Pete, you got them wire cutters?"..."Yeah, I got 'em."..."Cut the goddam fence."

The ground suddenly dropped away, and Jim stumbled and fell. He was in a shallow draw where the bullets couldn't reach him. For a moment he lay still, panting for breath.

"C'mon, cut the goddam fence."..."I'm tryin' to."

Footsteps pounded the ground out in front of Jim, and he knew one of the men was looking for him on foot. Lord, if he had only taken John Holcomb's advice and carried a gun. He could at least shoot back. Now he was helpless. Hell, he couldn't even throw a rock at them in the dark.

Well, he couldn't just lie there and wait for someone to walk up and shoot him. He had to move. But quietly.

Jim was afraid to stand up, afraid he would be visible. He moved out of the draw, but tried to stay as low as the sagebrush around him. The brush seemed to be taller to the west, and he moved in that direction. He was moving parallel with the fence.

"What's the matter? Can't you cut that goddam wire?"..."I got it now, I got it."

The tight fence wire went *twang*, and Jim could visualize it springing back in both directions. He heard another *twang* as the second wire was cut. Two more wires to go, and they would be hunting for him on horseback.

Got to get as far away as I can, Jim thought. Keep movin'. Crouching, and at times touching the ground with his hands, he kept going. He heard two more shots but the bullets didn't come near him. He believed with some satisfaction that the gunmen had lost sight of him. They would have to hunt for him.

Then he heard a shout that made his heart jump into his throat again.

CHAPTER 11

"There he is. Over there." A bullet clipped off a sage branch near Jim's head. Another hit the ground with a thud right in front of his face. He flattened out.

Footsteps pounded toward him. Another shot. Jim hugged the ground, his mind working.

How dumb can you get? he silently asked himself. A movin' man is a hell of a lot easier to spot than a still one. How damn dumb can you get. Stay still.

No, you can't stay still now. They know where you're at. Got to move again.

Twang. One more wire to go.

Stay low, but get up and run like a rabbit. Jim got up and ran, zigzagging, bending low.

"I see him, I see him." A bullet *thunked* into the ground. There was another shot, then Jim heard a dull click as the pistol hammer fell on an empty shell casing.

Now, he silently told himself—run while you've got a chance.

The last wire was cut, and shouts and hoofbeats came from behind Jim.

"He's over that way. Get him."

Jim ran. No use trying to stay low now. They could see him. He ran. He wished he had time to stop and take the spurs off his boots. Wearing them and running was like trying to run in a bog. He ran the best he could. Hoofbeats were coming closer. Any second now they would catch him and put a bullet in his back. Jim could almost feel it.

He clenched his teeth and ran.

"Can you see him?"..."No, but I know he's right over there."..."I saw him a couple seconds ago. He's right over there."..."We'll get him now."

They can't see me, Jim thought. For a few seconds, at least, I'm out of sight. Stay out of sight. But there's too many of 'em. They'll ride their horses over every inch of this ground. If I stay here, they'll find me. What the hell should I do? Crawl? No, I can't get away from here crawlin'. What the hell should I do?

Again, the ground dropped away from Jim's feet, and he half fell and half slid into one of the arroyos he remembered seeing in that part of the country. When he landed at the bottom, he discovered he was in an arroyo about six feet deep with steep sides.

The horses could make it into the arroyo eventually, but by the time they found a way, he could be long gone. Gone? Where? In here, I'm out of sight. This is the best place for me.

No, they'll ride the length of this damn gulley and find me. Got to keep movin'. They'll soon know I'm in here, but maybe if I climb out and hide in the brush they'll waste time lookin' in here.

"Look out, here's a 'royo."..."I'll bet he's down in it."..."Get down there. Come on, gig that horse."

What to do, Jim asked himself. Which way to go? Quit the arroyo?

"Joe, you get across this 'royo and see he don't run out the other side."..."Gotcha."..."We got him trapped now."

So much for that idea, Jim thought. Now what?

He believed, if he didn't have his directions turned around, that the arroyo ran north and south, and would have to cut across the road. No, it didn't cut across the road because there was no bridge or culvert or anything on that road. That meant it petered out somewhere this side of the road. How far?

Jim walked in a crouch down the arroyo toward the road. He only hoped he could get to the road before they saw him. He heard hoofs scrambling over the rocks, and he knew, sadly, that horses could see better in the dark than he could. They could find their way. It occurred to Jim that the horses would probably spot him before the men did, but, he thought wryly, at least they wouldn't point him out.

Now he heard a horse coming up behind him. It would be only a few seconds before it caught up with him. He had to run. He had no choice—he had to run.

Run he did.

A shout. A bullet screamed off a rock over his head. "Here he is. I got him now."..."I see him too. He's a dead man now."

Jim's teeth were clenched and his mind was screaming. Run. Come on, feet. Run.

Bullets ricocheted with sickening sounds all around Jim. His hat was knocked forward over his face. He grabbed it, shoved it back where it belonged as he ran.

He stumbled. He got up and stumbled again. Then he realized he had reached the end of the arroyo. It was shallower here, but steep. He would have to climb out hand over hand. He climbed.

"Do you still see him?"..."I know where he's at. He's right ahead of us. There he is."

Jim reached the top, flattened out on his belly, and rolled. Loud curses came from behind him.

"How the hell did you miss him?"..."I don't think I missed him."..."How the hell do we get out of here?"..."We'll have to go back a ways."..."Hey, Joe."..."Yeah."..."He's up on top where you're at. Do you see him?"..."I'll find him."

Jim lay on his stomach and heard every word. He knew he had to keep running. The hoodlum named Joe would ride right over him if he didn't. He got up and ran.

"I see him. I'll get him now."..."Shoot 'im."..."I've only got one more shell in this gun. I'll catch him."

Hoofbeats came from behind Jim. He ran. The hoofbeats came closer. He could hear the horse sucking wind. He ran, but he knew he could not outrun a horse. He was about to be caught and shot. It was a good try, he thought, but now I'm about to die.

Visions of death raced through the cowboy's mind. He could see his body, crumpled, riddled with bullets. He wondered, as he ran, if his killers would ever be caught and hung. He was breathing hard from the exertion, and one exhalation came out with a partially suppressed cry of anguish. He didn't want to die.

Then he almost ran into a fence post, seeing it just in time to stop. The fence was right in front of him. The *fence*. A horse can't get through that.

Jim hit the ground rolling. He rolled under the fence, got up, ran low across the road and rolled under the other fence. Now he had two fences between him and the horseman. A shot smacked a fence post and knocked splinters off it.

And suddenly Jim felt like laughing. He was going to live. The horsemen couldn't get to him without cutting their way through two fences, and that dumb jasper had just fired his last shot. Hell, if they cut through those fences, he could just go on up the fence and duck under it again.

Someone shouted, "Don't wait to cut the wire. Get down and get after him."

Sure, Jim felt like yelling, I can run as fast as you can, and you ain't goin' to get another shot at me in the dark. But instead of yelling, he stayed quiet.

Which way to go? It cain't be more'n two or three miles to the Holcomb ranch. That's where I'll go. No, wait. That's where they'll think I went. Hell, I'll go back toward town.

Keeping low and traveling as quietly as he could, Jim walked back down the fence.

The farther toward town Jim walked, the farther behind him the excited voices were, and eventually he was out of hearing range of the hoodlums. He crawled through the fence and walked on the road, where the footing was better. His plan at first was to walk back to town and hunt up the sheriff, but he decided it would be better if he could get to the Holcomb ranch and have John Holcomb accompany him to the sheriff's office. Yeah, that would be better. Just make himself hard to find until the hoodlums gave up, then walk to the ranch.

He wondered where his brown horse was. He knew the horse wouldn't go far dragging bridle reins. But he feared the horse had been injured when it rammed Red Shirt's horse broadside and fell to its knees.

While he was thinking about it, the horse suddenly loomed up in the semidarkness before him. Jim stopped. He couldn't be sure of what he was seeing. It was a horse, all right, but whose?—and could there be a man on its back? Jim saw as he crept closer that it was a riderless horse—and it was his horse.

The animal was grazing on the grass that grew alongside the road between the two fences. Jim picked up the reins and led the horse a few steps. "You seem to be all right," he whispered. "You're a tough ol' pony. Now let's see if we can find that hole in the fence."

He led the horse along the north side of the road until he came to where the fence had been cut. He led the horse through and mounted. Knowing the animal could find its way in the dark, Jim pointed it toward the ranch buildings and said, "Let's go home, old feller."

Jim was disappointed in Sheriff Walt Umbaugh. He was short and paunchy with a plump face, a bushy mustache and bushy eyebrows, and he carried his six-gun in a holster that was fastened to the same belt that held his pants up. The holster was so deep that only the butt of the gun showed. Jim hoped the man never had to do any fast shooting.

But the sheriff had pale blue eyes that appeared to look right through a man, and he talked with a slow, thoughtful drawl.

"You're sure you can identify them, son?"

"At least one of them," Jim said. "The one that was in front of me and had his gun aimed right at me."

Umbaugh turned to John Holcomb. "How come you're just now telling me about that barbwire and that stampede?"

Holcomb shrugged as he stood in the sheriff's office at the courthouse with a crutch under his left armpit. "I don't get around so good these days, Walt, and we have work to get done."

Umbaugh grabbed his high-crowned brown hat and slapped it down over thick gray hair. "I'll go out to the Hash Knife and see who I can see. You say one of the men that stampeded those colts was riding a horse branded with a double-B bar?"

"Yeah," Jim said.

"But you don't give me much of a description of the men. The way you describe them they look like a hundred other men."

Jim shuffled his feet. He could never feel comfortable talking to a lawman. "That's about the way they looked. The man in front of me last night was not quite as tall as I am and he wasn't fat and he wasn't thin. He wore a red shirt and a hat with a rolled-up brim."

The sheriff snorted. "Most men have more than one shirt, and he could change hats too."

"I'll know 'im if I see 'im," Jim said. "I could ride out to the Hash Knife with you."

"No. I don't want you pointing a finger at anyone and maybe starting a fight. If I see anyone that fits the description, I'll ask him some hard questions. I'll find out what he was doing last night."

Umbaugh went to the door and Jim and John Holcomb followed him outside the courthouse. The sheriff wore low-heeled shoes and no spurs. Jim wondered if he rode a horse or drove one hitched to a buggy. As the sheriff walked away toward the livery stable, Jim allowed, "Hell, we're just wastin' time."

"Prob'ly," Holcomb said, "but ol' Walt can fool you sometimes." He climbed awkwardly, pulling himself with his hands, to the seat of the light wagon. When he was seated, Jim handed him the lines, then mounted one of the sorrel colts he had just broken to ride.

The colt didn't like the sights, sounds, or smells of the town, and it walked down Main Street behind the wagon with its head up and its ears twitching. But it made no effort to bolt. Jim sat in his Texas saddle easily, as if he were riding an old gentle horse. He knew that any nervousness he displayed would be transferred to the young horse.

He preferred to keep his horse behind the bit, cowboy style, instead of on the bit, English style, simply because it was easier and more relaxing that way. After all, cowboys lived on horseback; they didn't ride for pleasure. But while his reins were slack, Jim held them in such a way that he could take up slack in a second if necessary.

Holcomb kept looking back at Jim, pleased at the way the colt behaved. He exchanged shouted greetings with people he knew on the street, and one old cowman yelled, "That one of yours John?"

"Yep, that's one of my four-year-olds." Holcomb had pride in his voice.

"Good-lookin' colt. What're you askin'?"

"Come over sometime and we'll palaver."

"Might do that."

They got back to the ranch before noon, and Jim ran in another colt, one he had not worked with before. Holcomb wasn't watching him anymore, satisfied that the hired cowboy knew his business. The colt, a big bay with two stocking legs, had been halter-broke and broke to lead, but had been handled very little. Jim got a halter on it and got it snubbed close to the snubbing post in the small square corral.

Using a long, plaited rope that had once been a three-strand catch rope which he had painstakingly untwisted and plaited into a flat, soft length, Jim tied a bowline knot around the horse's neck, low, next to the shoulders. He got behind the animal, and by flipping the end of the rope got the colt to step over it with a hind foot. The rope was between the colt's hind feet then, and Jim, keeping a safe distance away, flipped it up between the hocks.

Instinctively terrified at having a foreign object anywhere near its legs, the animal kicked, reared back on the halter rope, and kicked again. Jim hung onto the rope until the animal quieted down, then walked up to the left shoulder, passed the end under the loop around the animal's neck, and slowly, carefully, let the rope slip down the hind leg until it fit into the pastern. Then slowly, carefully, Jim pulled the foot forward.

At the first pull, the colt kicked and danced away again, jerking the rope out of the cowboy's hands. Jim patiently picked up the rope and started over.

Soon he had the left hind foot pulled forward to where the colt could barely touch the ground with its toe. He tied it there. Now the animal could not kick or buck, but it could hobble around, although with a great amount of discomfort. Jim believed that a colt hobbled so that it could move—but uncomfortably—would soon learn to stand still.

At first, the horse fought the scotch hobble, but soon discovered that fighting was hard work, and it was not being hurt anyway. That was when the sacking-out process began.

Using an empty burlap bag, Jim rubbed the horse all over,

talking quietly. Then he waved the sack over the horse's back and head. The animal ducked its head and snorted when the sack touched its ears, but otherwise stood still.

Jim backed away from the horse, then ran at it, waving his arms and hollering. The colt was naturally fearful and fought to free itself. But after a few such experiences, it realized it was not being hurt and it stood still.

Next, the cowboy crawled onto the animal's back, and again the animal struggled. But as before, it soon found it easier not to resist. Jim crawled over the horse, slid off its rump, jumped back on and waved the sack over its back, touching it with the sack and talking. "Told you it wouldn't hurt. See there. Chases the flies off, don't it."

Then came the saddle. Jim had found an old saddle in the barn that was lighter in weight than his Texas saddle, and he threw it on the horse's back, jerked it off and threw it on, again and again. He didn't place the saddle carefully on the colt's back—he threw it on the way he would throw a saddle on an old broke horse. The colt had to, sooner or later, get used to having a saddle thrown on it, and the sooner the better, Jim believed.

Finally, Jim cinched the saddle up. He tightened both the cinch and the belly strap on the double-rigged saddle. There again. Jim disagreed with many horsemen who believed it better to let the colt get used to one cinch at a time. Jim thought that since it was all new to the colt anyway, the animal would become accustomed to a double-rigged saddle as quickly as it would to a single rigging.

When he tightened the cinch, the colt let out a long groan and began leaning to the left. Since a tight cinch makes any horse not accustomed to it feel like lying down, Jim expected that, and he slacked off. Then, after the horse was standing straight again, he completed tightening the cinch.

The cowboy was almost through working with that colt that day, but he wanted to accomplish one more thing: He wanted the colt to carry the saddle.

He took off the halter and slipped on the bosal. He tied the reins to the saddle horn with enough slack so that the colt could run but couldn't put its head down to buck. If it tried to put its head down and buck, the bosal would bite it under the jaw and it would punish itself.

Now Jim had to get the colt to move.

He attached a long, light, cotton rope to the bosal, untied the hind foot, and opened the gate between the square corral and the round one.

It took the animal a minute to realize it was free. It took two steps and went straight up.

The horse kicked with both heels and squalled at the idea of having something on its back, but the bosal kept its head up. When it eventually quieted down, Jim hazed it into the round corral and closed the gate.

He picked up the end of the light rope with one hand and held a long buggy whip with the other. He flicked the whip at the colt's rump and made a barely audible clucking sound at the same time, and soon he had the colt trotting around him on the end of the light rope.

Then he began saying "ho, ho, ho" barely audibly, and shaking the light rope gently. The rope, attached to the bosal, caused the bosal to irritate the horse's jaw. It was uncomfortable, and the animal shook its head, broke into a gallop, slowed to a trot, a walk, and finally stopped. Instantly, Jim quit shaking the rope. The punishment ceased at the instant the animal stopped.

Within a few minutes, Jim could point the whip at the animal's rump, make a clucking noise, and get it trotting around him. He could say "Ho," shake the rope and get it to stop.

Moving quietly and carefully, he unsaddled the colt, pulled the bosal off and turned it out into the pasture. "See you again tomorrow," he said as the animal trotted away.

In less than two hours, Jim had made considerable progress toward gentling the colt, had taught it to carry a saddle without bucking, and had taught it to go and whoa on cue.

Holcomb had never seen a colt worked on a lunge line before and he congratulated Jim on bringing that technique to the Holcomb ranch. "Where," he asked Jim while Maggie Holcomb placed food on the table, "did you learn to do that?"

"Oh, I seen it in a circus once, about a year ago in Fort Worth. A man in white britches worked horses that way in the ring, and got them to do all kinds of things. I got to thinkin' that it might be a way to take the buck out of a colt before you get on his back."

"You're doing it, Jim. Not one of the colts you broke so far has bucked. Boy, that's the way to do it. If you can keep them from blowing up, you're that much ahead."

Jim grinned. "With that slick fork saddle of mine, they better not buck. If any of 'em gets to pitchin' with me, you watch him and tell me which way he went."

Holcomb laughed. "I'd rather hire a horse breaker than a bronc rider any day."

"Tell you somethin', John," Jim said. "That lunge line is good for a lot of things. If you have to turn the colts out before they're well-broke, all you have to do when you run 'em in again is work 'em on that lunge line a few minutes, and it'll all come back to 'em."

Holcomb slapped his bandaged left leg. "Damn—excuse me, Maggie—dam, I can't wait to try it."

"That sure looks good," Jim said as a platter of homemade bread and a bowl of butter was placed on the table before him. "Don't it, Chacho?"

The boy showed his white teeth and said, "Yesss."

CHAPTER 12

Jim had just turned out his third colt of the day when Sheriff Umbaugh drove into the yard in an open buggy pulled by one horse. He climbed down and hitched the horse to a hitchrack near the kitchen door. As soon as he saw John Holcomb and Jim approaching, he started shaking his head negatively.

"There was no one at the Hash Knife that looked like the men who tried to kill you," he said. "Jake Tooley's only got four men workin' for him now. Two of them are building fence and two are breaking horses. He said they were all in the bunkhouse last night."

"Did you see a bay horse with a double B bar on him?" Jim asked.

"No, son, but that horse could have been turned out anywhere."

"Yeah," said John Holcomb, leaning on his crutch, "and those gun slingers could be anywhere too. Just because you didn't see 'em don't mean they weren't around somewhere."

Umbaugh pushed his hat back. "That's so. But it could be the men who shot at your hired hand was trying to rob him and don't even belong around here."

"No," Jim said, "they wanted to kill me and make it look like a robbery. I could tell by what they said, about me bein' found with my pockets inside out."

"Now why"—the sheriff squinted at Jim—"would anyone want to kill you?"

"For the same reason they stampeded the colts: To keep John

91

here from gettin' 'em broke and sellin' 'em to the Army and beatin' out the Hash Knifed."

The sheriffs pale eyes bored into Jim's for a moment, and it made the cowboy glad he was not trying to lie. Then Umbaugh raised his hat, reset it, and looked down. "I don't know. It's hard to believe Jake Tooley would do a thing like that. He likes to fight and beat up men, but I can't believe he'd have someone killed."

Holcomb shifted the crutch out in front so he could lean on it with both hands. "I hear tell, Walt—I don't know if it's true—but I heard tell Jake Tooley's got financial problems the same as I have. He's got a bunch of colts over there he'd like to sell, and if he can, well, he's just like me. He's prob'ly desperate, just like I'd be if anything happened to Jim."

"That rumor's going around," Umbaugh said, hooking his thumbs inside his belt. "But there's another rumor going around: He's got a buyer for his outfit if he wants to sell."

"A buyer?" Holcomb asked. "Who?"

"I hear it's the town marshal, Delmar Chitlow."

"The marshal?" Holcomb grunted with surprise. "Why would he want to buy a ranch?"

Umbaugh snorted, and Jim detected disgust in his answer. "Maybe he wants to do something legitimate for a change."

The sheriff's words puzzled Jim, but he asked no questions.

"Anyhow, I hear Jake Tooley won't sell," Umbaugh added.

"I'd be surprised if he did," Holcomb said.

The sheriff squinted at the afternoon sun. "I might as well get on back to town. I'll ask around and see if anybody's seen those gunsels."

"Care for a cup of coffee, Walt?"

"Now that's mighty nice of you. I sure would."

Jim turned his back on the two and went to the corrals and his next young horse.

He had the colt scotch-hobbled and was sacking it out when he saw the sheriff's buggy leave. For a moment he thought he was seeing double. There were two buggies side by side on the road near the Holcomb ranch house. Then the buggies separated, and one pulled away from the house while the other came toward it. The one drawing closer had a top on it, and Jim could see that the driver was a woman. Curious, he let the colt's hind foot down and peered through the corral poles.

The driver turned out to be Miss Priscilla Newhouse.

Maggie Holcomb hurried out to the yard to greet her, wiping her hands on an apron as she hurried. "Why, Miss Newhouse. How nice to see you."

"I thought I'd take a drive today," the lady banker said, "and bring these out." She handed Maggie Holcomb a large paper bag.

"What on earth...?"

"It's clothes. For the boy. I had to guess at his size." Maggie Holcomb opened the bag and took out several garments and a pair of shoes. "Why, isn't that nice."

"I've always felt that I ought to do something for that child. I wish I hadn't waited so long."

Chuckling, Maggie Holcomb held up the shoes. "I may have to wait until the snow comes before I can get these on him. Right now I don't think he'd appreciate shoes."

Miss Newhouse laughed with her. "I didn't think about that." She looked around the yard, saw Jim and waved. Jim waved back at her. The two women went into the house.

Pleased, Jim turned back to the colt tied to the snubbing post. "There's some bad folks in the world but there's some good ones, too," he said. "Now, young feller, let's pull that foot up again. I'd like to keep my head on my neck, if you don't mind."

The colt rolled its eyes and snorted.

It was two days later, when Jim went to the house for supper, that Maggie Holcomb had become worried. "Have you seen Ramon?"

"Ramon?" Jim asked.

"That's his name. Ramon Garcia. I got that much out of him. But I can't find him anywhere."

"Why, no," Jim said. "He wasn't in the bunkhouse when I went in to wash up. Is his mare gone?"

"I don't know. Where do you suppose he might be?"

"I'll go look and see if his horse is gone," Jim said, and left.

When he returned, he too was concerned, but he tried not to show it. "The mare's gone. He's gone off somewhere. But don't worry."

"Where could he be? You don't suppose he decided he doesn't like it here?"

Jim tried to make his voice sound casual, unconcerned. "Naw, nothin' like that. He likes it here."

"Could I have been too strict with him? I didn't mean to be."

"Naw. He'll show up."

Maggie Holcomb couldn't eat her meal. She couldn't sit still. She repeatedly got up and looked out the kitchen door into the yard. "Where could he be? He's just a boy."

"He couldn't get lost if he wanted to," John Holcomb said. "That kid knows this country as well as anybody."

"That's just it, John. He was brought up wild and free. Perhaps he doesn't take to my teaching. Perhaps he would rather live the way he did before we brought him here."

"He likes you, Mrs. Holcomb," Jim said. Suddenly, Jim snapped his fingers. "Come to think of it, the livery stable man told me that Chacho sometimes goes up to the mountains for a couple days at a time."

"Where? Where does he go, Jim?"

"I don't know. The stableman don't know. He just gets on that mare of his and disappears. But he always comes back. He's hungry but healthy when he gets back."

"But he's just a boy."

"That kid learned to take care of himself the same time he learned to walk, Mrs. Holcomb. Don't worry, he'll be back."

Maggie Holcomb sat at the kitchen table with her chin in her hands. "I wonder where he is. I wonder if he's all right."

Jim was riding one of the young horses out on the vega next day when he saw the boy coming. He rode out to meet him. The boy looked exhausted, but he showed his gleaming teeth when Jim rode up.

"Where in hell you been, Chacho? Mrs. Holcomb is havin' fits."

The boy pointed to the mountains.

"I figured that, but where? And why? What makes you go up there all the time?"

Still pointing, the boy said, "I go. *Viejo*. Grandpa."

"What?" It made no sense to Jim. "Grandpa? Your grandpa's dead. What's he got to do with it?"

"Grandpa say. I go."

They rode side by side to the gate that opened into the ranch yard.

"Your grandpa told you to go?"

The boy nodded. "I go. Grandpa say."

Jim dismounted and opened the gate. He led his mount through and started to mount up again, then paused. Maggie Holcomb was hurrying toward them, holding up her long skirts.

"Better get off that horse, Chacho, before you get pulled off."

The boy slid off the mare's back, and was immediately smothered with hugs.

Maggie Holcomb hugged and patted him, and finally held him out at arm's length. "Are you all right? You're not hurt?" Assured that he was healthy, she scolded him. "Why did you do it? Don't you know you had us worried sick? Where did you go?"

The boy only looked blank.

Jim picked up the mare's reins. "I'll feed 'er, Chacho." He started to walk away, leading the two horses, then turned back. "I wouldn't be too hard on 'im, Mrs. Holcomb. Somethin', I don't know what, but somethin' makes him think he has to go up there. He thinks he just has to."

By mid-September, Jim had twenty-six of the colts broken and ready to sell. He still had not been bucked off, but he had been kicked several times, and four of the young horses had fallen with him while they were fighting their heads. One of them had fallen over backward that day onto Jim's right foot and leg, and Jim was limping when he went to the house for supper that night.

"You need a rest, Jim," Maggie Holcomb said.

"John, why don't you suggest he go to town for a day or two."

"You can go anytime you want to, Jim," John Holcomb said. "I can pay you a couple bucks."

"There's a dance at the schoolhouse tomorrow night," Maggie Holcomb said. "Why don't you get cleaned up and go to that dance. You might meet a nice girl."

Jim almost blushed. "Aw, I never learned how to dance. All I get to do is watch other people dance."

"I can teach you."

"Naw. But I think I'll go to town. Maybe get a haircut and some epsom salt to soak this foot in."

Jim heated some water that night on top of a stove made from a steel drum, which sat in the middle of the one-room bunkhouse, and took a bath out of a bucket. The boy was busy trying to read from a first-grade reader Maggie Holcomb had given him. Several times he had to carry the book to Jim and point at the words with his finger. Jim read the words to him and got him to repeat them.

"You keep learnin' like that and we're gonna have to call you perfesser," Jim quipped. "You're gonna be the best-educated blanket-ass in the United States."

"Blanket-ass?" the boy said, puzzled.

"Now don't you go repeatin' that. I shouldn't of said it. But if you go to a white man's school, you'll prob'ly be called that a lot of times."

Jim opened up his tarp-covered bed and started to crawl into it, then wrinkled his nose and said, "Phew. I was gonna take these blankets to the laundry, but now I think I'll burn 'em."

The boy smiled at the expression on Jim's face. "Phew," he repeated and chuckled.

"Yeah," Jim said with a half-grin, "if you didn't have Mrs. Holcomb washin' your blankets for you, your bed wouldn't smell so good either." Jim crawled between his blankets and settled his head onto the pillow. "You can blow out the light whenever you want to. And wash your feet. You don't want to live like a damn pack rat just because I do."

Again, the boy's face screwed up in puzzlement. "Damn pack rat?"

Raising his head from the pillow, Jim shot a scowl at the boy. "It's damn strange the way you repeat everything I don't want you to repeat. Mrs. Holcomb's gonna skin me alive."

The boy had sensed that the word "damn" was one he was not supposed to learn and this piqued his interest. "Damn strange," he said, and grinned, his white teeth shining in the lamplight.

Jim settled down on the pillow and his voice was muffled when he said, "Aw go to bed, you little booger."

"Damn go," the boy laughed.

San Lomah was quiet when Jim rode his brown gelding down Main Street, so quiet that the *clip-clop* of the horse's hooves was the loudest noise in town. Not wanting to leave his horse tied all day to a hitchrail, he rode down the full length of the street to see what there was to see, then turned back toward the livery barn. He passed the bank just as Miss Priscilla Newhouse was about to enter. She waved and yelled, "Good morning, Mr. Kinslow. How are things at the ranch?"

"Fine, Miss Newhouse, just fine." Jim had an urge to rein over, dismount and visit with her, but he wasn't sure she would appreciate that, so he went on.

At the livery barn, the owner invited Jim to put his horse in the feedlot, but said it would cost twenty-five cents to keep it there all day. Jim handed over the coin and quipped, "I never thought I'd pay to park a horse, but it's worth it."

The stableman said he hoped Jim would retrieve the horse before dark, because he had taken to padlocking the gates at night. Jim said he would.

His right leg was still swollen around the ankle and walking was uncomfortable to Jim, reminding him that he needed medication. He went into the mercantile and bought a five-pound box of epsom salt and two cotton blankets.

Back at the livery, he wrapped the salt in the blankets, rolled up the blankets, and tied them behind the cantle of his saddle. Then, walking with a slight limp, spur rowels dragging on the boardwalk, he headed for the barbershop.

As before, Jim's hat didn't feel right when he left the barbershop, and he lifted and reset it several times before he found an acceptable position for it. He decided that walking would be less difficult on the sore ankle if he took his spurs off, and after he did so he headed again for the livery barn. Activity was increasing on the street. Trace chains rattled and wheels squeaked as an empty freight wagon went by. Two women wearing long dresses and wool shawls went into the mercantile. A lone rider appeared at the west end of Main Street, and at first glance Jim thought the rider was injured. He was slumped over in the saddle and his head bobbed at every slow, trotting step the horse took. But when he drew closer. Jim saw it was the strange-looking gent with the white goatee, who obviously was not accustomed to sitting on a trotting horse.

The horse was heading for the livery barn where it knew it would find feed and rest, and it was eager to get there. The man appeared to be exhausted to the point of collapse. Curious, Jim followed him to the barn.

There, the man slid sorely out of the saddle, and leaned against the horse a moment to regain some strength in his legs. He walked shakily outside to a wooden water trough and sat on the edge of it. The stableman came over and studied him.

"What happened, Doctor Sanderson?" he asked. "Get lost?"

"Yes," the man said, barely audibly.

"I told you, if you get lost just give that old horse his head. He knows where to come to get that saddle off his back."

"Yes, I did," Doctor Sanderson said with a sigh. "The animal knew which direction to travel, but it didn't know the trails." He stood up, carefully, and took two steps to test his legs.

"Yeah, that's the trouble," Jim got into the conversation. "A horse never gets his directions turned around, but in the mountains you have to know where the trails are. If you don't you'll climb a lot of high hills. I'll bet he took you over some rough country."

"Why, yes"—the man's voice was still unsteady—"that is precisely what happened. It was so steep..." he stopped to clear his throat. "...I was afraid to travel in the dark."

"What're you doin' up there?" the stableman asked. Doctor Sanderson merely fluttered his hands. "Can you make it to the hotel?" Jim asked. "Want some help?"

The older man looked at Jim from under white bushy eyebrows. "Thank you very much, young man. You're very kind. But I think I can walk now."

"You sure?"

"Yes. It's not far. Thank you very much."

They watched the older man totter away toward the hotel. He walked hunched over, and he looked not only exhausted but like a man who was totally defeated.

The stableman lifted his hat, ran his fingers through straight dark hair, and mused, "Wonder what he's been doin' up there?"

"Lookin' for gold, maybe?"

"No. There's been some prospectin' up there, but nobody's found anything. Besides, if he was looking for a vein he'd have to carry some diggin' tools."

"He don't carry anything, does he?"

"Yeah, he carried some binoculars. Come to think of it, he didn't have 'em just now, did he?"

"No, I didn't see any."

"Must of lost 'em."

Jim squinted at the morning sun. "Whatever he does, I'll bet he won't be doin' it anymore."

"At least not for awhile," said the stableman.

CHAPTER 13

Jim thought about going to the sheriff's office to see if the sheriff had learned anything about the men who had tried to kill him. But he decided against it. Talking to lawmen wasn't his favorite pastime, and he was almost certain of what the answer would be.

He was standing on Main Street idly watching the people go by when he saw Jake Tooley. The big, burly rancher was riding in from the east with another man, obviously a cowpuncher from the way he sat his horse. Jim watched them ride by and noticed that Tooley still had that six-gun strapped low on his right hip.

And that reminded Jim that he had forgotten something. He had forgotten to carry the Colt .45 that John Holcomb had loaned him. "Damn," he muttered under his breath, "and after I promised myself I'd tote it."

Tooley stared hard at Jim as he rode past, but said nothing. Jim stared back at him.

Time seemed to drag as Jim waited until midafternoon for Maria to report for her duties at the St. Louis Emporium. He stood at the bar and nursed his beer, not wanting to drink too fast and get drunk. One thought kept going through his mind: he had been told he could take a couple of days off. He could stay up as late as he pleased and sleep as late as he pleased next morning. Maybe tonight would be the night with Maria.

The bartender came over and stood in front of Jim "It's slow now," he said in a conversational tone, "but it'll be lively tonight just before the dance, and when the dance starts it'll be slow again. Everybody'll be over there."

"Oh, yeah," Jim said, "I heard there was goin' to be a dance somewhere tonight."

"At the schoolhouse. That's the only room in town big enough to have a dance. Except for the courthouse. You going over?"

"I might go and listen to the music," Jim said. "Say," he added, pretending it was an afterthought, "is that Mex girl, Maria, still here?"

"Yeah, she'll be in pretty soon." The bartender glanced down the bar at two men who were his only other customers, than leaned closer, "Do her a favor and don't take up all her time, will you. She'd spend all her time with you if she could, but the boss don't like it. Wants her to circulate."

"Is that so?" Jim sat his empty beer mug down and wiped his mouth with the back of his hand. He tried to act uninterested, only curious. "Who is the boss, anyway? I never did know."

"The marshal. Delmar Chitlow."

"Huh?" Jim couldn't help showing surprise.

"Yeah. He owns the Buckhorn Bar, too."

"The marshal owns the saloons?"

"Yeah. There's a man knows how to make money." The bartender pulled up one of his sleeve garters. "He allows the gamblers to fleece the working men around here and he gets a percentage. Anybody that gripes about bein' cheated gets run out of town. And he allows the whores to stay out there in his cabins—providing they pay him a hell of a high rent."

"Well, I'll be damned," Jim said. "How come the town trustees or whatever they're called allow him to do that?"

"Oh, they don't care as long as he lets the big shots get by with anything they want and keeps the rest of us peaceful. And believe me, he keeps the town peaceful. Killed a couple of men that wanted to shoot it up."

"He did?"

"Yep. I saw him shoot one man last winter, and I heard he killed another one before I came here."

The bartender walked away, drew two beers from a wooden keg and sat them in front of his other two customers, and came back.

"That man's smart. Give him a few more years and he's going to be as rich as that Colonel James out at the Rafter H."

"Give me another, will you." Jim pushed his empty mug forward. "I guess Colonel James is the richest man around here."

"That's what they say. Only he was born rich. Got his money from his folks back in Virginia, or some place like that. Old Chitlow came from nothing. He had to use his head."

The bartender went to refill Jim's mug. Jim knew he was hearing the truth. Anyone who wanted to know what was going on within two hundred miles had only to ask a bartender. Bartenders heard it all.

An unpleasant memory came to him, and he looked down at his boots and muttered, "Well, I'll be damned." He remembered the marshal's smug, authoritative, spiteful face. And he remembered how it was to be locked up in jail. He also remembered how he had baited the marshal, and wondered why he hadn't been severely beaten. Or shot. Maybe because the lady banker had shown an interest in him, he decided.

Jim also remembered Sheriff Walt Umbaugh's seeming disgust with the marshal.

"Lord," he muttered.

"What's that?" the bartender asked, returning with Jim's refill.

"Oh, nothin'. I was just thinkin'. It takes a man like the marshal to hire a poor girl like Maria to do what she does."

"It's profitable," the bartender said as he left to wait on a new customer.

Jim was halfway through his second beer when Maria came in. She saw him and headed for him immediately. "Jimmee," she smiled, taking his arm and standing close to him. "Nice to see you."

"Howdy, Maria." Jim put his hand on her shoulder. "How's the world treatin' you?" He slid his hand across her back, gripped her other shoulder and pulled her to him, against him. She put her arms around his waist and hugged him.

Maria was wearing the same satin sheath dress she always wore with the same artificial rose between her breasts. This time she had her dark hair combed to one side and held there with the same turquoise clip. She was overpainted, but pretty just the same. To the cowboy, she looked wonderful.

"Maria." It was the bartender. He frowned and nodded toward the other customers.

"I go now, Jimmee. I'll be back." She forced herself to smile in the direction of the other customers and went to a man in bib overalls. He grabbed her around the waist and pulled her roughly to him. "C'mere, you purty li'l thing."

She forced a giggle and allowed him to paw her.

Jim felt jealousy rising within him. He fought it down, knowing he had no right to be jealous, knowing he would make an ass of himself if he tried to stop the man's pawing. He stared into his beer mug and growled to himself, "Goddamnit. There ain't no justice."

The sight of another man pawing Maria was more than Jim could stand, and he went outside. He was feeling morose and wishing he were somewhere else. He couldn't help thinking about Fort Worth and the good times that could be had there. He silently vowed that when he got the Holcomb colts broken he would draw his pay and head south. He would have enough money then to go to Fort Worth and have all the girls he wanted. But still, when he thought of Maria, a twinge of sadness went through him. "Dammit," he muttered. "Goddamit all, anyway."

His blue funk deepened, and he had just about decided to get his horse and go back to the ranch when suddenly the sight of a familiar figure riding toward him on the street gave his spirits a boost.

Skeeter Jones saw him too. "Slim Jim. This must be the day the coyotes come to town."

"Hell, when I heard you was comin' I knew they'd let anything in. How in the hell you doin'?"

"I'm as happy as a man with good sense," Skeeter said, dismounting. "How's that skinny frame of yours? I heard you had to outrun bullets the other night."

"I didn't know I could run so fast," Jim grinned. "I'd of made a Texas jackrabbit ashamed of himself."

Skeeter's forehead wrinkled and his face turned serious. "Whoever done it might try again, Slim. It wasn't robbery like the sheriff said, was it?"

"Nope. It was somebody who didn't want John Holcomb's colts

broke."

"Who could that be? Jake Tooley?"

"That's a good guess."

"He's a dirty bullyin' sonofabitch, Slim."

"Well," Jim said, hopefully, "the sheriff and everybody is onto him now. Maybe he won't try it again."

"Hail, I wouldn't turn my back on 'im. He's totin' a six-shooter ever' place he goes now. If I was you, Slim, I'd start totin' a gun too."

"I aimed to, but I forgot."

"I'll still loan you my old .44 if you want it. You was purty good with it."

"John Holcomb gave me a Colt .45. I hung it up in the bunkhouse and forgot it."

"Well, anyway," Skeeter said as his face came alive, "tonight's the night of the big *baile*. Let's git some supper and go over there."

"Aw, I never learned how to dance."

"Me neither." Skeeter grinned lasciviously. "But I sure like to hold the girls while they dance."

"Well, then, let's get some chuck, and I'd better go get my horse. I was goin' to stay all night, but I think I'll go on back to the ranch after the dance."

The one-room school building was brightly lighted. Kerosene lamps hung in every corner and three or four were hung on each wall. Light spilled out the windows and illuminated horses hitched to buggies, horses hitched to light wagons, and horses carrying saddles. Men and women walked into and out of the building, the women dressed in their fanciest gowns and the men in denims and boots. Some of the men had whiskey bottles stuck in their hip pockets.

A squeaky fiddle was being tuned and a piano tinkled. There were laughter and loud greetings as neighbors recognized each other.

Skeeter caught the spirit of the dance even before he dismounted. "Hail, Slim, them folks're gonna be dancin' up a storm purty soon. Let's go git in the middle of it."

They tied their horses to a tree a hundred yards from the building, and Skeeter asked idly, "What've you got in the blankets,

Slim?"

"I bought some new soogans and some epsom salt."

Skeeter chuckled. "Hail, Slim, that stuff'll make you shit like a goose."

Jim chuckled with him. "I ain't goin' to drink it, I'm goin' to soak my foot in it. I got a beat-up ankle that won't quit."

"Looks like you got enough of it to give an enema to the whole Union Army."

"It don't come in littler boxes."

"Well, hail," Skeeter changed the subject, "even with a bum ankle you can try to dance."

"At that, I can prob'ly dance as good as you."

Skeeter spat on his hands, rubbed them together, and looked toward the open door. "Wail, let's git in there and git at it."

Inside the brightly lighted room, the two young cowboys looked around and were disappointed. There were about sixty people in the room, and at least forty-five of them were men. As in most small western towns, the men in and around San Lomah outnumbered the women four or five to one. Strangely, the men were gathered in one end of the room and the women in the other. But Jim and Skeeter soon saw why. The men had their bowl of punch and the women had theirs. Occasionally, one of the men would pour whiskey from a bottle into the men's punch.

"Hail," Skeeter whispered to Jim, gloom in his voice, "looks like if we're gonna dance, we'll have to win a footrace."

"That sure leaves me out," Jim said.

The two young cowboys stood against a wall and studied the people. There were women of all ages and sizes, and all talking cheerfully. "Man,"—Skeeter was exuberant again—"I'd like to cut out that little heifer in the yaller dress. Or that one next to the winder. Or, say ain't that the lady banker? The one that got you out of jail?"

Jim looked where Skeeter pointed. It was Miss Priscilla Newhouse, her hair combed out and tied with a blue ribbon. She still wore no makeup, but her face had a healthy glow. She was smiling and talking animatedly with two other women.

"That's her, all right," Jim said.

"Goddam. That is one damn good-lookin' woman."

105

"She'd do," Jim agreed.

"Do?" Skeeter turned, facing Jim. "Why hail, Slim, I'd go barefooted all winter just to hold her hand."

Jim laughed. "She's not hard to get acquainted with."

"Oh yeah. Let's see you just walk up and start talkin' to 'er."

Jim had to back down. "I would, but..."

"Yeah?"

"Wait till the music starts, and I'll ask 'er to dance"

"You said you didn't know how to dance."

"Well, I'll have to watch other people and see if I can figure it out."

Across the room against the far wall, an overweight woman in a flowery-print gown sat at a piano while a skinny man with a prominent adam's apple and a drooping mustache tuned a violin.

When the music started, so did a minor stampede. The men didn't run as Skeeter had predicted, they scurried to the group of women. They tried to be polite, but they were afraid to waste time talking, afraid someone else would cut in. "Evenin' ma'am, would you care to..." is as far as one cowboy got before another man somehow managed to get between him and a pretty girl in a yellow dress.

Skeeter had joined in the stampede, and he too came back empty-handed. "I scooted as fast as I could without makin' a plumb fool of myself," he complained, "but there was three fellers ahead of me."

The piano was loud, and the fiddle could barely be heard above it and the noise of shuffling feet on the wooden floor. But the music had a rhythm. The musicians started out with a rousing "Under the Double Eagle," and Jim found himself tapping the floor with his good foot.

Skeeter punched Jim on the arm to get his attention and nodded toward the door. "Look who's here."

Jim looked, and commented, "At least he ain't got that pistol on him."

"No, but ol' Tooley's got a mean look on his pan. He'll start a fight with somebody before the night's over."

"Yeah. Big as he is, I'll bet he don't have no trouble gettin' a dance."

"Wail, if he picks on you tonight, he's gonna have four fists in his face, I'll promise you that."

"Same if he picks on you," Jim vowed.

The big, heavy-shouldered rancher went directly to the men's punch bowl and took a sip out of the dipper. Jim and Skeeter couldn't hear what he said, but they saw him scowl, take a pint whiskey bottle out of his hip pocket, and dump half its contents into the bowl. Someone slapped him on the shoulder and they both laughed. The two young cowboys could hear Tooley's "haw-haw" above the other noises.

The music stopped then and the men again gathered around the punch bowl, taking turns dipping the liquid out and filling their own cups.

"The way they're pourin' that stuff down their throats, it's weaker than I thought or they'd all be fallin' down drunk," Skeeter mused.

"Let 'em fall down drunk," said Jim. "That'll even the odds."

"Hail, come to think of it, that's right," Skeeter allowed. "Hail, if I had a bottle of whiskey I'd pour it in there myself."

Again the music started and again the men raced each other to the women. Within ten seconds there wasn't a woman in the room who was alone, and most of the men came back to the punch bowl disappointed.

Jim continued leaning against the wall, but Skeeter tried for a second time to find someone to dance with. "Hail, goddam," he said as he came back.

"We might as well go to the St. Louis Emporium," said Jim. "Maybe I can hook up with Maria. No sense standin' around here."

"Yeah. Let's go. Only thing that's gonna happen around here is two men are gonna try for the same girl and one's gonna take a poke at the other."

"No," Jim said, looking toward the door, "I doubt that. The marshal's here."

Marshal Delmar Chitlow had come in alone, taking off his high-crown gray hat and hanging it on a wall peg. He stood near the door with his arms crossed over his chest and looked over the crowd. His glance fell on Jim, then moved on. The silver-colored star on his shirt pocket glinted in the lamplight. The six-gun on his hip and the steely look in his eyes offered a warning to all potential troublemakers. He was the only man in the room carrying a weapon.

"Wail, we ain't even gonna see a fight now," Skeeter said. "Let's go."

As before, when the music stopped the men gathered around the punch bowl. And suddenly Skeeter had an idea. He grabbed him by the arm.

"Let's git outside. I got an idea."

CHAPTER 14

Skeeter was so eager to tell Jim about his idea that he half-pulled him out the door.

"What is it, Skeeter? What's this big idea of yours?"

"Come on. Let's git over to our horses."

"Why? What's...?"

"Come on."

Once they reached the tree where their horses were tied, Skeeter stopped and faced him. Jim stared at him curiously.

"Now," Skeeter said, "the problem is too many men, right?"

"Uh huh. So?"

"Too many men and not enough women," Skeeter repeated, "and the solution to that problem is to git rid of some of the men. Right?"

"Uh huh. You've had brainstorms before, though, and if you think I'm goin' to start a fire or somethin'..."

"Hail no, Slim. Nothin' like that. I got a better idea."

"Well, what is it?"

"Just listen to me a minute, will you? Just listen."

"All right, talk."

Skeeter was so excited he almost couldn't keep his voice down, and he repeatedly looked around to make certain no one else could hear him. "Now. The problem is how to git rid of some of them men, right? Now, what've you got rolled up in them blankets on your saddle?"

"I told you what I've got. I've got some epsom salt."

"That's right." Skeeter glanced around again, and managed to drop his voice. "What is epsom salt good for?"

"To soak sore bones in."

"What else?"

Jim pondered the question. "Well, it'll sure clean out your ol' guts in a hurry."

"There." Skeeter had a smug look on his face. "See what I'm tryin' to tell you?"

When the realization came to Jim, his face fell slack. His mouth dropped open. He whispered, "You couldn't...you wouldn't. In the punch? You wouldn't."

Skeeter just stood there grinning smugly and let Jim think it over.

And Jim, when the shock wore off, began to like the idea. "How can we? Boy, that'd sure send 'em to the bushes. Can we do it?"

"We'll figure a way."

"Damn, Skeeter, let's do it." Jim went to his horse, untied the roll of blankets, took out the box of epsom salt, handed it to Skeeter, and retied the blankets. The brown gelding stood patiently, but looked back at Jim as if to ask when they were going home.

"Now the problem," said Jim, "is how to pour this stuff in that bowl without gettin' caught. They'd kill us if they caught us."

The smugness disappeared from Skeeter's face. "Hail. I never thought about that. Thank on it, Jim."

"I'm thinkin'."

Jim put his head down and began walking around in a circle, deep in thought. Skeeter did the same. "Hail," Skeeter repeated, "there ain't no way we can git them yahoos away from that punch long enough."

"No way," Jim agreed.

They walked, studying the problem. Inside the school building, the musicians played a lively schottische. Women laughed and men whooped and hollered.

"Hail," said Skeeter.

"Damn," said Jim.

Jim widened his circle, grumbling. His left foot kicked an

empty whiskey bottle and sent it clattering. "I just can't think of a way. Can you, Skeeter?"

"I can't thank of a thang."

"Too bad," Jim said. "You had a good idea. It would've been funny."

"Yeah, but we need another idea."

Jim's foot hit the whiskey bottle again, and he bent over and picked it up. He started to throw it out of his way, then stopped suddenly.

"Say," he said thoughtfully. "Maybe. Just maybe."

"What?"

"The men are always dumpin' whiskey in that punch, right?"

"Right."

"Suppose one of us was to empty a bottle in it? Would they pay any attention?"

"Prob'ly not. Why?"

Jim held up the empty bottle. It was a quart size. "How much epsom salt will this hold?"

Skeeter's face brightened. He giggled gleefully. "Enough to give 'em all the scours."

Immediately, Jim grabbed the box of epsom salt, dropped to his knees, and opened it. "You hold the bottle and I'll pour."

They spilled about half the salt onto the ground, but they filled the bottle with the remainder.

Skeeter chuckled, "Man, there's gonna be a lot of dirty drawers tonight."

"A feller'll have to be careful where he steps around here," Jim said.

"All right." Skeeter stood up. "It was my idea, so I guess I ought to do it." He unbuttoned two buttons of his shirt and placed the bottle inside, down next to his belt.

"I'll help."

"Shall we go?"

"Let's do it. But be damn careful. If anybody gets wise, be ready to run like hell."

The two young cowboys stepped cautiously through the open door and stood quietly, checking out the crowd. The marshal gave them a thorough looking over, and Skeeter, for a terrible moment, feared the marshal would demand to see what was inside his shirt. But the lawman finally looked away.

"Whew," Skeeter whispered to Jim, "I thought for a minute there I was gonna dirty *my* drawers."

"Me too. He don't like us anyhow. Wish he'd leave."

"He don't act like he's goin' to. Let's git it done."

"Wait. The music is goin' to stop pretty soon and they'll all be over here. Wait till it starts again."

The music ended with a plaintive squeal of the fiddle, and the dancers stood still and applauded. The fiddler carefully placed his instrument on top of the upright piano and headed for the men's punch bowl. The woman pianist stood up and headed for the women's punch bowl.

"Oh hail," Skeeter whispered, "they're gonna take a rest. The men'll all be over here now."

The fiddler said something about the bowl being nearly empty, and one of the women made her way through the crowd with a gallon pitcher of punch, which she poured into the men's bowl.

A bow-legged rancher wearing new Levis complained that she was diluting the refreshments, but he got no sympathy from her.

"You men are drinking too much anyway," she said.

Someone said he'd go get another bottle, and another tasted the punch, smacked his lips, and said he hoped somebody had a bottle because this tasted like sugar water. The crowd discussed it for a minute, then gradually moved away, preferring to commingle with the women. They visited and laughed, and above the noise came Jake Tooley's "Haw-haw."

"Now's the time," Skeeter whispered.

"Yeah, let's do it."

Skeeter glanced around and made his way—trying to act casually—to the punch bowl. Jim went with him. At the bowl, Skeeter unbuttoned his shirt and took out the whiskey bottle. Jim positioned himself between the bowl and most of the crowd.

"Now there's a good man," said the rancher in new Levis when he spotted Skeeter's bottle.

"Yeah." Skeeter had a scared and sickly grin on his face.

"Thought I'd, uh, spike it up a, uh, a little."

The rancher started to walk over, and Jim hurriedly moved to a spot between him and Skeeter. Skeeter dumped the contents of the bottle into the bowl.

The rancher stepped around Jim and clamped a hand on Skeeter's shoulder, and for a moment Skeeter's face went white. But with his other hand, the rancher picked up a tin cup, handed it to Skeeter, and said, "It's your whiskey, so you ought to get the first drink."

"Wait, uh, yeah," Skeeter stammered. "Yeah, I guess that's right." He took the dipper, stirred the liquid, and poured some into the cup. He glanced at Jim, licked his lips, and put the cup to his mouth.

Jim was horrified and he felt like yelling, "Don't," but he knew he had to keep quiet. Skeeter took a tiny sip, smacked his lips, said "Not bad," and walked away.

The rancher filled another cup and soon three more men gathered around the bowl. Skeeter made his way to the door, and, glancing around to make sure he was not being watched, threw the liquid from his cup out the door. Then he and Jim positioned themselves against the far wall to see what would happen.

Another man came up and emptied a bottle into the punch, which someone then tasted and allowed it was just right. And soon a crowd gathered, the men taking turns filling their cups.

Skeeter glanced at Jim but kept his face straight. Jim glanced at Skeeter, deadpan. They watched.

Men stepped back as Jake Tooley made his way through the crowd. Someone handed him a filled cup. Tooley drank it all, said, "Ahhh," wiped his mouth with the back of his hand, grabbed the dipper, and filled the cup again.

Skeeter glanced at Jim, and this time he couldn't hold back a smile and a "Humph." He immediately cleared his throat and wiped the smile off his face. Jim glanced at Skeeter and had to clamp his lips shut to keep quiet. When that didn't work he had to put his hand over his mouth. But he managed to disguise what he was doing by scratching his jaw and looking up at the ceiling.

Tooley poured the remainder of his pint bottle into the bowl and bellowed to the crowd that now the punch would taste like a man's drink. Then he helped himself to another cup full.

The two young cowboys over against the wall suddenly went into coughing convulsions. Skeeter's face was red and tears streamed down his cheeks as he coughed and hacked to camouflage his laughter. Jim had to turn his back to Skeeter and face the wall, also coughing and sputtering.

One of the men paused with his cup halfway to his mouth, looked over at Jim and Skeeter curiously, then finished his drink. Skeeter let out a loud guffaw before he could clamp his hand over his mouth. Jim almost strangled, and his cheeks puffed out like two balloons. Skeeter's shoulders shook and he danced around as if he were having a seizure.

A short time later the music started again, and the man who had tried many times to dance with the girl in the yellow dress finally got her in his arms. But only for a second. He was roughly shoved aside by Jake Tooley. He and Tooley glared at each other for a moment, then the man turned away. Tooley danced with the girl. His "Haw-haw" drowned out the music at times.

When Skeeter saw that, he stopped his hacking and coughing. "Just wait, you son of a bitch," he muttered, "and you'll be dancin' the backyard trot."

The first man to feel a gurgle in his stomach was, fortunately, standing near the door. A strange expression came over his face, and he ducked outside. Soon another bow-legged gent followed him. Then another. The music continued, but women were being abandoned.

When the music ended, Tooley bowed awkwardly to his pretty partner, and made his way back to the punch bowl. He filled a cup and drank it down.

"I'll bet we can get in on the next dance," Jim said.

"Just pick a girl. Which one do you want?"

"Ain't decided yet. How about you?"

"That gal in the yaller dress. She's as cute as a spotted pup."

"Watch ol' Tooley," Jim said out of the side of his mouth. "He's about to have an enema."

Tooley, over by the punch bowl, was rubbing his stomach and looking a trifle ill.

"I thank I'll hooraw 'im a little." Skeeter grinned, and headed

Tooley's way.

The crowd around the punch bowl had thinned out considerably when Skeeter stepped in front of the burly rancher. Tooley scowled at him.

"You know what I don't like about you, Tooley?" Skeeter said, keeping a straight face.

"Huh?" Tooley said.

"I said, 'Do you know what I don't like about you?'"

"You lookin' for a busted jaw?" Tooley straightened up to his fullest height and balled his big fists.

"I'll tell you why," Skeeter persisted.

The big man stood with his fists ready, knowing he could handle the young cowboy in a slugging match. But then his stomach gurgled, and he felt an urgent call from nature.

"You're full of shit, that's why."

Tooley bellowed, "Why, you little...I'll, uh..." A painful expression came over his face. He sputtered. "I'll, uh—" Suddenly, he wheeled and ran through the door.

Jim couldn't help it then, and the laughter exploded from him. He laughed so hard his knees were weak and he had to lean against the wall for support. Skeeter joined him.

"Did you see...ol' Tooley's...face?" Jim sputtered between guffaws.

Skeeter too found talking difficult. "He...he...had his pants halfway down...before he got out the door."

"He looked like a man...with the...St. Vitus's dance."

Across the room, Marshal Delmar Chitlow stood with his hands on his hips, staring at the two young cowboys. He knew they were up to some kind of orneriness, but he hadn't figured out what they were up to.

When music filled the room again, Skeeter wiped his eyes with a shirt-sleeve, sniffed his nose, and managed to control his laughter. "Now's my chance," he said as he headed for the pretty girl in the yellow dress. He had no competition, and he flashed a grin at Jim when he whirled the girl about in the middle of the floor.

Jim looked around and saw several unattached women, and he wanted to try dancing. But the music was a fast waltz, and he decided to wait for a slower piece.

Skeeter was grinning from ear to ear when he rejoined Jim. "Now that's what we came here for. Her name's Genevieve and her dad's a blacksmith. I'm gonna dance with 'er again and ask 'er if I can call on 'er sometime. Say," he said, noticing Jim's quiet mood, "when're you gonna give it a try?"

"Soon's they play somethin' slow," Jim said. "I ain't gettin' around too fast on this ankle, and I don't want to make a fool of myself."

"Hail, if you can walk you can dance."

The next number was a slow fox trot. Skeeter again danced away with the girl in the yellow dress, and Jim watched Skeeter's feet. Finally, by mustering all the courage he had, he decided to ask someone to dance. He looked over the available women and spotted Miss Priscilla Newhouse.

With his heart in his throat, Jim approached her. "Good evenin', Miss Newhouse, would you, uh..."

"Good evening, Mr. Kinslow. I would love to dance with you." She lifted her arms and Jim took her right hand in his left, held it out, and put his other hand on her waist. He shuffled his feet uncertainly, not knowing how to start and determined not to favor his sore ankle. "I, uh, have to apologize, Miss Newhouse. I never done this much."

"Don't worry, Jim. May I call you Jim?"

"Yes."

"Fine. Call me Priscilla, will you?"

Jim was looking down at his feet, trying to figure out the steps. "Sure," he answered.

She moved closer so that her body was touching his and murmured, "Just relax and move with the music. You'll learn."

The young cowboy's knees turned to butter. He had never in his life known anything so soft, so feminine, so desirable.

"You're doing fine, Jim."

At the appropriate time, he uttered a weak "Thank you," and turned to go. But she held his arm. "Stay and visit awhile, Jim. The punch will wait."

"Sure, Miss Newhouse—I mean, Priscilla."

Jim felt uncomfortable, and that feeling was aggravated when

116

Skeeter walked past and winked at him.

"Margaret tells me you are doing wonderful work at the H Bars," she said. "I'm so happy about that. They owe you a great debt. Are you nearing the end of your work?"

"Yes ma'am—I mean, Priscilla. It won't take much longer. John'll have thirty-eight good young horses to sell."

"The horse market is still good," she said. "This will give them the capital they need to catch up on the mortgage payments and make a few improvements on their property."

"Yes," Jim said, finding her easy to talk to and feeling less uncomfortable. "He's got a good bunch of three-year-olds that'll be ready to break and sell next year, and a crop of two-year-olds to break and sell the year after that."

Her eyes were frank but lively with interest. "I believe the Holcombs will do fine now."

"First they have to sell these four-year-olds," Jim said.

"But that should be no problem. Some Army officers will be here in October; and all john has to do is show that the colts are broken properly, and he will get a good price for them. He will need you to show them."

"I'll stay till then."

"Where will you go then, Jim?"

"Back to Texas, I guess. I'm a southerner. I don't like the cold."

"You don't have to leave, Jim. There are opportunities in the livestock industry here. I—the bank—can help."

"Thank you, Miss Newhouse. Priscilla. But I don't know exactly what I'll do."

"Think about it, will you."

"Yes, ma'am. Priscilla. I'll do that."

"And don't forget, I owe you a debt. If there is any way I can repay you, just holler. Understand?"

"Yes ma'am."

CHAPTER 15

The next number was another slow foxtrot, and Jim managed to keep his feet moving slowly with Priscilla Newhouse in his arms and without stepping on her toes, and again he felt as if he were made of rubber. But when that number ended, the musicians hardly took a breath before they went into another schottische. Jim knew he couldn't manage that one.

He had to step aside when a well-dressed man bowed before Priscilla Newhouse and asked for the dance. She excused herself to Jim and danced away in the other man's arms. Jim watched them a moment. The man was dressed in a gray coat and vest with a cravat at his throat. He wore matching gray pants and gray spats. His mustache was neatly trimmed and his black hair was neatly combed straight back. He had the appearance of a successful man.

Envy welled up in the young cowboy, and when he looked down at his scuffed boots and faded denim pants, he was almost ashamed of himself. He found Skeeter at their favorite place against the wall. "Well anyhow, I danced a couple of times," he said, trying to keep jealousy out of his voice.

"Me too," Skeeter said. "But she had to go home. Her folks left and she had to go with 'em."

"We might as well go too."

"Yeah." Skeeter glanced around, caution in his eyes. "Some of these men've come back from the bushes and they're beginnin' to look us over."

"Let's git, then. But slow. Try not to look guilty."

"I'm tryin'," Skeeter assured Jim soberly. "Believe me, I'm tryin'."

Carefully, slowly, doing their best to look innocent, the two young cowboys made their way out the door and to their horses. There, they mounted, said "Adios" to each other, and went their separate ways.

It was way past Jim's usual bedtime when he settled in between his new blankets, but it seemed he had no more than dozed off when John Holcomb was shaking him awake.

"Wake up, Jim. Hell's busted loose."

"Huh?" Jim sat up, blinked in the lamplight, and rubbed his eyes.

"They run 'em off, Jim. Came in the night and run off all my young horses."

"Huh?" The hired cowboy blinked stupidly, trying to shake the sleep out of his eyes. "Who?"

"You know who. I heard you come in last night, but I figured there was no use goin' after 'em in the dark so I let you sleep. It'll be daylight soon. We got to get after 'em."

Suddenly, what John Holcomb was saying got through to Jim's sleep-drugged mind. He sat up with a jerk and reached for his shirt.

"They headed north, toward the high country. We can track 'em. It ain't rained in a month."

Jim dressed cowboy-fashion. Not until he had his shirt buttoned did he swing his legs out from under the blankets. Working hurriedly, he pulled on his boots then stepped into his pants. He was still buttoning his pants as he half-ran out the door of the bunkhouse, Holcomb hobbling along behind him.

The boy was awake, sitting up, blinking.

"Did they leave anything at all?" Jim asked.

"They left the team and saddle horse I kept up, but that's all."

Jim hurried to the barn corral and was relieved when he saw the one saddle horse that Holcomb had been keeping up. The horse was an older, gentle sorrel gelding.

"He'll do," Jim said, pulling his saddle off a rack in the dark barn.

"You got to wait till daylight, Jim. Might as well take a bite of breakfast."

"When did they run 'em off? Did you see who it was?"

"Right after dark. I heard 'em and grabbed my rifle, but it was too dark and I was afraid I might hit one of the colts."

"Did you see who it was?" Jim repeated.

"No, but I can make a damn good guess. I saw three men and there might have been more."

"It wasn't Jake Tooley. He was at the dance last night."

"Then it was his hired help."

"Where would they go with 'em? Can they git over the mountains?"

"They could, I guess. They could haze 'em up to Willow Creek, up there about six miles, then follow the creek west. They could come down out of there on the other side of town, then they could go south to New Mexico or west to Durango."

Jim pulled the cinch tight on the sorrel and led the horse out of the corral. He shivered in the cool, predawn air. "Maybe I can stick a couple of biscuits in my pocket. And some cold meat, if you've got any."

"Sure, sure. Help me harness and hitch up the team, Jim, and I'll go for help."

"Judgin' from what I seen of that sheriff, he wouldn't be much help. Those rustlers'll be so far gone by the time he can get a posse together, he'd never catch 'em. I'd better git on their trail."

"You're right, but you can't do much by yourself. You can bet they'd shoot you on sight."

"I can trail 'em and see which way they're goin'. If they're goin' west they'll have to pass town somewhere, and the sheriff can get on their trail without comin' back here."

"Yeah, that might be the best thing to do. But hell, what if they're goin' east?"

Jim paused before buckling the hame strap on one of the harness horses. "Damned if I know what I'll do. Just see which way they went and hope."

Jim walked to the house, leading the sorrel. He found Maggie Holcomb up and mixing a batch of pancake batter. In spite of her

120

protests, he didn't wait for breakfast, but instead stuffed a handful of cold biscuits into his shirt pockets. While he was doing that, John Holcomb came out of another room carrying a rifle in a saddle boot.

"Take this, Jim. And keep your eyes peeled. Anybody that would steal horses would kill a man."

Jim took the rifle. "Don't worry, I will."

It was still dark, but daylight was just beginning to show itself on the eastern horizon when Jim reached the northern limit of Holcomb's fenced pastures. He got down to open the gate, saw that it had been left open, glanced to the east, and wished daylight would hurry. He dropped on his hands and knees and groped with his fingers for hoofprints. He knew that if he took off in the wrong direction he would lose the trail right there. He had to be sure of which way the young horses were driven before he went farther.

"You'd think a blind man could follow the tracks of that many horses," he said to the sorrel. "We know they went north this far, but maybe they went west from here, stayin' just under that high ridge. They could of got around town in the dark. Or they could of gone east. There ain't another town east of here for a hell of a ways."

He stood up, glanced again at the eastern horizon. "They'd have to cut some fences if they went east, but that wouldn't bother 'em. They'd have to cut some fences if they went west too—unless they got up in the high hills where they ain't any fences."

Jim squatted again and looked at the ground. "Come on, daylight."

Within a few minutes, he was able to barely see the tracks and he mounted the sorrel. "All right, now, we can wait awhile and follow the tracks, or we can move on and take a chance of goin' in the wrong direction. Let's think about it a minute.

"John once said there's a trail goin' north right up into those mountains and he said it joins another trail up there somewhere that follows a creek to the west. There ain't no trail goin' east, he said. Nobody's goin' to try to drive a bunch of horses over these mountains where they ain't no trail. So if they went north from here, they went up to that creek and now they're foggin' it to the west around the town."

Jim mulled that over, then, "Know what, ol' horse? I'm bettin' they went right up into those hills. Let's lope, ol' horse."

They didn't go far before they reached a narrow trail that followed a dry creek bed uphill, and by that time the light had improved enough that Jim could see he had guessed right. Jim put his hand on the stock of the rifle, which he was carrying in a leather boot under his right leg. He liked the feel of it, and wondered whether he should carry it in his hand in case he had to use it in a hurry.

No, he decided, that would probably be useless. If they saw him first he wouldn't even know where the bullet came from. And there was a good chance they would see him first. Unless they needed all hands to fog those colts along, one man would be watching their backtrail.

The thought of being picked off from ambush sent a cold chill up Jim's back and forced a groan from his lips. "Lord. What in hell am I doin', anyhow? They ain't my horses. How damn foolish can a man git?"

Jim made another decision. He would just follow the tracks to where they came down out of the mountains, then he would ride like hell for San Lomah and the sheriff's office. At least he could tell the sheriff which way they'd gone.

He rode on, climbing steadily. At places where the trail wasn't too steep he urged the sorrel into a trot. He only glanced occasionally at the ground in front of him, but his eyes were continually studying the hills, boulders, and trees far ahead.

"Damn," he muttered to himself. "If they git those colts strung out, one man in the lead and a couple more poppin' 'em from behind, they can travel almost as fast as I can. Come on, ol' horse."

It was midmorning when Jim reached Willow Creek, which was nearly dry this time of year. He had ridden over one high ridge and found the creek in between two ridges. It was almost hidden in dense willow bushes, but once he made his way through them, he saw that the trail went west, and he knew he was still following the stolen horses.

He allowed the sorrel to drink in the creek, then went on. Then he saw something that made him stop and wonder. More horse tracks. The size of the herd had doubled here. The herd of stolen horses had met another herd. Jim pushed his hat back and wiped a shirt-sleeve across his forehead.

"What the humped-up hell's goin' on? Did those gunsels steal horses from somebody else and gather 'em all up here? Naw. There's nobody else in this part of the country to steal horses from. What...? Uh oh, I see."

CHAPTER 16

What Jim saw were smaller tracks. Colt tracks. Young colts. This year's colt crop. "Hell, those fellers run into a bunch of John Holcomb's mares and colts.

"That's just dandy. Now they've got just about every head of livestock John Holcomb owns." The hired cowboy urged his mount into a gallop, his mind racing. He had to stop them somehow. He rode recklessly, the sorrel dodging boulders and jumping gulleys. He brought the horse to a sliding stop when he saw the mare and colt near the trail ahead of him.

The animals had obviously broken out of the herd and gotten away from the thieves. Then Jim saw another mare and colt farther ahead. He could guess what had happened. The young horses had gotten mixed with the mares and colts, and the whole bunch had milled together until the colts were separated from their mothers.

Jim grinned wryly. "That made 'em hard to handle. Instinct tells 'em to come back to where they last saw each other, and it'd take a whole crew of cowboys to keep 'em strung out and goin' in the right direction. I'll bet those yahoos were more than glad to cut the mares and their colts out of the bunch."

The cowboy was chuckling over that when he heard a wild whinny from up on the far ridge. He looked in that direction and got his first look at the Rafter H stallion.

The horse was on top of the ridge, watching Jim and the mares. Though Jim had never seen the horse before, he recognized him immediately. In the first place it was a stallion. It had to be, the way it was prancing nervously up there and the way it repeated its wild whinny several times. And in the second place it was no mustang. The stallion was obviously of good breeding, and it was of a larger breed than most cowponies.

For a moment, Jim sat and stared. "Now there's a horse. Just look at that brute."

The stallion galloped along the top of the ridge a short distance, then wheeled and galloped back, watching Jim, watching the mares. Suddenly, the cowboy's eyes narrowed. Something was not normal.

"He's not settin' those forefeet down right. No wonder. A horse'd have to have feet like a mule to run around in these rocks very long."

Another whinny from farther down the narrow trail brought Jim's mind back to the job he had set out to do. The whinny turned out to have come from another mare that had been let out of the herd, and Jim knew that the thieves were allowing the mares and colts to get away, not wanting to be slowed down by them.

And knowing that the thieves had been slowed by the unwelcome additions to their stolen herd gave Jim hope that he could catch up with them.

Then what?

John Holcomb had counted three of them and said there could be more. Three men could handle the stolen horses. If there were four, that would leave a man to watch behind them.

Jim shivered and looked ahead fearfully when the realization came to him that he could be in someone's gunsights right now.

And was it really necessary to keep on the trail? He knew now where the thieves were headed. Or did he? They had to come out of the high country west of San Lomah and head south from there. Or west.

Maybe, Jim thought, the smart thing to do was to go back the way he had come and then go to town and alert the sheriff.

No, that wouldn't do. John Holcomb had already alerted the sheriff by now. But *dammit*, the sheriff couldn't know which way the thieves were headed. If he got a posse together and they tried to follow the trail as Jim had, they would be so far behind they would be no help at all.

Jim sat his horse trying to decide what to do. The Rafter H stallion whinnied from atop the ridge, wanting to join the mares but afraid to do so as long as there was a human being in sight.

What good am I doing by following them? Jim asked himself silently. He doubted he could stop them. His one rifle against their three or four gave them all the odds. All he could do was get himself killed. And for someone else's stock.

The smart thing to do was to turn the sorrel around and go back, and Jim had just about decided to do that when another thought occurred to him. The young horses were all the Holcombs had between them and bankruptcy. Without them they had no income and they couldn't pay Jim for the work he had done. The cowboy reached another decision.

"It's John Holcomb's horses and my money," he said aloud. "Let's lope." The sorrel was rested now, and was easily urged into a slow gallop down the trail that paralleled the creek.

The creek ran between two high ridges for two more miles then crossed a wide meadowland, and that was where Jim found the rest of the mares and colts. Hi guessed that the rustlers had gathered all the horses into a bunch there and had cut out the mares and their colts to get rid of them. That had made it easier to get the stolen horses strung out and traveling. But, Jim smiled a grim smile, all that took time. He was gaining.

Except for small dips and rises, the trail was fairly level, and Jim kept the sorrel on a slow gallop. He could tell by the tracks that the stolen herd was being kept on a gallop most of the way. However, there were places where some of the young horses had tried to quit the trail and had had to be chased back. That, too, had taken time.

Jim lifted the rifle out of its boot and carried it in his right hand. While he rode, his eyes took in every rise in the terrain and every boulder large enough to hide a man.

Because he was watching carefully, he saw the puff of smoke before he heard the shot. He dismounted on the run and let the sorrel go on as the shot echoed back and forth between the ridges and hills. Another shot followed the first one within two seconds. The first bullet went over Jim's head and the second screamed off a rock near his feet.

Jim dove headfirst behind a small pile of boulders, carrying the rifle. He skinned the side of his face when he hit the ground but he didn't even notice.

He wanted to stay there, safely, behind the rocks. He could still hear the deathly scream the bullet had made when it ricocheted. A shiver went through his body. A man could get killed. How many times was he going to be shot at before he got John Holcomb's colts broke and collected his pay—if he ever did.

Just stay here, he told himself. You can't get shot behind these rocks. Nobody but a damn fool would risk his life for somebody else's horses.

If he stayed there long enough, the man who shot at him would move on and follow the stolen horses.

Then what?

Aw hell, he muttered to himself, I've thought about it and thought about it and I'm not quitting now. But what to do?

If he as much as looked over the rocks he was hiding behind he would be a target. He worried it over in his mind. He knew the shots had come from a rise about four hundred yards ahead.

Four hundred yards. It took a pretty good shot to hit a man at that distance. But one of the shots had come mighty close. The shooter was no greenhorn. What to do?

Jim remembered the old frontier trick of putting his hat on the end of the rifle barrel and holding it up a few inches above the rocks, just to see what would happen.

He felt foolish, but he tried it. Nothing happened. He moved the hat a little, the way a man would move. Still nothing happened. Finally, moving with caution, Jim looked around the edge of one of the boulders. He saw nothing except his sorrel horse grazing a hundred feet away.

He's gone, Jim thought. He saw he couldn't hit me and he went on. I can probably leave these rocks now without gettin' shot at. Maybe. That horse is right out in the open. I'd be a good target goin' after that horse. Jim squatted on his heels and thought it over.

Aw, he's gone. He prob'ly figures he's scared me off. Sure. It's safe to go after that horse now. I ain't goin' to walk back to the ranch.

And come to think of it, if all he wanted to do was stop me, why didn't he shoot that horse? I couldn't follow 'em on foot. He didn't wait to see what happened, that's why. He took two quick shots and left. Sure, that's what he did. Git on out there and get on that horse.

Sure. But what if I'm guessing wrong? I could be dead before I took five steps.

Again, a shiver went through the cowboy. But he had to do it. He couldn't stay there and cover up his head. His knees trembled and his throat went suddenly dry as he slowly stood up.

Keeping his eyes on the rise ahead, Jim walked to the horse, knees weak. The horse allowed him to walk up and pick up the reins. Holding the rifle and the saddle horn awkwardly in his right hand, Jim climbed into the saddle. What now? he asked himself for the tenth time.

He saw that the ridge to the north was parallel to the creek, and he decided it would be safer for him up there. They would be looking for him on the trail. Up there, he could look down at them. That is, if he could catch up with them. Climbing that ridge would take time, and the country up there would be rougher and harder to travel.

But he had no choice. The man with a rifle would be waiting for him somewhere ahead, and next time he wouldn't miss.

Jim reined the sorrel uphill.

By traversing the hill and by allowing the sorrel to stop twice and blow, he got to the top of the ridge. Up there, he could see in all directions, and he saw the thieves and stolen horses far ahead, following the creek.

Jim's first thought had been to let the sorrel rest a minute, but when he saw the stolen horses ahead he touched spurs to the animal and rode along the ridge, traveling in generally the same direction. He could only hope that the ridge continued paralleling the creek. It was rough going. Jim had to ride around huge piles of boulders and rock outcroppings while the men and horses on the trail below had much easier terrain to travel.

"Sorry, ol' horse. We can't lose 'em now," Jim said to the hard-working sorrel.

He rode at a gallop when he could, and slowed to a trot in places where the going was too steep or rocky. He was glad that

Holcomb had managed to shoe the horse before the accident had left him unable to do that kind of work. The sorrel was a good horse, but Jim wished he had ridden his faster, tougher brown gelding.

Most of the time, Jim was able to keep the stolen horses in sight, but he couldn't catch up with them. He counted four riders, and he was almost certain it was the same four who had tried to stampede the young horses into a tangle of barbwire and who had tried to murder him on the road from San Lomah. The distance between them was too great to see their faces, but one of them wore a red shirt. Hell, they had to be the same four. It was no coincidence that the exact same number of men were involved in three separate incidents.

Tooley's men? Sure. Ol' Tooley was at the dance and had an alibi, but Jim was willing to bet it was Tooley's idea to steal John Holcomb's young horses. Tooley knew Jim was at the dance and that John Holcomb, crippled and helpless, was the only man left at the H Bar Ranch.

"Some day," Jim muttered to himself, "there's goin' to be a reckoning."

The sorrel was tiring. Jim was using his spurs more and more. Still he couldn't catch up to the stolen horses. He was accomplishing nothing. He couldn't stop them. If it came to a gunfight, the odds were heavily on their side. All they had to do was leave one man behind to trade shots with him.

But the compulsion to follow them stayed with Jim, and all he could hope for was a break somewhere ahead.

Then he saw the break. The creek, while it was now going downhill, skirted a high hill to the south, cutting between the hill and the end of the ridge Jim was on. Jim hoped that by spurring the sorrel he could get to the end of that ridge, to where it dropped off sharply, at the same time the thieves started around the bottom of it.

"Sorry, ol' horse," Jim said as he raked his spurs along the animal's sides.

Riding hard and feeling sorry for his mount at the same time, Jim got ahead of the thieves to where the ridge dropped off into the creek. He figured they were just about straight north of San Lomah at that point, but far up in the hills. He knew the creek and the trail had to come out of the mountains somewhere, but he didn't know at what point.

Jim heard the bullet whistle over his head before he heard the shot. Again, he dismounted on the run, gripping the rifle. A volley of shots followed him as he ran in a crouch to the shelter of a rock outcropping. They had seen him and they were all shooting at him.

Rifle slugs *spanged* off the trees and smacked against the rocks. Chips flew off the trees.

Jim guessed that they intended to keep him down until they could get the stolen horses around the end of the ridge and on down the trail. They were succeeding. With bullets hitting the rocks and trees all around him, Jim didn't have the nerve to stick his head up. He crouched behind the outcropping, feeling a little like a turtle pulling its head into its shell.

He heard not only gunshots but shouts and the rumble of running hooves, and he knew they would soon be gone.

Get up and shoot, Jim told himself. Fire a few rounds. Do something. Did you come this far, ride the hell out of a good horse, just to let 'em scare you off? Get up, you skinny-assed, bow-legged Texas coyote.

To see if the rifle was loaded, Jim jacked the lever halfway down, cursing himself. Damn fool. Carrying a rifle without even checking to see if it's loaded. He was relieved to see that it was. The rifle was a Winchester, caliber .44-40. A good gun.

The volume of shots from below slowed. Now's the time, Jim told himself. He stood up, exposing himself from the waist up, saw a man on a horse below him, aimed quickly and fired. The recoil felt good against his shoulder and cheek. But he had fired too hastily.

Another half-dozen shots hit the rocks and trees around him, and he ducked down out of sight. Dammit, he cursed, I never claimed to be a gunfighter. Hell, I'm a workin' man. I never took a shot at anybody before. I don't want to kill anybody.

But dammit, those sons of bitches tried to kill me. They tried twice. No, three times now. And they ain't through yet. Jim levered another shell into the firing chamber. Next time take aim, he muttered.

CHAPTER 17

When he exposed himself the second time, Jim picked out a target, took two seconds to aim, and squeezed the trigger. The man half-fell off his horse and his hat went spinning. A wry grin turned up a corner of Jim's mouth. But then the man pulled himself back upright in the saddle, and another volley of shots came Jim's way.

A searing pain flared up on his left side, and he dropped behind his shelter. With shaking fingers he unbuttoned his shirt and saw a red welt along his rib cage. The bullet had creased his side, and it hurt, but there was no entry wound.

Anger surged through Jim as he looked at the wound. "Those sons of bitches." He stood up and fired again. He saw with satisfaction that the stolen horses had gone on down the trail while the four men were busy shooting at him.

To get to the stolen horses, the men would have to ride through a gap created by the hill on the south side of the creek and the end of the ridge to the north. If Jim could keep them from getting through it he could...

Could what?

Well, maybe—Jim's mind was working—maybe those colts will scatter when they hit the flats, and those sons of bitches, if they get by me, will have a hell of a time gatherin' 'em up again. If I cain't stop 'em, I can sure as hell slow 'em down—if I live long enough.

Jim walked on his knees to the edge of his shelter, then raised up onto one knee, resting his left elbow on it, and took aim at the man in the red shirt. The rifle barked and jumped in Jim's grasp. The man pitched sideways off his horse and fell on his face. The horse jumped into a run. The man stayed where he had fallen.

The other three men returned the fire but their shots were fired from nervous horses. Jim levered another shell into the firing chamber and squeezed off another round. One man ducked low over his horse's neck, but Jim knew it was the sound of the bullet, not an impact, that had caused him to duck.

The bullet had another effect. The thieves had been headed for the gap until the shot caused them to hesitate. If they continued riding they would have been good targets for Jim's rifle. But they stopped, dropped off their horses, and fired uphill at Jim.

Jim had to take cover. The men were in the open and they had nothing to lose by taking careful aim. Their bullets spelled death for anyone who got in their way.

Jim was safe behind his cover, but he knew that if he didn't return the fire the rustlers would soon be gone.

He raised up, fired hastily, and ducked. He counted to five and did it again. He could only hope that his rifle contained a few more shots. A heavy volley from below forced him down again.

Gunfire ceased then, and Jim guessed that they were waiting for him to show himself. Minutes passed. Jim took a quick look to see what they were doing, and ducked when another volley came his way.

Time passed. It was a stand-off, he realized. If they headed for the gap Jim could pick them off. If he raised up and took careful aim they would pick him off. More time passed.

Then a heavy volley raked the trees and boulders around Jim and quit as suddenly as it had started. Jim licked his lips for courage and raised up.

Two of the men were on horseback and riding hard for the gap. Jim sighted down the barrel of the Winchester.

Before he could squeeze the trigger a bullet knocked chips off a rock near his head. Chips stung his face and spoiled his aim. The two men rode to safety while another, still on foot, took aim at him and fired again.

The man's first shot had caused Jim to duck and the second did no harm. Jim counted to five and stood up again, and again a bullet came dangerously close. Then he saw the strategy of the three riders.

Two of them rode for safety while the third kept Jim from taking aim. Then one of the first two dismounted, crawled back to where he could see Jim without showing much of himself, and fired while the third one mounted and rode for safety.

It worked. Now they were all three out of Jim's sight.

In a short time they would be out of the mountains and down on the plains where they would gather the stolen horses and quit the country. By the time Jim got down off the ridge and onto their trail he would be far behind. And by the time he got the sheriff and a posse after them they would be far enough ahead that they would be hard to catch.

Disappointment and discouragement swept over Jim like a wave of nausea. "Dammit all, anyway," Jim muttered.

Well, he had trailed them this far, and he might as well go on, he decided. He found the sorrel behind a small hill, mounted, and reined the animal downhill.

He rode recklessly, sending the horse plunging down off the ridge, knowing that if it tripped it would somersault the rest of the way down. The horse miraculously reached the bottom of the ridge still on its feet.

The man in the red shirt had died instantly, Jim saw as he rode past. Blood was still pouring out of a hole as big as a silver dollar on the left side of the dead man's back. Red Shirt, or whatever his name was, hadn't felt a thing.

When he rode through the gap, Jim could see where the trail ran through a few piñons and cedars far below and petered out on the flatland. He saw the stolen horses already out of the hills and onto the flats, and he saw the three men riding hard a mile behind them. The riders would soon reach the flats, and then they would have ten thousand square miles of unfenced country to lose themselves in.

Jim's disappointment deepened.

But suddenly the three riders reined their horses to a stop. They milled, as if uncertain what to do.

It was then that Jim heard the far away *pop-pop* of gunfire from below. The three riders were being shot at.

They milled confusedly a few seconds longer, then spurred their

133

horses back uphill, toward Jim. They hoped to escape the shooters by heading back to the high country.

Jim dismounted and dropped to one knee. "They'll have to get by me first," he muttered. He took careful aim and fired, but the distance was too great to hit anyone. He jacked the lever down and discovered that he had fired his last bullet.

But the three riders didn't know that and they stopped, looked up Jim's way, then split up, riding hard through the piñons, two going west while the third went east.

More shots came from far below, and Jim could see two men in a gully firing rifles. He recognized them both—John Holcomb and Sheriff Walt Umbaugh.

Holcomb was sitting with both feet out in front of him, an awkward position for shooting, but the only one his bandaged leg would permit.

Smoke puffed from Holcomb's rifle barrel and a second later the sound of the shot reached Jim's ears. The rider heading east fell from his horse, got to his knees, and collapsed face down.

John Holcomb was getting revenge.

The other two riders disappeared, however, and Jim was disappointed when he saw no one chasing them. He saw Holcomb's team and wagon and knew that that was the only way Holcomb could travel. Jim looked for a saddle horse down there but saw none. It was obvious that the sheriff had ridden in the wagon with Holcomb.

There was no one to go in pursuit of the two escaping horse thieves but Jim, and Jim decided he wouldn't do it. He had ridden a horse half to death already, had suffered many narrow misses—in fact, one narrow hit—and it was the sheriff's job to chase horse thieves, not his.

He stood up, and yelled and waved his hat to let the shooters below know it was him, then mounted the hipshot sorrel.

He allowed the horse to take its time, and he got to where Holcomb and the sheriff were waiting about thirty minutes later. He noticed as he rode that the stolen horses were grazing and had not scattered too far. Rounding them up would not be too difficult. John Holcomb would get his horses back.

Holcomb was standing, leaning on his crutch, when Jim rode

up. "I got one and two got away," he said without enthusiasm. "Is that all of 'em?"

Jim dismounted wearily and loosened the cinches. "No. There's another one back up there, dead."

"You hurt, son?" the sheriff asked, eyeing the blood on Jim's shirt.

"Just a scratch."

"Let's have a look."

"No, I've been scratched worse by barbwire."

"Can you gather these ol' colts and haze 'em toward home?" Holcomb asked.

"Yeah, but I could sure use a fresh horse. This ol' pony has gone about as far as he can go."

"We'll have some help here any time now," Sheriff Umbaugh said, glancing back toward town. "I was just getting out of bed when John here came rattling up in his wagon and yelling like an Apache. I didn't take time to get anyone, but I sent a man after some help and climbed in the wagon and high-tailed it out here. There'll be some help coming along pretty soon."

Jim saw that the two harness horses hitched to the wagon were standing with their heads down and were wet with sweat.

"How did you know where to come?" he asked the sheriff.

Holcomb answered. "It took some fast thinkin', Jim. We knew they wouldn't go east in the mountains, because it's too hard to drive horses over those steep hills. And we figured they wouldn't go east under the mountains, because they would run into too much deeded land and wire fences. And we guessed they wouldn't drive stolen horses anywhere near town last night, 'cause there was a dance and too many men comin' and goin'."

Holcomb paused to see if the sheriff agreed with him. "But we knew that if they got up in the high hills and followed Willow Creek they would come down here west of town, and then they'd have nothin' but government land an' no fences clear to Mexico."

"It was a good guess," the sheriff added.

Holcomb looked down a moment than gave the sheriff a good-natured slap on the shoulder. "Aw, hell, Jim, I might as well admit it. It was Walt that figured it out."

"We heard shooting up there," the sheriff said. "What happened?"

"Oh, we traded some rifle bullets," Jim said.

Umbaugh stared curiously at Jim a moment, then said, "Well, whatever happened, you slowed them down. If you hadn't, we wouldn't have got here soon enough and they'd be halfway to the Mexican border by now."

"Yeah, we couldn't of chased 'em very far in the wagon," Holcomb said.

Though weary, as much from the tension as from the riding he had done, and though his bullet wound stung, Jim was pleased. Now he knew that his long day's ordeal had accomplished something. Now he no longer felt like a fool.

He grinned a shy grin. "I've got money tied up in those horses too, you know."

Umbaugh saw riders coming, and said, "Looks like a small army. Too bad they didn't get here sooner."

They waited until a half-dozen heavily armed men rode up, their horses blowing from the run. The sheriff told them in a few short sentences what they needed to know, and four of them spurred their horses up into the piñons and rocks, looking for any trail left by the two fleeing horse thieves. Two of them stayed behind upon request of the sheriff, and Jim could see by their outfits and the way they sat their horses that they were cowboys.

"Would you gentlemen mind helping him here gather those horses and drive 'em back to the Holcomb ranch?" the sheriff asked.

One of the men was a Rafter H cowboy who recognized Jim. "Hell no," he said cheerfully. "You just show us which way you want 'em to go, Jim."

They let Jim take the lead on the jaded sorrel, and with catch ropes swinging, they kept the young horses following him. It was dark by the time they got to the lane east of town where there were fences on both sides of the road. Holcomb had gone ahead with his tired team, promising he would leave the gate open.

Until then, Jim hadn't even thought about food, but now his grumbling stomach reminded him that he hadn't eaten since the day before. He ate the cold biscuits he had carried in his shirt pockets.

"I can take 'em from here," he allowed. "You fellers might as well go on back."

"All right, Jim."

"Have one for me at the St. Louis Emporium, will you?"

The cowboy chuckled. "I might even have two or three. Hope you like hard whiskey."

"In case you don't," the other cowboy put in, "I'll have some beer."

The young horses were tired too, and when they came to the open gate Jim didn't have to race ahead of them and turn them in. They turned into the gate voluntarily. They seemed to know they were going home, and they seemed to be glad to get there.

The sorrel was glad too. He managed to pick up his tired feet a little faster as they went through the gate.

"Just a little farther, ol' horse, and we'll be home. I'll git this saddle off your back, and you can roll in the dirt and scratch where it was, and then you can put your nose in some good feed."

The horse broke into a slow, shuffling trot.

CHAPTER 18

During the night, while Jim was mulling over the day's events in his mind instead of sleeping, he reached another decision: He would try to catch the Rafter H stallion.

"That old brown horse of mine ain't a racehorse," he told the Holcombs while Maggie Holcomb set breakfast on the table, "but he can outrun most horses. And I've got 'im standin' on good steel."

"You might be right." John Holcomb said. "I wish I could go with you. If that stud is sore-footed as you said, and your horse is shod, you just might be able to get within roping distance of him. I sure wish I could go with you."

Maggie Holcomb said breakfast was ready, and the men, the boy, and Maggie Holcomb busied themselves eating. As was the custom with cowboys, the men ate silently. But when the meal was finished, John Holcomb allowed that the young horses ought to rest a day or two before Jim resumed working with them, and he leisurely tilted his chair back on two legs and rolled a cigarette.

"When are you going to try it, Jim?"

"Tomorrow. I'll be up in those hills shortly after sunup. I know where that horse is now, and I won't have to hunt for 'im."

John Holcomb thumped his bandaged leg. "I wish I could go with you."

It was cold in the high country before sunup, and Jim shivered and wished he had worn a warm jacket. The wound on his left side hurt a little when he moved his left arm, but he didn't have to move the arm much to handle the reins. And even when he did, he could stand a little pain. He felt silly when he remembered how Maggie Holcomb had scolded him for his shyness and finally persuaded him to raise his shirt tail enough that she could apply the antiseptic she had concocted with warm water and powdered merbromin.

The brown gelding was feeling good and traveled along at a brisk walk, even when it had to climb the steep trails. "Save your strength, ol' feller," Jim said. "Your day's work ain't even started yet."

Jim took his borrowed catch rope down and threw a few practice loops at the rocks and bushes. He had done no roping from horseback at all since he had left the Rafter H, and he could only hope that his aim would be good when the time came.

A buck deer with a wide rack of antlers bounded like a large rubber ball across a small park ahead of him, and Jim allowed as how he would like to bring the rifle up there one day soon and get some fresh meat. "That one looks fat and juicy," he said to the horse, and then he remembered that he had again forgotten to strap on the .45. "I could prob'ly knock 'im down with a pistol," he mused, "but, oh well, that ain't what I'm here for."

The sun was high enough to warm up the air by the time Jim reached the high mountain valley where he had seen the mares. He reined up at Willow Creek, dismounted, loosened his saddle cinches, and let the brown horse rest and cool off after the hard climb. "Hope they're still in here and I hope that stud is with 'em. If he is, I'll bet he'll head up that same ridge again. If he don't, and if he heads down this valley along the creek where the runnin' is good, we'll have a hell of a time catchin' him."

The horse cropped the high country grass as if it was the best feed he had ever tasted. Soon Jim tightened the cinches again. "Well, ol' feller, are you ready for some hard runnin'?" He stepped into the saddle, tied the end of his catch rope hard and fast to the saddle horn, and rode forward cautiously.

The mares were there, and they raised their heads and watched him come. The stallion was there too, and he immediately took off running.

The rocky ridge was to Jim's right, and he lifted the brown gelding into a slow gallop along the left flank of the valley, hoping to scare the stallion into running up the ridge again. It worked.

Jim grinned. "He's a ridge-runnin' fool, ain't he. Look at him go."

The horse was running up the side of the ridge, scrambling at times to get over the rocks. The animal was not pretty.

It had the intelligent head, deep chest, and sloping shoulders of a thoroughbred, but its mane and tail were long and matted and weighted down with burrs and pine needles, and its dark bay coat was scarred in places.

The horse turned east, to a territory where there were no trails, and disappeared over the ridge just as Jim rode the brown gelding on a gallop to the bottom of it. He pulled the gelding down to a walk as it climbed the hill.

"Save your wind. He won't get away."

Instead of going straight up the hill as the stallion had done, the cowboy traversed the hill, making a switchback, and came out on top at the same place the stallion had. There, he stopped and allowed his mount to get its wind. "He ran along the top of this ridge," Jim said aloud, looking ahead, "but this ridge drops off up there somewhere. He had to get down."

He lifted the brown gelding into a slow gallop along the ridge, looking ahead and watching the ground for tracks. Suddenly, he reined up. "Yep. That ol' horse is smart. He seen he had to get down and he picked this spot. It's a good place, but he couldn't keep from leavin' tracks."

Instead of racing after the stallion, Jim stood in his stirrups and studied the valley below. It was covered in places with dense willows, and Jim guessed a small stream ran through them, similar to Willow Creek over the ridge to the south. He guessed too that the horse was standing in the willows, hiding.

"Let's just wait here a minute," he said as much to himself as to the horse he was riding. "That ol' pony, if I'm guessin' right, is curious. He'll have to look at his backtrail sooner or later to see if we're still after 'im."

Sure enough, the willows stirred in one spot, and a pair of bay equine ears poked above them. "Uh huh," Jim murmured. "He ain't so smart after all. An old cow would've laid down in that brush and we'd never of found 'er. Let's go. But easy. Maybe we can get closer before he takes off."

He rode down off the ridge, keeping his eyes on the spot in the willows where he knew the thoroughbred was hiding. "He'll hear us anytime now and take off like a striped ape," Jim mused.

Again, he had guessed right. The willows suddenly rippled and the stallion's head could be seen making its way through them. The animal instinctively left the willows, ran out into the open, and scrambled up another ridge on the other side of them.

This disappointed Jim. He had hoped the animal would stay in the willows where a horse could not run its best, and where he could keep track of it, and, hopefully, get closer. But now he had to beat his way through the thick willows and climb another ridge. "Well, ol' feller," he said, "I didn't expect it to be easy."

At the top of that ridge, him reined up and stood in his stirrups. The horse had disappeared. Looking around, Jim discovered that the country was a series of valleys and ridges, but up to the north, perhaps two or three miles away, the country seemed to drop off and change colors.

While the hills and valleys here were covered with green trees and brush, the country off to the north seemed to be brown and gray. Jim could see no sign of life in the valley below him, and he guessed that the horse was traveling north. He touched spurs to the brown gelding and galloped in that direction.

He knew he had guessed correctly when the top of the ridge flattened out and he could see tracks left by the stallion. "Now's the time to run," he said to his mount. "We can't let him get too far ahead."

Alternating his gaze from the ground immediately ahead to the country far ahead, Jim rode the gelding at a full gallop. He rode that way for several minutes before he spotted the stallion a half-mile ahead.

The ridge sloped gradually from there to another valley, this one wider, and Jim could see that on its north end the valley disappeared into a dozen or more acres of brush.

The race was on, then, and Jim rode recklessly. "Go get 'im, feller. Sic 'em." The brown gelding went willingly to work, and soon it was flattened out and running at breakneck speed. Both stallion and horseman sped down the top of the ridge, down its sloping end, and onto the valley floor, the stallion maintaining its half-mile lead.

Jim held the catch rope in his right hand, hoping that he eventually would get close enough to throw a loop around the stallion's head.

"Damn. We can't catch him down here," he said. "We got to get him in the rocks."

Running as only a thoroughbred could, the stallion skimmed over the cinquefoil and followed a course parallel with another small stream. The brown gelding did its best, but the thoroughbred pulled farther away.

Jim knew there was no use in spurring. It would only shorten the horse's stride. Jim carried no whip and he wouldn't have used one anyway; he knew his mount was running its best. "Go get 'im, feller," Jim hissed. "Get after 'im, boy."

They covered the mile length of the valley, the stallion gradually spreading the distance between them, and then they were in thick scrub oak, so thick that the horses had to push their way through.

And still the race continued. The brush tore at Jim's clothes, ripping the side of his shirt. It tore at his face, and he had to duck his head and let the brim of his hat take the beating. By doing that he lost sight of his quarry. His hands on the reins were scratched by the brush, and he was almost dragged out of his saddle several times. He wished he had worn chaps and a heavy duck jacket, but then realized he was glad his mount did not have to carry the extra weight.

The cowboy cursed and endured the beating he was taking and continued urging his mount on. Then they broke out of the buckbrush into a kind of country that Jim had never seen before. He reined up for a moment to get his bearings, and saw the stallion racing over rocky but grassless ground three-quarters of a mile ahead. He sent the brown gelding racing after it.

The terrain supported little vegetation and was rocky and full of shallow gulleys. Steep bare hills rose on either side. Jim paid no attention. He kept his eyes on the thoroughbred, and saw that they were finally gaining.

"Atta boy. The rocks're slowin' him down. Keep goin', feller. Keep them long legs a-goin'."

The brown gelding was blowing hard, running on sheer will power, jumping the gulleys. And it was gaining. Up ahead, the stallion jumped a gulley, stumbled, and went down on its knees, but bounded up immediately and went on.

"His feet're givin' him trouble. We'll get him." The brown gelding was slowing, its heart pumping, its lungs almost to the bursting point. But the stallion was slowing too.

The distance between them narrowed, a quarter-mile. Two hundred yards. The race continued.

Jim built a loop in his rope, made certain the end was tied hard and fast to the saddle horn.

A hundred and fifty yards.

They were running along a dry stream bed now, but the ground was still rocky in places. Ahead a mile or so, the country rose into a steep cliff, and the dry stream bed entered a narrow canyon. "We got to get him before he gets in there," Jim muttered. "If I rope him there, we'll have a hell of a wreck."

A hundred yards.

The cowboy was whirling the loop over his head now to put some power behind his throw—when the time came to throw. The distance narrowed.

"A little closer, feller. Just a little closer."

The brown gelding was reaching with its nose for the stallion's left hip, and Jim had the loop whirling over his head, looking for a shot.

Both horses had run almost as far as they could run, and both had slowed considerably.

"Two more yards, feller," Jim pleaded. "Give me two more yards."

The saddle horse tried. Its nose, with nostrils flaring, reached a little closer.

"Another yard. Come on, ol' feller. Just give me another yard, will you."

The saddle horse staggered, but continued on.

"Please, feller. Don't quit now." The cowboy gritted his teeth in desperation. "I promise, you'll never have to work another day. Just one more yard."

And then Jim was in position. His mount had its nose almost to the stallion's left hip. All right, cowboy, Jim muttered to himself, you'll only get one shot. Don't miss. He whirled the loop twice more and pitched it straight out, like a man throwing a baseball.

The loop shot out flat. The honda—the eye in the loop—hit the stallion just below and behind the left ear. The noose sailed around its head.

Instantly, Jim grabbed the body of the rope with his throwing hand and jerked it upward. The noose was pulled snug around the stallion's neck right behind the ears. It was a perfect catch.

"Atta boy," Jim congratulated his mount. "You put me right up there, feller. Atta boy." He lifted the reins. "All right. Slow down, but don't jerk 'im too hard. We don't want to hurt 'im. These thoroughbreds're easy to hurt, you know."

When the stallion felt the pull on its neck, it dropped its head between its front feet and took a long jump. Jim brought the gelding to a stop and played the horse on the end of the rope like a fly fisherman plays a trout. The animal squealed, jumped, and bucked.

"Easy, ol' horse," Jim said. "Easy now."

Finally, the stallion stopped, faced its captors, and stood still, spraddle-legged, head down, blowing hard. Jim allowed his saddle horse to stand still and blow.

Both animals were so winded they were unsteady on their feet, and once the gelding staggered and almost fell over. Jim was sorry for it, but he didn't dare dismount and loosen the cinches. Not yet.

Gradually, the animals' breathing slowed, and the stallion tested the rope again. It reared, pawed the air, and tried to turn away. The rope jerked it back facing its captors again. It reared and took four steps on its hind legs toward Jim. For a moment, Jim feared he was going to be knocked out of his saddle, but the horse dropped to all fours and tried to turn away.

"Easy, ol' horse. You're s'posed to be a broke horse, you

know."

The stallion was facing Jim again, and Jim turned his mount around to see if the stallion would lead. It pulled back, then lunged forward, and Jim turned back.

"You forgot all about it, didn't you, ol' horse. I guess we'll have to remind you of it."

Whooping, Jim spurred the gelding forward, and the stallion wheeled and tried to run. Jim brought the gelding to a sudden stop and the stallion was jerked around hard.

"Want to try it again?" Jim spurred forward again, but this time the stallion held its ground. "It's comin' back to you, ain't it, ol' horse."

Man and stallion eyed each other a moment, and Jim dismounted. He tied the reins to the rope so that his saddle horse could not turn away from the stallion, then started walking forward.

"What would you do, ol' horse, if I scratched your neck? Would you keep your feet on the ground?" Jim inched forward. The stallion watched him and snorted.

"They told me you was a broke horse. You was raised in a barn, you know." Jim talked quietly, steadily. "Remember that good grain you used to eat? And that good hay?" He was close enough. He reached out.

The stallion backed up until the rope tightened. "It ain't so bad bein' a tame horse, is it? Better'n pawin' the snow for every bite of grass you get in the winter, ain't it?"

Cautiously, the cowboy touched the stallion on the neck. The animal snorted and rolled its eyes, but stood still. Then Jim was rubbing the horse's neck and shoulders. "It's comin' back to you, ain't it, ol' horse. Would you let me lead you now?"

Still moving carefully, Jim untied the rope from the saddle horn and fashioned a halter out of it. "I hate to tie knots in a good catch rope," he said to the stallion, "but this time it's worth it. You're worth it."

The halter made, Jim stepped to one side and gave the rope a slight pull. The stallion followed him. "Well, I'll be damned. You are a broke horse. Well, I'll be damned."

The cowboy stood back and looked critically at the stallion.

"You sure need them feet trimmed. And that mane and tail. But when I get you trimmed and curried, you'll be a hell of a good-lookin' horse. And"—pride welled up in the cowboy—"you'll belong to me."

The horse stood just over fifteen hands, and Jim judged it to weigh around thirteen hundred pounds. It was a dark bay with a black mane and tail and black lower legs, and two white spots, one around the right hind pastern and the other a diamond-shaped blaze between the eyes.

Jim led the horse around a while, then led it up to his saddle horse. The brown gelding was breathing normally now, and Jim stepped into the saddle. "Let's head for home," he said, squinting at the lowering sun.

CHAPTER 19

It was not until he was on his way back that Jim took a good look around. The country was drastically different from the mountainous terrain where the chase had begun. Instead of tall pines, the trees here were short piñons and cedars; instead of sloping ridges the hills rose almost straight up.

The cowboy found himself inside a huge bowl with one edge chipped away to form a deep V. He headed for that V, which was almost hidden by the dozen or more acres of scrub cedars.

The stallion was leading well and both horses were trotting along steadily, and the cowboy's eyes often widened in wonderment at the terrain. The cliff that formed the eastern side of the bowl seemed to be made of a different material than the other sides. It was of soft sandstone and was dotted with holes created over the centuries by wind and rain. Jim was looking up at the cliff when he rode past a short narrow pocket reaching back into the cliff a hundred feet. He stopper and stared in amazement.

The end of the pocket rose vertically for a hundred yards or more. But what amazed Jim was the erosion hole in the end of the pocket. It was larger than most and instead of being the usual round hole, this one had nearly-square corners. Jim guessed that at one time the hole had been square, and he guessed that it had been manmade. He was certain of that when he saw that a narrow bench ran horizontally under the hole, and that crude stair-steps had been hacked out of the cliff leading to the bench.

It was spooky in the dim light, and the cowboy could not help looking over his shoulder, half-expecting to see ghosts of long-dead Indians. He rode on, feeling a scary chill on the back of his neck.

The sun had already disappeared over the rim of the bowl to the west, and Jim rode at a steady trot until he came to the buckbrush. He made his way through that, then struck a steady trot again and maintained that speed until he came to the gate at the Holcomb ranch. It was long after dark when he rode up to the corrals and dismounted. But Jim was not in the dark long. Two lanterns came bobbing toward him, and when they got close he saw that they were carried by John and Maggie Holcomb. The boy was with them.

"Is that him." John Holcomb asked, excitement in his voice. "Did you catch him?" He raised the lantern and looked closely at the captured stallion. "Yes, by God—excuse me Maggie—it is him. How'd you do it, Jim?"

"Just ran him down."

Maggie Holcomb was excited too. "Isn't he big. He's not pretty, though."

"He'll look better when Jim gets him curried and trimmed, won't he, Jim. Did he give you much of a run?"

"All I wanted," said Jim. "He almost ran the legs off this poor old horse of mine. If he hadn't made the mistake of runnin' onto some rocky ground, I never would of caught 'im."

John Holcomb squatted and studied the stallion's hooves. "Yep. That's what done it. Look at them—those—feet. Most horses wouldn't even try to run with feet like those."

"He's got a lot of heart," Jim said. "He never gave up till he knew he was caught."

They put the stallion in a corral by itself, threw some hay into the corral, then gave Jim's brown gelding the same kind of care. "I'll get to work on those hoofs first thing in the mornin'," Jim said.

After supper, when the dishes were stacked and cigarettes were rolled, Jim told the Holcombs about the country he had chased the stallion into. He told about the square hole in the cliff and the stair-steps leading to it. He said he would go back there within the next few days and take a closer look. "But when I go back I'm goin' while the sun is up high. It's spooky around there in the evenin'."

148

"I got as far as the buckbrush once," John Holcomb mused, "but I didn't go no farther. Looked to me like there was no end to that brush."

"I wouldn't of gone into those scrubs if that horse hadn't led me there," Jim allowed.

"Do you know what I think?" Maggie Holcomb wiped her hands on her apron and sat at the table with them. "I think that cave was created by wind and rain erosion like the other holes in the cliff, and then someone, Indians probably, chiseled it out to make it larger, and squared the entrance."

"That's the only possible explanation," John Holcomb said, striking a wooden match on the sole of his boot. "It sure bears looking into."

The boy sat at the table with them, his chin in his hands, his ears taking in, and his mind cataloging, everything that was said— everything that he could understand.

"It had to of been a long time ago," Jim said, "'cause the corners ain't too square and the steps ain't too square anymore, either. I'm not sure a man can climb those steps."

"Of course," Maggie Holcomb agreed. "If that cliff is sandstone it would erode very easily, and the wind would, over the years, round off the sharp edges."

They talked far into the night, way past the boy's bedtime, but the boy's eyes never quit shifting from one adult to the other as they spoke.

The Rafter H stallion stood quietly as Jim, using heavy nippers and a rasp, trimmed its hooves. The hooves were badly overgrown and broken, and Jim allowed they would have to grow and be trimmed again before they could be shaped properly. John Holcomb was able to stand on one foot at his forge and make some light shoes out of pieces of windmill steel, and Jim tacked the shoes on, using only six nails for each shoe.

"They'll have to be pulled off and the feet trimmed again in about a month," he said. "It'll take several trimmin's and shoein's before those hoofs are shaped right."

Next, Jim went to work on the horse's mane and tail. He combed and brushed the mane until it lay on one side, and he yanked hairs, a few at a time, from the tail until he got it shortened to a point just below the hocks.

By noon, he had the stallion looking like a cared-for domestic animal.

The two men ate a cold lunch alone that day. Maggie Holcomb had gone to town in the light wagon. She had taken the boy with her so she could continue his English lessons while the team pulled the wagon to and from San Lomah.

John Holcomb had been strangely quiet, as if he had something on his mind, and finally he spoke about it. "I've got to get some money out of the colts soon, Jim." He seemed to be a man with worries who just had to talk to someone, and his employee was the only human present. "Maggie took our last dollar with her to buy some flour and baking soda."

He glanced at Jim, saw that Jim was interested, and went on. "The bank won't extend its note again. We've got ten days to raise some cash or the bank'll sell this place right out from under us. I tried to sell some of my mares and colts last spring, but nobody wanted to buy horses they couldn't put to work."

Jim filled two cups with coffee and sat. "I didn't think Miss Newhouse would do that to you."

"She ain't got a thing to say about it. It's the directors' decision."

"Well, John, you got as good a bunch of young horses as there is anywhere, and in a few days they'll all be ready to use."

"Oh, I know I can sell 'em somewhere sooner or later, but the question is whether I can raise some money soon enough."

There was silence. Finally, Holcomb stood up, placed his crutch under his right armpit, and forced a note of optimism into his voice. "It's gonna be close, but if the Army gets here when they're s'posed to, we'll make it." He went outside.

Jim drained his coffee cup and joined him in the yard. "I guess I'll have to go to town and borrow ten bucks to pay for that stallion. Since you ain't got the money to pay me, I'll borrow it. And I'd better do that right now."

"Yeah," Holcomb agreed. "You can't wait too long to lay legal claim to that horse."

Maggie Holcomb had told all listeners in the mercantile about the Rafter H stallion, and the word had spread rapidly from there. When Jim rode one of the stallion's colts down the main street of San Lomah that afternoon, he was pointed at and stared at. Strangers yelled greetings to him, and merchants came out of their stores to watch him ride past.

At the bank, Miss Priscilla Newhouse scurried from behind her desk to greet him, and bank employees stopped what they were doing and stared.

"Jim, I just heard about it," Miss Newhouse exclaimed. "Wonderful. And," she said, becoming serious, "I heard too about how you trailed those horse thieves. I'm just awfully glad that you are a friend of mine." She shook hands, but this time she took Jim's hand in both of hers and refused to let go for a long moment.

Jim was embarrassed. He had never before in his life been the center of attraction, and he did not know how to handle it. He kept his hat pulled low, afraid to look out from under the brim, afraid he would find someone staring at him. He stammered, "I just came to, uh, to..."

"Come on into a private office, Jim. We can talk there." He followed her, and felt better when he was out of sight of the bank employees.

"I just wondered if I could, uh, borrow ten dollars, ma'am."

"Of course. More, if you want it." She sat at a desk and opened a drawer. "May I ask why, Jim? Not that it matters," she added hurriedly. "The money is yours. But I'm terribly curious."

"I want to buy that horse, Miss Newhouse. The word is that Colonel James promised to sell him for ten dollars to the man that could catch him."

"Oh, I see. Of course. I heard that too"

"I hope he don't go back on his word."

"Oh, he won't. I know Colonel James quite well, and he'll keep his word. I'm sure of that." She handed Jim a gold eagle. "Is that enough? Do you want more for anything?"

"No, thank you," Jim said. "Do you want me to sign something?"

"Oh, no. Let's just make this a loan between friends, shall we?"

Jim turned his hat around in his hands. "Well, I didn't mean to...I mean, I wanted to do it a business way."

She came from behind her desk and touched him on the arm. She stood close and smiled up at him. "Won't you let me do this as a friendly gesture?"

As always, when Miss Priscilla Newhouse stood close, Jim's knees turned rubbery. He couldn't help wondering what it would be like to take her in his arms. He had to get out of there before she read his mind. "Yeah. Yes. And I sure do thank you. I—" Didn't she know what she was doing to him?—"I have to go."

He put his hat on and turned to the door. "Thanks again, Miss Newhouse. I'll be sure to pay you back."

"Good-bye, Jim," she said softly to his back.

On the street again, Jim didn't even get to his horse before he received two offers of free drinks. One offer came from a former coworker at the Rafter H and he accompanied the cowboy to the Buckhorn Bar. There, three other cowboys surrounded him and wanted to know how he'd done it. Jim told the story over again and concluded with, "But I want to tell you, if that horse had good feet under him, nothin' could catch him." He realized that he could drink the rest of the day and most of the night without spending a dime if he wanted to. But he had other things in his mind.

Jim rode the stallion that evening when he got back to the Holcomb Ranch. He rode the animal with a snaffle bit because he guessed that that was what it was used to. He was puzzled for a moment when he found that the horse would not neck-rein the way cowponies were taught to do, and that it had to be turned by pulling on first one rein and then the other. It had to be turned by "plowlining," as Jim described it later to John Holcomb, but he knew he could soon "put a rein" on the horse.

The horse kicked up its heels a few times but soon settled down, and when Jim rode at a gallop to where John Holcomb was leaning against a wagon, he was grinning from ear to ear.

"Now this is a horse," he said. "Man, I can just feel the power in this old boy. I want to tell you, I'm horseback."

John Holcomb grinned with him. "I sure like the way he moves. I can see why the colonel paid a lot of money for 'im."

"And he's goin' to be mine," Jim said.

He was on his way to the Rafter H by daylight next morning, feeling as good as he had ever felt in his life. He lifted the stallion into a long-legged, easy lope, and knew the horse could keep up that gait for miles and miles. He skirted the town of San Lomah because he did not want to be stopped and engaged in a conversation, and he reached the main gate to the Rafter H shortly before noon.

It was a proud young Texan who rode up to the main house and dismounted. His arrival had attracted three ranch hands who came up to look the horse over. One of them said he would fetch the colonel.

"No," another said in answer to Jim's question, "Skeeter's gatherin' cows out of the high country and won't get back till dark. Yeah, ol' Ziegler is with him."

Jim had never met the owner of the Rafter H. Even though he had worked for him, he had spent his time first at the ranch's horse camp to the south, where he broke horses, and later with the roundup wagons, where he had gathered and branded calves. He was surprised, then, when he saw the colonel come out of the main house and walk toward him.

The colonel was the well-dressed, well-groomed gent who had danced away with Miss Priscilla Newhouse at the schoolhouse dance.

"Jim"— Colonel James held out his hand—"I've never had the pleasure of meeting you." They shook hands, and the colonel's attention went immediately to the horse. "Yes, it is Duke the Third. He's a little worse for wear, but there's no mistake. It is he."

"He's a lot of horse, Mr. James," said Jim.

"How in the world did you catch him?"

Again Jim told the story, and again he concluded with the fact that had his saddle horse not been shod and had the stallion not been sore-footed, the race would have been a hopeless one.

"I can't believe that. It is certainly good to see him again. What do you intend to do with him. Jim?"

"Buy him, Mr. James."

"Mmmm, and how do you propose to pay for him?"

"With cash, Mr. James. I've been told that you promised to sell him for ten dollars to the man that caught him."

Colonel James smiled. "That I did. I hate to lose him, but a promise is a promise. Do you have ten dollars?"

"Yessir." Jim dug the gold eagle from his pants pocket.

"Very well. If you will wait one moment, I will write you a bill of sale." Colonel James went back into the house. The stallion threw its head up and whinnied wildly at a small bunch of horses in the distance.

"He got used to the wild life," Jim said to one of the ranch hands. "In a way I feel sorry for him."

The ranch hand grinned a lascivious grin. "Considerin' what his duties are, I wouldn't mind tradin' places with him."

"Here you are, Jim." The colonel handed Jim the bill of sale. "Now tell me, how are his colts?"

"They're mighty purty horses, Mr. James. They broke out good."

"I assume they are for sale."

"Yessir. That's why John Holcomb raised 'em."

"And they are all broken now?"

"They will be in a few more days, sir."

"Will you deliver a message for me, Jim? Will you tell your employer I want ten of them? Ten of the best. Tell him that whatever offer he gets from anyone else, I'll better it."

"Sure, Mr. James."

"And, him, tell him for me that this is the least he can do. After all, he got the services of my stallion for nothing." The colonel rubbed his chin, his brow furrowed, then added, "No. Don't tell him that. I wouldn't want my words to be misconstrued."

"Yessir."

"And tell him I'll send some men for them in two or three days."

"Yessir."

It was late afternoon when Jim rode around the outskirts of San

Lomah. But his hopes of getting back to the Holcomb ranch without attracting attention were dashed. He was on the wagon road going east when he looked back and saw a rider trying to catch up with him.

It would have been bad manners to ride on, so Jim reined up and waited. Then he wished he had not. The rider was wearing a pearl-gray Stetson, a tied-low six-shooter, and a star on his shirt pocket.

Jim groaned. What now? He had a bill of sale for the horse. Besides, he was outside town, out of the marshal's jurisdiction. What could Marshal Delmar Chitlow want with him now? Jim could think of no reason the marshal would want him, but he had learned from hard experience that the law could not be trusted. Not by a hired man, anyway.

Chitlow reined up beside Jim, his horse blowing from the run. "I just want to talk to you for a minute."

"Yeah?" Jim's eyes showed distrust.

"That's the Rafter H stud, ain't it?"

"Yeah."

"What do you want for him?"

"Want for 'im?" The cowboy was surprised. "Why?"

"I want to buy him. He does belong to you now, doesn't he?"

"Yeah, but... What do you want with him?"

"That's my business," the marshal snapped. "Name a price."

Jim looked down and combed the horse's mane with his fingers. "Well, I don't know. Ain't thought about it." He looked up and met Chitlow's hard gaze. "I just don't know."

"You have no use for a horse like that. A stud horse would be nothing but a lot of trouble for a drifting cowboy."

"That's right," Jim agreed, "but he wouldn't be much use to a town lawman either." Jim had decided that he would not be bullied.

The two men scowled at each other a moment, then finally the marshal looked down. A tight, forced smile turned up the corners of his mouth under the mustache.

"All right, I'll tell you. I'm going to buy a ranch. I've got my eye on two ranches, and I'm going to buy one or the other real soon. Both have some mares, and I'll have plenty of use for that horse. Now, will you sell him to me?"

Jim studied his face and found him serious. "I still don't know, Mr. Chitlow. I'll have to think about it. To tell the truth, I don't have any idea what this horse is worth."

The stallion and the marshal's horse met noses then, and the stallion squealed and pawed the ground.

"See what I mean?" the marshal said. "A stud isn't what a cowboy needs. He'll always be fighting other horses unless he's given special care."

Jim pulled his mount away from the other horse. "I know what you mean. I'll think about it."

"All right, you think about it. But before you accept any offer, you give me a chance to make a bid."

Jim didn't answer. He rode on.

CHAPTER 20

The Holcombs were worried again, and this time it wasn't just Maggie Holcomb. "He's gone again," she said, her forehead wrinkled.

"Left right after you did," John Holcomb said. "Soon as you were out of sight he caught his mare and rode north."

Jim dropped into a wooden chair in the kitchen. "Gone up to the mountains again, I'll bet. He'll be back, prob'ly in time for supper."

"It's almost dark now," Maggie Holcomb pointed out. She turned her worried face to him. "He's just a child, Jim. One day he is going to ride off and get hurt and not come back."

"He can take care of himself," Jim said, trying to assuage her worries.

"I know he's been taking care of himself since he was a baby," John Holcomb put in, "but too many things can happen. He's just a little kid. That mare of his is getting old, and that's rough country. She could turn over on him."

It was the first time that John Holcomb had expressed any worry over the boy, and this pleased Jim. Maggie Holcomb went to the door and looked out. "It's dark now." She looked back at the men with a tortured expression. "He's not coming back tonight. He's up there all alone, and—I can't help it—I'm worried."

"Listen," Jim said, still trying to calm their fears, "he's done this a lot of times. Even before anybody worried about him. He always came back. He'll be back. Maybe not tonight, but he'll be back."

"I just don't understand, Jim," John Holcomb said. "Why does he do it? Does something compel him to do it?"

"Yes," Jim said, matter-of-factly. "Somethin' does. Somethin' tells him he has to go up there."

You're not talking about Indian spirits or anything like that?" John Holcomb asked.

"I don't know, John. I just know his grandpa told him about somethin' in those hills, and he has to go up there."

"He could be chasing a legend," Maggie Holcomb put in, her voice strained.

Suddenly, Jim snapped his fingers. "That's it. He's chasin' a legend. And I'll bet I know where he went."

"Where, Jim?" Maggie Holcomb's face was white.

"To that cave I told you about. He heard every word. The legend has to do with that cave. That's what he's been lookin' for."

"And you found it by accident," John Holcomb commented.

"Oh, I wish he would come back tonight. I won't sleep all night," said Maggie Holcomb.

"If I could get on a horse I'd go look for him," said John Holcomb. "If I could just bend this damn knee a little."

"I'll go," Jim said. "No use lookin' for 'im in the dark, but I'll go soon's it's daylight."

Supper was eaten without enthusiasm, and Jim lay awake most of the night, listening, hoping the boy would return. He was up before daylight, saddling a night horse and running in the colts. By sunup, he had caught one of the colts, had saddled it, and was heading up the canyon trail. He had skipped breakfast "I'll find 'im, Mrs. Holcomb," he had said. "Don't worry. I know where to look."

At midmorning, Jim reached the grassy valley where he had seen the H Bar mares. They were still there. And it was there that Jim found the boy. Rather, the boy found Jim.

They saw each other coming, and both urged their mounts to greater speed as they rode toward each other.

The boy was smiling broadly and holding something high above his head. As they came together, Jim saw that the boy's hands and knees were skinned but otherwise he appeared in good health. Then Jim looked at what the boy was holding.

"What the hell is it, Chacho? A cross?" He took and examined it. "That's what it is. A purty one." He turned it over in his hands. "Never saw anything like it. Where'd you find it, Chacho? In that cave?"

The boy nodded vigorously, smiling.

"Wonder if it's gold?" Jim mused. "Damn, look at them purty rocks. Like colored glass. I ought to go up there and look around myself. But"—he fixed a stern look upon the boy—"we've got to get back before Mrs. Holcomb has a conniption fit."

As before, Maggie Holcomb saw them coming and ran across the yard to them, holding up her long skirts. John Holcomb followed as fast as he could on his crutch.

"I ought to give him a whipping," John Holcomb said after he had taken his turn at patting the boy on the back. "But how can I? Even if he was my own kid, I couldn't punish him. We're just too glad to see him."

It was not until they were in the house and the boy as eating his oatmeal that Jim remembered the cross. He held it up. "What do you think of this?"

John Holcomb took it and turned it over in his hands. "Lordy. That's the fanciest cross I ever saw. Wonder what it's made of."

Maggie Holcomb took her turn examining the jewel-encrusted piece. It was blackened with age, but when she scraped it with a paring knife, the dirt peeled off, revealing a dull yellow color.

"It's gold, I'll bet," John Holcomb said.

"Are you sure, John?" Maggie Holcomb asked.

"Yep. I'm almost certain."

"Wish we could be absolutely certain." She turned to Jim. "Do you know anything about gold, him?"

"No," Jim replied between bites of wheatcakes, "but I know somebody that does."

"Who, Jim?"

"That lady banker, Priscilla Newhouse."

"Of course. She would know," Maggie Holcomb said. "And she would know what to do with it."

"Besides," John Holcomb added, "she can be trusted. I wouldn't trust just anyone with a thing like this."

It was agreed that Jim and the boy would go to town and show the cross to Miss Newhouse. Jim wanted to leave right away, but Maggie Holcomb would not hear of it. The boy needed rest. Tomorrow would be soon enough.

"All right," Jim said. "I can turn a few figure-eights on a couple of colts yet today."

He got to the door before he remembered something else important. "I almost forgot, what with everything else happenin'. Colonel James said to tell you he wants buy ten of your broke colts. Said he'd pay more than anybody else. Said he'd send some men after 'em in a few days."

John Holcomb's mouth dropped open. It took Maggie Holcomb a moment to absorb Jim's message, then she went to her husband and hugged him. "Did you hear that, John?" She stood back and studied her husband's face, a wide smile on her lips. "That's our mortgage money, John."

Turning to Jim she exclaimed, "We've been worried, Jim. We've skipped as many payments as the bank will allow. This is wonderful news. This is our mortgage money."

"Or"—John Holcomb had the worry wrinkles on his forehead again —"it's Jim's wages. We owe it to him."

Jim was happy to be able to bring them good news. "It's your mortgage money," he said as he went out the door.

Miss Priscilla Newhouse looked up from her desk when Jim and Chacho entered the bank. She smile and waved them over. Jim removed his hat, no longer caring if he was stared at. He had other things on his mind.

"Could we talk to you in private, Miss Newhouse?"

"Certainly." She stood up and led the way to the private office, closing the door behind them. She smiled down at the boy. "How are you? I'm glad to see you."

Chacho was not sure what she said, but he returned the smile. Jim took the cross from under his shirt and handed it to her.

"We're hopin' you can tell us if this is valuable."

Priscilla Newhouse gasped. "Oh, my..." She took the artifact and handled it tenderly. "My goodness. Where on earth did you get this?"

"Chacho found it," Jim said.

She dropped into a chair behind the desk and looked up at Jim. Her eyes were wide, and she spoke in a reverent whisper. "Where? Where on earth did he find it?"

"In the mountains. Do you know what it is, Miss Newhouse?"

"In the mountains?" she whispered. "Did he just...did he just find it?"

"No," Jim said. "He's been lookin' for somethin' up there for a long time."

Her voice was almost hoarse. "Do you know...do you know what this might be?" She studied the cross and looked up at Jim again. "Do you know what this might be, Jim?"

"No, Miss Newhouse. We're hopin' you might know somethin'."

She cleared her throat to get her voice back to normal. "Well, I'm not sure, but I know someone who—excuse me a moment, will you." She stood up, went to the office door, opened it and shouted, "Charles."

A pimply-faced teenage boy hurried up.

"Do you know Doctor Sanderson when you see him?"

"Yes ma'am."

"He's staying at the hotel. Run and fetch him. Tell him it is extremely important that he come over here immediately. Hurry, will you?"

"Yes ma'am." The youth left on the run, and Jim watched him through the plate-glass window as he ran all the way to the hotel.

Miss Newhouse sat down again, a crease between her eyes. "I'm almost afraid to say this, Jim, but this could be something Doctor Sanderson has been searching desperately for."

"I knew he was lookin' for somethin' up in the hills," Jim said, "but why would a doctor be lookin' for this?"

161

"He's a doctor of philosophy, Jim. He is from the Smithsonian Institution."

Jim said, "Oh," although he did not understand.

"He is an archeologist, Jim. He has been trying to prove, or disprove, an Indian legend. He has been convinced in his own mind that the legend is true."

"A legend? That's what Mrs. Holcomb guessed that Chacho here was lookin' for."

"Then it must be true."

They saw Doctor Sanderson coming. He was walking as fast as a man could walk without running, the teenage boy leading the way. By the time he entered the office, he was out of breath. Miss Newhouse said simply, "Thank you for coming, Doctor. I thought you might be interested in this." She handed him the cross.

He gasped, as Miss Newhouse had, when he saw it. He turned it over and over in his hands, sat in a chair opposite the desk, studied it further, and looked at Miss Newhouse, a pained expression on his face.

"Where?" he gasped.

She nodded at Chacho. "The boy found it."

Doctor Sanderson turned to the boy. "Where...?" That was all he could get out. He held his hand over his heart, still gasping for breath.

"Doctor Sanderson, are you all right?" Miss Newhouse went to him, worried.

"Yes," he said. Just let me get my breath. I'm...I'm all right."

He continued examining the cross, turning it at different angles with shaking hands. He asked for a magnifying glass. Miss Newhouse had to go to another office, but she did find one. He examined it further through the glass. Finally, he looked up, first at Miss Newhouse, then at Jim and the boy. His breathing had slowed, but he was excited. "It's Jesuit. It's Incan gold."

Nobody spoke for a long moment. Then Doctor Sanderson asked, "Tell me, is there more?"

"Is there, Jim?" Miss Newhouse asked.

Jim turned to Chacho. "*Mas?*" He took the cross and pointed at it. "*Mas?*"

162

The boy nodded yes.

"*Cuanto?*"

The boy held his arms wide.

"He said there is more, a lot more," Jim said to Doctor Sanderson.

"That's it, then." His voice rose. "That's it. Where did you find it?"

Miss Newhouse cleared her throat. "Well now, Doctor, I think we should take care of some legal formalities first."

"Certainly, certainly." The archeologist was on his feet, dancing excitedly. "It's the boy's discovery. But I just can't wait. What do you want me to sign?"

"It will take only a few minutes. We have legal counsel next door. If you will excuse me a moment, I'll tell him what we need." She left.

The doctor couldn't take his eyes off the artifact. He examined it again through the magnifying glass, chortling more to himself than to anyone else. "It's magnificent. It's...it's just magnificent."

"Uh, Doctor Sanderson," Jim said, uncertainly, "Miss Newhouse said somethin' about an Indian legend. Is it true?"

"Yes. This proves it. This has to be part of a lost Jesuit treasure. They brought it with them when they were driven out of New Spain about the middle of the last century." Doctor Sanderson kissed the cross with a loud smack, then danced a jig. "They wouldn't believe me. Now they'll believe me."

Miss Newhouse returned, waving a sheet of paper gently to dry the ink on it. She sat at her desk and pursed her lips, taking on a businesslike attitude. "This should do it. You understand, Doctor Sanderson, we are just protecting the child's interests. This merely gives him full claim to whatever discoveries he made, or that you make with his help."

"Certainly, certainly." He grabbed the paper, read it hastily, and asked, "Where do I sign?"

"Right there, Priscilla Newhouse pointed with her finger, dipped a pen in an inkwell, and handed it to him. He signed with a flourish.

"Now," he said to Jim, "will you show me where you found

163

this?"

Jim looked at Priscilla Newhouse for advice. She nodded. "It's all right, Jim. This paper gives all credit and monetary rewards to Ramon Garcia or to his appointed guardian. We'll have to have a guardian appointed, but that will be no problem."

"I can draw you a map, or Chacho can take you there," Jim said to Doctor Sanderson. "I can draw you a map so you can't miss it."

"A map will do nicely. I'll get some help and some packhorses and get started right away."

"Sit here, Jim." Priscilla Newhouse stood up and offered Jim her seat behind the desk.

Jim took the pen and a sheet of paper from the top of the desk, and—face screwed up in concentration—drew a crude map. "You have to start just north of the Holcomb ranch house," he said. "That's the only trail I know of, and it only goes partway. You have to hack your way through a dozen acres of buckbrush, but after you get through that you just follow a dry creek bed and keep lookin' off to your right. You'll see a bunch of holes in the cliffs. Mrs. Holcomb said they were caused by wind and rain. But this one is bigger than the rest and it's almost square."

"Yes, yes." The archeologist nodded emphatically, studying the map. "Seems clear enough." He turned to Miss Newhouse. "I must get started immediately."

"It'll take you a good seven or eight hours to get there," Jim advised. "And that's from the ranch. You'd better wait till mornin'."

Disappointment clouded the archeologist's face. "Very well. But I must arrange for someone to help me and be ready at the crack of dawn. I'll need two saddle horses and a packhorse."

"Jim," Miss Newhouse asked, "could you..."

"I wish I could, Miss Newhouse, but the Army is comin' to look at John Holcomb's horses in a few days and I've got to work with 'em some more."

"I see. Well, Doctor Sanderson, I'm sure you can find someone."

"Yes, yes," he said excitedly. "I must hurry and make the arrangements." He left, walking rapidly toward the livery barn.

CHAPTER 21

Breakfast was over at the Holcomb's H Bar Ranch by the time the sun came up. The hired cowboy had caught the first of four colts he planned to work with that day, and was cinching a saddle on its back when two men leading two packhorses rode into the ranch yard.

John Holcomb, who was hobbling across the yard on his crutch, recognized one of the men immediately, and grinned. "Clebe, you old rounder, what in hell you up to nowadays?"

Clebe Howell, former H Bar employee, returned the smile. "Workin'. For a few days, anyway. Meet my boss, Doctor George Sanderson."

Doctor Sanderson reached down from his horse and shook hands with john Holcomb. "It's a pleasure to meet you, Mr. Holcomb. I hope you don't mind our trespassing on your land."

"I've been hearin' about you, Doctor. You can cross my land anytime."

"He hired me," Clebe Howell said, "because I know where that trail is and where it goes, but I'll have to follow Jim's map most of the way."

Holcomb noticed that the pack horses carried only two small bedrolls, a few groceries, a skillet, and digging tools. There was plenty of room in the pack panniers for anything the archeologist might want to bring back.

"We must be going," Doctor Sanderson said. "Nice meeting you."

The hired cowboy worked all day with four young horses, and by evening he had them turning with a light flick of the rein at a trot. "In a couple more days I'll have them turnin' at a run," he promised.

The next day, two representatives of the U.S. Army showed up. Even Jim could tell they were military men as soon as he saw them coming. They rode their Army saddles erect, sitting straight up, heels down, letting their right arms dangle lifelessly while they handled their reins with a military grip in their left hands.

Their boots were shined and looked as if they had never stepped in horse manure, and the flat-brim hats sat on each officer's head at exactly the same angle. One man was short and stout while the other was medium height and slender, but otherwise they looked exactly the same in their tunics with epaulets and brass buttons, and their gloves with long wide cuffs.

"Mornin'," John Holcomb said as they rode up.

"Good morning, sir," the short, stout one replied.

"Do I have the honor of addressing Mr. John Holcomb?"

"Yes sir." Holcomb tried to copy the officer's formal manner.

"We have been advised that you have some young horses for sale."

"That I do."

"And we have been advised by a Miss Priscilla Newhouse in San Lomah that the horses are broken to ride."

Holcomb waved toward the vega where Jim was turning figure-eights on a young horse. "Gentlemen, I have had the good fortune of employing one of the finest horsemen in the west, and he is just now putting the finishing touches on the last of the colts."

Turning in their saddles, the two officers squinted across the distance and watched Jim. "He seems to be handling the reins lightly," the slender one said to Holcomb. "That is definitely a merit. The Army takes a great deal of care with horses' mouths."

"Would you like to see the colts?"

"Not today, sir. We have promised a Mr. Jacob Tooley that we would inspect some horses on his ranch today. We came here this morning to ascertain that you, too, have horses for sale."

Holcomb pulled his hat brim down to shade his eyes from the morning sun. "Tell me, gentlemen, how many horses is the Army

166

interested in buying this fall?"

"Possibly thirty-five head, sir."

"I have thirty-eight, but I have already promised ten to a neighbor. That leaves twenty-eight for sale—and, gentlemen, I can promise you that they are the finest and best-trained young horses that you will find anywhere."

"I'm sure they are, sir," the officer replied without rancor but without enthusiasm either. It was his way of letting the civilian know that he had heard such promises before. "Today is, I believe, October four. We will return at oh eight hundred hours on October seven." The two officers turned their horses around. "Good day, sir."

Holcomb watched them leave, and said to himself, "Stuffy pair of jaspers, but if they've got the bucks to buy horses, I'll treat 'em like long-lost brothers."

Dr. George Sanderson was a weary man when he slid out of his saddle that evening in the yard of the H Bar Ranch, but his face with its goatee was animated and his eyes were merry.

"Would you care to come in the house?" Holcomb asked. "We'll put the coffeepot on."

"Thank you," the archeologist said. "That is very kind."

Maggie Holcomb poured coffee for Doctor Sanderson, Clebe Howell, her husband, and Jim Kinslow as they all sat at the kitchen table. Chacho sat with them. "Did you find anything interesting, Doctor?" she asked.

Doctor Sanderson sipped his coffee and leaned back with a happy sigh. "It was everything I had hoped for, Mrs. Holcomb. The story is there just as plain as anything."

All eyes and ears were turned to him.

"We found four skeletons and they are not the remains of Indians. Arrowheads are still there between the ribs of two of them. The story is clear, and it is just as the legend has it."

Clebe Howell shivered visibly. "It might be a scientific discovery to Doctor Sanderson here, but them bones give me the shivers. I felt like somebody was a-watchin' us."

Doctor Sanderson chuckled. "Nonsense."

"Tell us the story, Doctor," Maggie Holcomb pleaded.

Doctor Sanderson took another sip of the coffee. "What

167

happened, dear folks, is this: About the middle of the eighteenth century, the King of Spain became jealous of the power wielded by the Jesuits in New Spain, now known as Mexico. The Jesuits were forced to flee to the north.

"They first destroyed many of their mission records, but they took their most valuable treasures with them. And—" Doctor Sanderson spread his hands—"with gold plundered from the Incan Indians put together with their own craftsmanship, their treasures were many.

"We know that some of them traveled to California and Arizona. What we did not know for certain, despite legends to the contrary, is whether they ever got as far north as Colorado. We repeatedly heard rumors that some of them did, but we could find no proof. Not until today.

"It is obvious now that a few of them, along with their Incan slaves did come this far north. But they did not survive. North American Indians—we don't know yet which tribe—attacked them. Or perhaps their slaves turned on them. We are not certain. But the Jesuits were killed. The Indians, having no use for the treasure at that time, hid it in that natural cave, and then all but forgot about it.

"But the story was passed on from one generation of Indians to another until it reached the ears of this boy here." Doctor Sanderson reached over and patted Chacho's head. "Tell me, young man, who told you the story?"

"He don't understand much English," Jim answered, "but he told me it was his grandpa that told him. He was raised by his grandpa, and his grandpa was a full-blooded Ute."

Nodding that he understood, Doctor Sanderson continued his story. "I can guess how it happened. The elder Indian had heard the legend and knew approximately, but not exactly, where the treasure was hidden. He realized that the treasure now had considerable value, and he wanted his young grandson to have it."

"And that," Maggie Holcomb added, "is why Ramon went by himself up into those mountains. He was looking for the treasure his grandpa told him about."

"It was very fortunate for him that he found it," Doctor Sanderson said. "It would have been discovered sooner or later, but he is a very fortunate young man. Tell me, did he just stumble onto it?"

"No," Maggie Holcomb answered. "Actually, it was Jim here who first suspected something interesting might be in that cave. He had chased a horse into that part of the country and was returning when he noticed something unnatural. He didn't have time then to investigate, but he told us about it, and Ramon overheard him."

"I see." Doctor Sanderson stroked his goatee. "Then it was the cowboy who made the initial discovery"

"Oh no," said Jim. "I just got suspicious. I had no idea what was in that hole in the cliff."

"What else did you find, Doctor?" Maggie Holcomb asked.

"We have two pack bags full of valuables. We have candlesticks, vessels, altars, crosses, and other items, all extremely valuable."

"How much do you think it's worth?"

The archeologist pursed his lips and stroked his beard again. "It would be most difficult to put a dollar value on it. The minerals and jewels alone are worth a great deal. But the real value is in the story they tell. The Smithsonian Institution will pay well."

Maggie Holcomb beamed, and John Holcomb and Jim grinned happily. She put her arm around Chacho's shoulders. "It looks like your future is assured, Ramon. You are a wealthy child."

"Know what I want him to do with his money?" Jim said. "I want him to get an education. Like Miss Priscilla Newhouse. It was because she has an education that she knew what to do. Don't let 'im grow up to be an ignorant cowpuncher."

"I can't forget," Jim continued, "the story I heard about the cowboy that was the first to discover gold over at Cripple Creek. He was so ignorant he sold his claim for fifty dollars, and he died poor while the two slicks that bought it from him got rich."

"If I have anything to say about it, he'll be the best-educated Indian in America," Maggie Holcomb vowed. Doctor Sanderson stood up. "Thank you very much for the coffee. We must be going. I must send a wire off to Washington, to my colleagues. We will soon have a team of archeologists here." He again spread his hands. "Please, please, I implore you, say nothing of this to anyone. Please. We just cannot have people tramping around up there looking for treasures."

"We can keep a secret," John Holcomb said. "But," he said, nodding at Clebe Howell, "how about you, Clebe?"

"I ain't gonna say nothin'."

"We have an agreement," Doctor Sanderson said. "I will pay him a bonus, a substantial one, if he keeps mum. But if the news gets out, I will hold him personally responsible, and there will be no bonus."

"I ain't gonna say nothin'," Howell repeated emphatically.

The next visitor to the Holcomb Ranch was Miss Priscilla Newhouse, who arrived early next day. She was excited. "The circuit judge will be back at home next week, and I'm sure he will appoint you and Mr. Holcomb legal guardians of Ramon," she told Maggie Holcomb as she alighted from her one-horse buggy.

"Nothing could make us happier," Maggie Holcomb replied.

"I assumed that you would want to be appointed," said Miss Newhouse.

"Oh, yes. We decided some time ago that if we could keep our ranch, our home, we would try to adopt Ramon. We have grown to love him."

"I'm sure the judge will agree to that. If there is any question, I am prepared to bring forth a dozen witnesses who will testify that no one else even attempted to care for the boy after his grandfather died."

"How about relatives? Now that Ramon has wealth, some of his relatives are bound to hear about it and try to become his guardians."

"Oh, I'm sure they will. But I don't think the judge will look kindly upon relatives who obviously cared nothing about the child when he needed them. Besides"—Miss Newhouse smiled a knowing smile—"news of his wealth won't get out for some time yet."

Events moved rapidly at the Holcomb's H Bar Ranch. At midmorning, the day after Priscilla Newhouse's visit, three men from the huge Rafter H appeared on horseback. Skeeter Jones was one of them, and another was the Rafter H foreman, Carter Ziegler.

Skeeter was carrying his old .44 six-gun in a worn holster on his right hip, and when Jim asked about it, he replied, "Ol' Tooley said he's gonna make a bloody mess outta me. He thinks I'm the one that spiked the punch at the dance. He don't know you helped, and I didn't tell anyone any different."

"Be careful of him, Skeeter."

"Don't worry. If he picks on me, I'll try to handle 'im with my fists, but if that don't work, well...I'll tell you, Slim, I ain't gonna let 'im beat on me just 'cause he's bigger than me."

Jim ran in the four-year-olds, and Ziegler picked out ten of them. He counted out one thousand dollars and handed the money to John Holcomb. "Colonel James said to give you a hundred dollars a head," he explained, "and he said that whatever the Army pays he'll pay five dollars a head more. He said to tell you that if he owes you more, he'll settle with you next week."

"The colonel is a man of his word," Holcomb said. "Tell him I'll be happy to do business with him anytime."

Skeeter had to have a look at the Rafter H stallion, and he too asked what Jim intended doing with the horse. "I was thinkin' you and me might ride back to Fort Worth when these colts are sold," he said, "But you cain't keep that horse in a corral with any other horse."

John Holcomb stood in front of Jim and counted out three hundred dollars. "Would you sell 'im right now, Jim?"

Jim looked at the money in Holcomb's hand but didn't take it.

"I know he's worth more than that, and you can probably get more. I'm the first to admit that. But I'm not wealthy."

"I'll sell him to you on one condition, John."

"Name it."

"You take that old brown horse of mine and pension him."

"You don't want 'im anymore?"

Jim dug the toe of his boot into the ground. "No. He's purty old, and that run I gave him catchin' this horse took somethin' out of him. He'll never be the same. I'd just like to see him turned out somewhere on good grass with some mares and colts."

"I'll do it, Jim."

The cowboy took the money, folded it, and put it in his pants pocket. "The horse is yours."

"I'll be damned," exclaimed Skeeter. "Three hunnerd dollars for a day's work. Man, that's more'n I made all summer."

Jim punched Skeeter on the shoulder and grinned. "Sell that 'ol pony of yours, or give him away, and let's you and me take the stage and the trains south."

Skeeter returned the grin. "I cain't wait to see ol' Fort Worth again. There's women there I ain't even touched yet."

The three of them chuckled at Skeeter's enthusiasm, and Holcomb quipped, "Somebody ought to warn Fort Worth you two are coming'."

The Rafter H men left, driving the young horses ahead of them, and within twenty minutes, Maggie Holcomb, with Jim's help, had the light team hitched to the spring wagon, and she, John Holcomb, and the boy seated in it.

"There's bread and butter and potato soup in the kitchen, Jim," she said. "We'll be home for supper."

"We just can't wait another day to hand that bank five hundred dollars," John Holcomb said. "That'll keep them happy until we get more funds from the Army." He chirruped to the team, and drove off.

Jim went to the corral where he had two of the Holcomb colts penned. He stood for a moment and leaned against a corral post. He gazed out over the vega where the grass had turned brown at summer's end, and at the creek, lined in places with poplar and cottonwood trees, all of which had shed their leaves. He looked to the mountains, at the blue haze that hung over them, at the buckbrush that had turned reddish down, and at the now-bare aspen trees on the higher elevations.

"Purty country," he said to himself, "but winter's comin' and it's time for this ol' southern boy to roll up his bed, sack his saddle, and move on..."

Jim allowed, when the Holcombs returned, that his work was done. "I don't know what else to do with these colts without cattle to chase."

"You can't make cowponies out of them without cattle," Holcomb agreed. "Jim, I need you one more day. The Army will want to see the colts ridden, and haven't got anyone else to do it."

"Sure. I'll go to town tomorrow and pay the bank the ten dollars I owe, and find out when the stage leaves in a couple of days, and I'll come back."

CHAPTER 22

Miss Priscilla Newhouse smiled, but refused to accept more than ten dollars from Jim. "It was just a personal favor," she said. "I can't accept any interest."

"Well, I can't force it on you, Miss Newhouse."

"It's Priscilla. Remember?"

"Oh yes." Jim grinned shyly. "Priscilla."

"I'm happy that you came by this morning, Jim. I've been wanting to talk to you."

"About what?"

"Jim, now that I have been able to piece together the story, I'm convinced that you are entitled to a share of the Jesuit treasure."

"Naw," Jim shrugged. "It's Chacho's."

"Now, let's look at this in a businesslike manner, Jim. Without your help, the boy might not have found the treasure. It would have been found eventually, I'm sure, but it could have been found by someone else. Doctor Sanderson, perhaps."

Jim didn't know what to say, so he said nothing.

"With your permission, Jim, I will see that you receive a fair share."

Shoving his hands deep into his pockets, Jim replied, "Aw, I don't know. I'm doin' pretty good, what with the money I got comin' from John Holcomb and the money I got for that stud horse and all."

"You're too easy to take advantage of, Jim. I'm sure no one will object. I'm sure everyone will agree that you are entitled to a share."

The cowboy merely shrugged.

"I would say at least ten percent, but I'll ask our legal counsel about that. Ten percent would be a lot of money."

Jim just looked at her vacantly for a moment, then let his gaze drop.

"Do you know what you could do with ten percent, Jim? Let's see now, I'm guessing that the full reward will come to around one hundred thousand dollars. Ten percent would be ten thousand dollars."

Jim's head came up then. "Ten thousand dollars?"

"That is my estimate. It could be more. Think about it. With ten thousand dollars you could buy some land and build a house, and go into the livestock business. The bank could help. Listen, Jim, I know a rancher who has four hundred dogie calves to sell. You could buy them, winter and graze them on federal lands in the mountains next summer, and sell them a year from now at a very good profit."

The cowboy said nothing, but his face showed interest.

"You wouldn't even have to put up your own money for the calves, Jim. The bank will lend you the money. If you lose, the bank loses. If you make a profit, which I am sure you will unless the weather is awfully bad, the bank will get its money back with interest."

Still no answer.

"What do you think? You don't have to be a drifter all your life."

She moved closer. "I realize this whole idea is something entirely new to you. But, Jim, you have to think big. Be bold." There it was again. Her closeness. The frankness in her eyes. His knees turned rubbery.

When he spoke, his voice was unsteady.

"I, uh, I might do somethin' like that, Miss Newhouse. Priscilla."

She smiled into his face. "That's the way to think. You can do it, Jim. I honest believe you can do anything you set out to do. You just have to formulate a plan and go to work on it."

"I, uh, guess I don't just have to go back to Texas, Priscilla. I always wanted to own property. Raise beef and good horses."

"Wonderful. This is your opportunity."

Her gaze locked onto his. He had that terrible urge again to put his arms around her, to pull her close. He could almost taste the sweetness of her lips. For a moment he couldn't help thinking about her on a ranch. His ranch. But no, he couldn't dare even think about it.

Could he?

She was looking into his eyes, smiling, inviting. Maybe.

"Let me, uh, think about it, Priscilla."

"Of course. Think about it, Jim. But think positively. Will you do that?"

He left the bank feeling unsteady on his feet. His mind was in a fog. He mounted his horse and rode out of town, seeing no one and hearing nothing.

At the top of a low hill on the east side of San Lomah, he dismounted and sat cross-legged on the ground. The horse cropped the grass, and Jim was pleased to notice that the young horse had learned to eat with a bit in its mouth. But he had to think of something other than horses.

Business. For the first time in his life he had to think about business.

Ten thousand dollars. He couldn't just blow it. He would never again have an opportunity to go into ranching for himself. And there was Priscilla. She couldn't be interested in a common cowhand, but a land owner? A businessman? Why not?

The way she had smiled at him and touched him had to mean something. Good lord, she was some woman. With a woman like that a man could do anything.

So it got cold in Colorado. He could learn to live with it. Raising calves in Colorado was different from raising calves in south Texas, but he could learn. Hell, she'd said herself he could do anything he set his mind to. And as the feller says, if you're going to accomplish anything in life you have to try. A man had to try. He stood up.

"I'll do it," he said aloud. "Ol' Skeeter'll have to go back to Fort Worth by himself. I'm stayin'."

He gathered the reins, stepped into the saddle, and rode at a trot back down Main Street.

At the bank, he wrapped the reins around a hitchrail and strode into the bank lobby, large spur rowels ringing. He saw Miss Priscilla Newhouse seated behind the desk in the private office at the same time she saw him. She waved him in, and he removed his hat and stepped through the office door like a man with a purpose. It wasn't until then that he saw Colonel James.

The owner of the Rafter H was seated in a chair opposite the desk. He stood up and offered his hand, but it was Miss Newhouse who spoke first.

"Jim, I'd like you to meet Colonel James, my fiancé." It was her last word that hit the cowboy like a ramrod. It sent his mind reeling, his temples pounding. His jaw dropped open and he could not speak. Colonel James spoke heartily. "We've already met. How are you, Jim?"

Almost unconsciously, the cowboy took the proffered hand and shook, weakly. He tried to speak, but all that came out was a strangling sound.

"Jim, are you all right?" Miss Newhouse came around the desk and stood before him.

He had to get hold of himself. He had to recover—like he always did after being thrown hard by a horse or after being knocked flat by a charging cow. He ordered his voice to speak.

"Uh, yeah. I'm all right." He shook his head and swallowed hard. "Felt kind of funny there for awhile."

"Are you ill, Jim?"

"Oh, no. I'm fine." He forced himself to grin. "I, uh, just came to ask you somethin', Miss Newhouse."

"What is it, Jim? Are you going to follow my advice?"

"No. Uh, I just wanted to ask you one more favor."

"Of course."

"I just wanted to ask you to send any money I might have comin' from, uh—" he glanced at Colonel James. "...You know, to me at Fort Worth, Texas. In care of general delivery."

She stepped backward and sat on the edge of the desk. "Jim, I'm disappointed."

He had regained his senses fully now. "I'm sure sorry, Miss Newhouse, but I'm too much of a southerner, I guess. Would you do that for me? I'd sure appreciate it."

"Of course I will, Jim, but—"

He had to get out of there and he had to get out now. "I've got to go. I sure do thank you, Miss Newhouse, for everything."

He wheeled and left. Miss Priscilla Newhouse watched him go, her forehead furrowed, her eyes sad.

Jim walked right past the horse he had tied to a hitchrail outside the bank. Then he remembered, went back, and mounted. He rode down Main Street, head down, shoulders slumped. He wished he could just draw his pay and leave immediately. He wished he didn't have to spend another day there.

He rode past the Buckhorn Bar without seeing it. He rode past the St. Louis Emporium without hearing Skeeter yell, "Slim Jim." Looking straight ahead, he rode on to the east side of town, to the same spot when he had reached a momentous decision earlier. Again he dismounted, dropped the reins, and sat cross legged.

A long groan came out of him, and he put his elbows on his knees and his face in his hands and stared at the ground. He saw nothing but Miss Priscilla Newhouse and Colonel James. He groaned again and cursed himself aloud. "How dumb can a feller get. I should have guessed. Them two was made for each other."

For an hour he sat there silently.

Finally, he stood up, picked up the reins, and got on the horse. He turned the horse toward the ranch where he could spend the rest of the day and the night feeling sorry for himself, then stopped.

"The world ain't goin' to quit spinnin' just because ol' Jim got disappointed. Like the feller says, when you get dumped on your ass, you can just set there and die, or you can get up and go on. A drink might help, Wonder if Skeeter's still back there."

He turned the horse around...

Skeeter saw him come through the door of the St, Louis Emporium. "Slim Jim, c'mere, you Texas bolt weevil." As Jim approached, he added, "Where'd you go? Last time I saw you, you looked like a man that's deef and dumb and cain't see or hear either. What happened?"

"Aw, nothin'." Jim bought a round of whiskey. He tossed his down in one gulp and refused even to blink as it burned its way down his throat. It helped to clear his mind.

"Ready to head south, Slim?"

"Day after tomorrow," Jim answered. "You?"

"Hail, I'm ready anytime you are. I drew my pay this mornin'."

"Wish I could pull out right now," Jim said, "but John Holcomb ain't got nobody else to show off his horses. Say, Skeeter, you don't want to stand around here all day tomorrow. Why don't you help me? John'll pay you for it. You can ride some of those colts, and well get done quicker."

"Sure, I'll help you, Slim. If I stay in town I'll just spend money—and I don't wanta spend my money till I get back to Fort Worth."

"That'll make an easy day of it. Then we can pull out."

"Man," Skeeter grinned. "I cain't wait to get back to good ol' *Ex*-change Avenue."

Jim felt a pull at his right shirt-sleeve. It was Maria.

"Jimmee," she smiled.

"Maria. How'n hell are you? Ain't seen you for awhile."

Maria was still wearing the satin sheath dress and was still heavily made-up. In spite of that, she was attractive. But her smile slipped and she shrugged. "Not good, Jimmee."

"Why? What's the matter?"

Her eyes rolled, taking in the entire room. Jim could see unhappiness in her face.

"Oh," he said, understanding. "I don't blame you. This must get mighty old after awhile." He put his arm around her shoulders and pulled her tight against his right side. "Saloon gals have it rough too."

A tight, forced smile crinkled her eyes. "I hear good things about you, Jimmee. I hear you catch wild horse."

"Yeah. I got lucky."

"Uh oh," Skeeter interjected, suddenly standing straight. "I just cain't keep away from that gunsel."

Following Skeeter's gaze, Jim saw Jake Tooley come through the swinging doors. "Pay him no mind Skeeter, and maybe he won't start nothin'."

Tooley glanced at the two young cowboys, but turned to the bar and ignored them.

The deputy marshal came in—the short man with the big pistol—and started talking to Tooley.

"Looks like he's got other things on his mind," Jim said, and turned back to Maria. "Little lady, let's you and me go over there to one of those tables and make some medicine talk."

"I can't, Jimmee. The boss say no."

"To hell with him. I've got somethin' important to say."

Her eyes studied his face. "All right, Jimmee."

Jim ordered another whiskey and carried it to a table in a far corner. Maria followed, but glanced back at the bartender, worried.

After they were seated and Jim had sipped his whiskey, he folded his arms on the table and leaned toward her. "Maria, how would you like to leave here?"

"Go where, Jimmee?"

"How would you like to go to Fort Worth? It's a big town, and a girl can find a better job than this. I'll pay the bills."

"Go with you, Jimmee?"

"Yeah. I've got enough money now to pay both our ways for quite awhile and I've prob'ly got more money comin'. A lot more."

She didn't answer, but studied his face, trying to determine whether he was serious.

They were so intent in their conversation that they didn't hear the angry words spoken at the bar. They didn't see Jack Tooley give Skeeter Jones a hard push, an open invitation to fight.

"You mean that, Jimmee?"

"I mean it, Maria. You just pack your bag and meet me at the stagestop day after tomorrow. Skeeter'll be goin' too, but he won't be sleepin' with us." Jim had to grin at those words.

But she still was not sure he was serious, and her brow wrinkled.

They didn't hear the bartender tell take Tooley and Skeeter Jones to go outside if they wanted to fight.

"I promise you, Maria, I won't let you down. I'm not talking about gettin' married or anything like that, but I promise I won't leave you stranded."

She stared at him, and a tear came to her eye. He put his hand over hers. "I'm sorry. I didn't mean to insult you or anything."

She sniffed her nose and wiped her eye with the tips of her fingers. "It's okay, Jimmee. I not sad. I just can't believe... Nobody ever done anything for me before."

"Oh, I'll get tired of the big town sooner or later and hire out on some cow outfit, but I promise I'll leave you with enough money to buy some clothes and take your time findin' a decent job."

They didn't see Jake Tooley and Skeeter Jones go out the back door to the alley behind the St. Louis Emporium.

"Yes, Jimmee. I go with you."

They heard the gunshot.

CHAPTER 23

Jim jerked upright in his chair and glanced around the room. "Skeeter," he muttered under his breath. "Where's Skeeter?" he asked aloud.

He knew the shot had come from the alley, and he ran to the rear door. He jerked it open just in time to see Jake Tooley stumble inside and hurry to the bar. "You son of a bitch," Jim yelled at him. Tooley ignored him and ordered whiskey in a shaky voice.

"Skeeter." Jim yelled the name before he was out the door. He saw his friend lying on his side in the alley dirt. Jim hit the ground on his knees beside him. "Good lord, Skeeter."

Skeeter's eyes were squinched tight, but they opened slowly when he heard his name called and sensed his friend nearby. He managed a weak smile. A red stain was spreading across the front of his shirt. One eye was swelling rapidly. The knuckles on his right hand were bruised.

"Skeeter, I didn't know... I didn't see what was happenin'."

"It was my fight, Slim."

Jim looked up at the small crowd that had gathered. He screamed at them. "Get a doctor. Run, get a doctor!"

A man left, running.

"A doctor's comin', Skeeter. Hell fix you up." Skeeter looked down at the blood on his shirt, and his face screwed up in pain.

"Aw, Skeeter."

The pain cleared for a moment, and the pale eyes opened again, looking at Jim. "Say, Slim." He made the S's whistle. "When you git back to Fort Worth—" The pain returned and Skeeter's voice choked off. He had to force himself to continue. "When you get back to Fort Worth...remember me to ever'body. Will you?"

"I'll do 'er, partner."

The pain cleared again, and a small smile came to Skeeter's lips. He brought his knees up to the fetal position. He died then.

"Aw, Skeeter."

For a long moment no one spoke. One man shuffled his feet. Another coughed. Finally someone said in a hoarse whisper, "He didn't even get to draw his gun."

Jim noticed then that Skeeter's .44 was still in its holster. Gently, he lifted it out and checked the cylinder. The gun was fully loaded.

He stood up slowly, the gun in his hand. "That son of a bitch," he muttered through his teeth. "That son of a bitch."

Moving hastily, desperate now, Jim burst through the alley door into the St. Louis Emporium. His eyes took in the room at a glance. "Where's Tooley," he bellowed.

The bartender motioned toward the street. "He's just getting on his horse."

Jim ran, large spur rowels ringing, and shoved through the swinging doors. He held the .44 down at his side. He saw Tooley gathering his reins, preparing to mount. Jim shouted one word, and he shouted it with a voice that had been strengthened by yelling at cattle, a voice that could be heard clear across town: "*Tooley!*"

The burly rancher was about to put his foot in the stirrup. He stopped, suddenly, looked fearfully at him, dropped the reins and stood beside the horse. "Now, listen..." His right hand hovered over the six-gun on his hip.

Jim cocked the hammer back, raised the gun straight out, and pointed it at Tooley's face. "You're gonna die, you son of a bitch."

"No. Listen..." The big man's voice was suddenly hysterical. "I didn't...you can't shoot a man without givin' 'im a chance."

The front sight covered the big man's nose, and Jim knew that all he had to do was squeeze the trigger, just twitch his finger, and Tooley would be dead.

"No," Tooley screamed. "Don't."

Someone behind Jim said, "You can't just shoot him down, cowboy. Turn him over to the marshal."

Slowly, Jim lowered the gun. Using both hands, he let the hammer down gently. "I guess you're right. Someone get the marshal."

Relief spread over the big rancher's face as Jim held the gun down at his side. Tooley turned away as if to leave. "I'll go get the marshal myself," he said over his shoulder.

Jim looked next door at the marshal's office, and was surprised to see a face in the window, looking out, a face with a mustache.

Suddenly, Tooley spun around. The gun was in his hand.

A woman screamed. It was Maria. "Jimmee, look out!" She meant her words as a warning, but instead they distracted Jim for a half-second. Tooley's gun barked—but the shot was fired hastily and the bullet tore into the ground between Jim's feet. Tooley cocked the hammer back for a second shot.

Jim acted without thinking. He did what he and Skeeter had once practiced doing for the fun of it. He jerked the gun up to hip level, barrel parallel, and pulled the trigger back. At the same instant, he rocked the hammer with the edge of his left hand.

The old .44 roared like a cannon. It bucked in Jim's hand, and smoke puffed out of the barrel. The acrid smell of burned gunpowder filled Jim's nostrils.

Tooley's face went blank with shock as the bullet hit him. The gun slid from his fingers onto the ground. The gun fired when it hit the ground, but the bullet thudded harmlessly into the foundation of the mercantile across the street.

The gunfire had spooked Tooley's horse, and it shied away, dragging its reins. Another horse had reared back, broken its reins, and was galloping down the street. Jim's young horse was dancing nervously at the end of its reins.

Jake Tooley grabbed his right shoulder with his left hand and staggered, but stayed on his feet. Fear spread over his face again as he looked first at his bleeding wound, then at the people on the sidewalk. And at Jim.

Jim cocked the .44 and prepared to fire another shot. He took careful aim.

"No, please." The big man appeared to be on the verge of tears. "I didn't do it. I didn't shoot your pal."

"What?" Jim hissed.

"I didn't shoot your pal. I don't know who done it. Please don't." Tooley swayed drunkenly, and Jim knew a smaller man would have fallen.

"If you didn't shoot him, who did?"

"I don't know. I swear I don't. I didn't see nobody."

"You're a liar."

"No. Please. It's the truth. I didn't do it."

Jim's finger tightened on the trigger. The big man saw death coming. "Please, don't."

They stood that way: Jim on the verge of killing Tooley, Tooley blubbering. Jim knew he had the bullying rancher completely at his mercy and would be justified in killing him. But a small doubt tugged at the back of his mind. Something didn't fit here. The knuckles on Tooley's right hand were skinned. Skeeter had a swollen eye. They had fought with their fists.

Jim looked around at the men standing on the boardwalk, at the marshal's office, at Maria, who whispered, "Don't, Jimmee."

Acting on impulse, Jim picked up Tooley's gun, and with one hand, flipped open the loading gate. He counted two empty cartridges—the two that had been fired on the street. He remembered running to the alley door and jerking it open to find Tooley hurrying inside. Tooley's gun had been in its holster.

Turning to the bartender who stood on the walk with other onlookers, Jim asked, "Did you see him reload?"

The bartender shook his head negatively.

Jim dropped Tooley's gun in the dirt. He knew then that Tooley had not shot Skeeter.

For the second time, he lowered the .44 and eased the hammer down.

Tooley stood still, gripping his right shoulder, tears on his face. He was a beaten man. Other men had seen him beg for mercy. Word would spread. Jake Tooley would never again bully anyone.

Jim placed the .44 inside the waist of his denim pants. He had to tighten his belt a hole to keep it there. Then he spun on his heels and marched directly to the marshal's office. He hesitated at the door for a second, then, with determination, he yanked the door open and went inside.

Marshal Delmar Chitlow sat at his desk. The deputy marshal, the little man with the big pistol, leaned insolently against the far wall. Jim's eyes went from the marshal to the deputy and back. He spoke slowly and deliberately.

"Why wasn't you out there?"

"Where?" the marshal asked, as if nothing had happened.

"Guns've been goin' off all over the place," Jim said through clenched teeth, "and you're supposed to keep the peace."

Chitlow tilted his hat down lower over his forehead, tilted his chair back on its hind legs, and laced his fingers behind his head. "Guns going off, huh? Who shot who?"

"You know damn well."

The chair came down on all four legs with a thud. Chitlow's right hand was a blur. A gun appeared in it. "Yeah, I know. You just shot Jake Tooley." A sneer spread beneath the mustache. "You're under arrest."

It happened so fast that Jim had no chance to react.

He was caught with his gun inside his belt, and he was helpless. The deputy chuckled. "We don't allow fightin' in this town."

Like a cornered rat, Jim glanced around the room, looking for a way to escape. There was none. The bore of the marshal's gun didn't waver.

"Get his gun," the marshal said to the deputy. The deputy giggled and moved toward Jim.

But before he got there, the door swung open again and Sheriff Walt Umbaugh strode in.

The sheriff stopped suddenly when he saw the gun in Chitlow's hand. He took in the room at a glance, and said, "I heard the shooting and came to see if you needed any help, Delmar. Looks like you've got everything under control."

"Everything's under control. This drifter here has been nothing but trouble ever since he hit town. I'm going to lock him up and throw away the key."

The rage that had built up in Jim exploded. "You lyin' bloodthirsty son of a bitch. You just killed a man and you're tryin' to blame it on somebody else."

"What?" The word was spoken in unison from two different directions. Marshal Chitlow jerked upright in his chair. Sheriff Umbaugh's piercing blue eyes bored into Jim.

"He killed Skeeter Jones, Sheriff. Just shot him from behind an alley door. Then he watched out the window while I blamed it on Jake Tooley, and he watched me and Tooley shoot it out."

"Shut up, drifter." The marshal's gunbore seemed to grow larger.

Umbaugh walked over to the marshal's desk and sat on the edge of it. His gaze was leveled at Jim. "What are you saying, son?"

Jim blurted it out. "I can guess what happened. He got word that Skeeter and Tooley were goin' out to the alley to fight. He shot Skeeter from behind his own alley door, and figured Tooley would get the blame."

Chitlow snarled, "Shut up."

"Well, now," the sheriff drawled, "maybe we ought to hear what he's got to say, Delmar."

"He's just making up stories to save his own hide. Jake Tooley shot that cowboy in the alley and this gunsel shot Jake Tooley."

Jim hissed, "You're a liar."

Chitlow stood up, raised his pistol, and aimed it at a spot between Jim's eyes. "What did you call me?"

Jim knew he was staring death in the face. He could almost feel the slug tearing into him, obliterating his features. In a split second he could become a lifeless, bleeding hulk on the floor. His heart jumped into his throat. His knees trembled. He forced himself to look the marshal in the eye. "I said you are a goddam liar."

The finger on the trigger tightened.

CHAPTER 24

Sheriff Umbaugh barked an order, "Wait. Now just hold on. It's not a capital crime to call someone a liar, Delmar, and you're not the executioner."

The gunbore held steady.

"I'm warning you, Delmar. You shoot that man and I'll see you tried for murder."

The gun was lowered. Jim was weak with relief. But the marshal turned his anger on the sheriff. "This is my jurisdiction, Sheriff, and this is my office. I'm ordering you to leave."

Umbaugh shook his head. "You're wrong about that. I'm the top law-enforcement officer in this county." The two men glared at each other.

Jim noticed that the sheriff's gun was still in its holster with only the butt showing, while the marshal held his gun in his hand. The deputy kept quiet.

"Now, son," Umbaugh said, turning his back to the marshal, "I'm not forgetting how you helped stop those horse rustlers. What makes you think Delmar shot your friend?"

"A bunch of things."

Umbaugh crossed his arms over his ample middle. "I'm listening."

Jim stood awkwardly on first one foot and then the other while memories of past events flooded his mind. He began slowly. "First off, he wants to buy a ranch. He told me that. He wants either the

Hash Knife or John Holcomb's H Bar. He's made a lot of money in this town and he wants to be a rancher."

"He doesn't know what he's talking about." Chitlow had sat back down in his desk chair, but there was venom in his voice.

"Go on, son."

Shifting his weight from his right foot to the left, Jim went on. "Tooley wouldn't sell the Hash Knife, and John wouldn't sell his outfit, either. But John was havin' troubles. He was way behind in his mortgage payments and he was bettin' everything on sellin' those young horses of his."

Jim paused, and looked from the sheriff to the marshal, and continued, "Somebody tried to stampede those colts into a tangle of barbwire, and then shot at me when I hazed 'em away. I figured it was Tooley's men, but now I don't think so. They wasn't ridin' Hash Knife horses. Oh, I saw one of 'em with Tooley in the saloon, but it was prob'ly just a speakin' acquaintance. I'm bettin' he was workin' for the marshal."

"Aw, he's just making all this up." Chitlow's voice was still full of malice. "He's done enough talking, and it's time he cooled his heels in the hoosegow."

The sheriff didn't even look Chitlow's way. "Go on," he said.

"The marshal figured if John's colts got cut up he'd be ruined and he could buy the H Bar. Or he could buy the H Bar if John couldn't get his colts broke to ride in time to sell to the Army. That's why he wanted to have me shot out there on the road that night. He wanted to make it look like robbery. And then,"—Jim had to pause for breath—"I'm bettin' he put the same four men up to stealin' John's horses."

"That's it." Chitlow's voice was rising. "That's enough. Take him, Shorty."

The deputy grabbed Jim by the arm and pulled him toward the jail cell.

"Not yet." The words were spoken sharply, and Sheriff Umbaugh left no doubt that he meant what he said. His pudgy face had turned hard. "Let go of that man."

The deputy released Jim's arms as if it were hot.

"All right, son," Umbaugh said, speaking softly now, "I was

aware that Delmar offered to buy the Hash Knife, and he could have been dealin' with the bank for the Holcomb ranch. But that doesn't make him a murderer."

"Shooting Skeeter does," Jim blurted out. "His plans fell through. John's goin' to sell his horses to the Army, and he's already sold ten head to the Rafter H. The Army wants more than John has left, so Tooley'll get some of the Army's money too. Both outfits are goin' to make money tomorrow."

"So what's all that got to do with the shooting in the alley?"

Jim's mind raced. He could picture in his mind how Skeeter was shot—he remembered seeing the deputy marshal in the St. Louis Emporium—but the reason for the shooting was still not clear. He had to figure it out and he had to figure it out now. Until a short time ago he had thought Jake Tooley was the villain, but now he knew it was Delmar Chitlow. He knew it in his own mind, but he had to convince the sheriff. He had to produce a motive.

"It was..." His mind raced. "It was..." Suddenly it came to him. "It was simple. This deputy told the marshal that Skeeter and Jake Tooley were goin' out to the alley to fight. The marshal saw his chance." Jim talked faster now, sure of himself.

"He didn't want to stop the fight, 'cause if Skeeter killed Tooley, he could buy the Hash Knife, and if Tooley killed Skeeter he knew I would shoot it out with Tooley.

"Listen, Sheriff"—Jim was excited—"he peeked around his alley door, and he was disappointed when he saw they wasn't goin' to shoot it out but was fightin' it out with their fists. He decided to shoot one of 'em and make it look like the other did it. He couldn't shoot anybody in the back 'cause that wouldn't look right, and it was Skeeter that was facin' 'im."

Jim had to pause for breath. He wasn't used to talking that much. "He knew there'd be more shootin', and no matter who lost he'd win. If I killed Tooley, he could buy the Hash Knife from Tooley's relations. If Tooley shot me, John wouldn't have anybody to show his horses tomorrow and the Army wouldn't buy 'em. He figured the bank would foreclose then and he could dicker for the H Bar. What the marshal didn't know is John sold ten head to the Rafter H, and that gave him enough money to hold the bank off for awhile."

His voice was becoming hoarse from so much talking, and Jim stopped. But he was feeling good. He believed he had built his case. He stood with his hands on his hips and waited for someone else to speak.

"You sure about all this?" Umbaugh asked.

"I'm positive. Hell, there's all kinds of people out there that'll tell you the marshal looked out the window while me and Tooley shot at each other."

Umbaugh swiveled his plump body around. "That's not like you, Delmar."

"Aw, he's just making it up," Chitlow said. He had forced himself to speak in a calm voice, and even to smile wryly. "He said at the beginning of his speech that he was guessing. He's got nothing to back up his little speech." Chitlow chuckled. "I was right here when that cowboy was shot in the alley. Shorty can tell you that. Ain't that right, Shorty?"

"Shore as hell is," Shorty replied.

"And," the sheriff asked, "you stayed in here while two men shot it out in the street?"

The marshal shrugged. "Well, you know how it is, Sheriff. I've got so much paperwork to do I just didn't hear what was going on. I didn't know what happened till this drifter came busting in here acting crazy."

"Uh huh." The sheriff turned to Jim. "If two men went to the alley to fight there must have been onlookers. There must have been witnesses."

Jim could see his case weakening. He shook his head negatively. "I don't know why—but there wasn't. I didn't know they was goin' out to fight, and maybe nobody else knew it except this deputy. But when I heard the shot I ran to the alley, and when I got there, there wasn't nobody else there."

"Uhmmm." Umbaugh looked down at his high-top shoes.

Chitlow chuckled again. "Well, Sheriff, it was quite a story, I have to admit. But you have to admit it was pretty far-fetched." He tilted his chair back and laced his fingers at the back of his head. "If there were no witnesses, how can he make an accusation like that?"

"There was a witness," Jim said.

Umbaugh's head came up sharply. "Who?"

"Him." Jim pointed at the deputy marshal.

"That's a lie," the deputy yelled.

The marshal's chair came down on all four legs. "Now listen, Sheriff, this has gone on long enough. He's talking like an idiot."

Looking down at his shoes again, the sheriff let out another "Uhmmm."

He had lost. Jim knew it. He had all kinds of reason for suspicion, but no proof. The deputy wouldn't talk, and Delmar Chitlow was too smart to be bluffed. He hadn't made his money by being stupid. Jim's spirits sagged. Now he was going back to jail, and this time he would stay there. Jim's future looked very bleak indeed.

But, dammit, he had done nothing wrong. It was Tooley who had fired the first shot out there on the street. Jim's muscles tensed and he estimated his chances of escape. The marshal had a gun in his hand again while Jim's gun was still in his belt. He had no chance at all of winning another shootout. But, dammit, he was not going to jail. No, by God, he was not going to jail.

Sheriff Walt Umbaugh stood with his thumbs hooked inside his belt. He seemed to be studying his shoes. Then suddenly, surprisingly, he spun around and faced the deputy, pointing a finger at him.

"It was you," he shouted. "You killed that cowboy."

The little deputy shrank back, surprise on his face. The sheriff took two threatening steps toward him, still pointing, and the deputy backed up to the wall.

"I didn't," the deputy said, uncertainly.

"You did it. I know it. Everybody knows it. You shot Skeeter Jones." Umbaugh's face had hardened into square determined lines. His eyes under the bushy brows bored into the deputy like twin torches. "You're going to hang for murder, Shorty. Sure as shooting, you are going to hang."

The deputy's hand went to his gunbutt, stopped there.

"I'm warning you, Shorty," the sheriff's voice boomed, don't draw that gun. I'm warning you."

Chitlow cut in, "Now just a goddam minute, Sheriff. You can't talk to my deputy like that."

Turning fast again, Umbaugh faced the marshal. "The hell I

can't. You think I don't know what's been going on in this town. Hell, this town is my jurisdiction too, and I know there's been some mean things happening."

The marshal opened his mouth to speak, but Umbaugh cut him off. "I knew you were making a lot of money with your gamblers and your whorehouses, and I knew you wanted to buy a ranch. I knew you allowed the merchants and landowners to do anything they pleased in this town while you locked up the working men just for spitting on the sidewalk. I knew you locked men up and kept them in jail without even telling the judge, then ran them out of town."

The sheriff's voice was sharp, cutting. "I know you killed two men in two years when it wasn't necessary. No lawman worth his salt would have killed those men. Besides, this young man's theory fits. It makes sense."

After letting his words sink in, and noting the surprise on Delmar Chitlow's face, Umbaugh continued in a milder tone. "And there's one more piece of evidence. That horse with the Double B Bar brand, the one Jim here saw ridden by a hoodlum out there in John Holcomb's pasture? I've been asking around, and a neighbor of yours saw that horse in your corral one day. You hired those hoodlums."

Jim stood transfixed. He was surprised and fascinated by the sheriff's behavior.

"So don't tell me what I can and can't do." Umbaugh spun around, facing the deputy again. His voice picked up volume and he bored in. "The marshal told you to do it, didn't he? You'd do anything the marshal told you to, wouldn't you? Admit it, Shorty, or you'll hang."

The deputy's gaze shifted from the sheriff to his boss. Jim interpreted that as asking for instructions. Umbaugh read the same sign.

"You did it, Shorty. I can prove it."

Doubt clouded Shorty's features. "You can't prove it."

"Shut up, Shorty," Chitlow barked. "Don't say a word."

"There was a witness, Shorty. You didn't see him, but he saw you."

The doubt was replaced by fear. "There wasn't."

"Shut up, Shorty." The marshal's voice carried an unspoken

warning.

The sheriff ignored him. "Oh, yes, there was. You were seen. You stood behind that door and shot that cowboy, and you did it deliberately. That's a hanging offense, Shorty. You're going to hang."

Shorty's lower lip trembled.

"You did it because the marshal told you to, didn't you? He threatened to take your badge away from you, didn't he? You'd be nothing without that badge, wouldn't you, Shorty?"

The sheriff took a step closer. Shorty seemed to shrink. Umbaugh kept up the pressure.

"You'd do anything the marshal told you to, wouldn't you? Oh, you're in all kinds of trouble now. You're going to hang."

"No." The word came out of the deputy as if it had been torn out. "No. I didn't do it."

"Shut up, goddam it," Chitlow barked.

Again, Umbaugh ignored the marshal. But then his voice dropped an octave. He talked calmly, with sympathy. "You're not really such a bad guy, Shorty. You only did what the marshal told you to, didn't you? Maybe you won't hang. Maybe you'll just go to prison. That is, if the marshal is convicted along with you. You don't want to take all the blame, do you?"

The words got no reaction from Shorty, but Chitlow jumped to his feet and stomped around in front of the sheriff, positioning himself between the sheriff and the deputy. "That's enough. You are not going to badger my deputy like that."

Umbaugh merely stepped aside to where he could focus on Shorty again, and when he spoke he resumed his hard line. He shouted, "Then, by God, you'll hang, Shorty. You're going to hang while the marshal watches, just like he watched you shoot Skeeter Jones." The hard eyes seemed to burn into the deputy. "You're going to hang by the neck with your feet dancing in the air."

A look of anguish appeared on the deputy's face. His mouth worked without a sound. His eyes rolled wildly.

Chitlow persisted. "I'm warning you, Sheriff."

Umbaugh continued, "You ever watch a man hang, Shorty? It's awful. A man dies slowly. You're going to hang, Shorty, unless you tell us all about it."

The words came out of the deputy in a rush, shoved together, almost incoherently. "Hemademedoit." Shorty's hand came up and a finger pointed at Chitlow. "Hemademedoit."

Umbaugh recoiled as if he had been slapped in the face. He glanced at Jim, at Chitlow, back at the deputy. "He made you do it?" The deputy nodded vigorously. "Hetoldmeto."

CHAPTER 25

"Well, I'll be damned," the sheriff said, incredulously. He rubbed the back of his neck and stared at his shoes. "I'll be double-doodly damned."

Jim was fascinated. He had never seen the kind of performance the sheriff had just given.

Umbaugh shook his head negatively. "I guessed wrong." He looked up at Jim. "I figured Delmar did it, and I was just trying to scare the deputy into spilling the beans to save his own neck."

"All right. Just stand right where you are." The marshal spoke rapid-fire, and his gun covered both the sheriff and Jim. "Now, I'm going to have to—"

"Have to what, Delmar?" The sheriff was calm.

"You know what I have to do. Both of you do exactly as I tell you."

The sheriff's gun was buried in that deep holster of his and Jim's gun was stuck in his belt. Jim wanted to move. His nerves cried for action. But he knew he had no chance of disarming the marshal.

The sheriff moved slowly, deliberately, toward Chitlow. "Give me the gun, Delmar. We don't want any more shooting."

"Stay back. Don't move." The marshal's gun swung over to cover the advancing sheriff. Jim was no fast-draw expert. He was no fighter. But he had handled livestock on horseback and on foot all his life, and there had been many times when he had had to move fast. Instead of reaching for his gun, he jumped at Chitlow.

He heard the marshal's gun go off in his ear at the same time the top of his head butted the marshal's face. He grabbed for the marshal's gun arm, and got hold of it. The two men struggled for the gun. The gun fired again, and Jim realized it was a double-action revolver, the kind that didn't have to be cocked. He got both hands on the marshal's wrist, but the marshal was beating him about the face with his free hand. Jim hung on.

Suddenly, the marshal went limp.

When Jim dared to look up, he saw Sheriff Walt Umbaugh holding his own pistol by the barrel, and he knew the sheriff had used it as a club. He twisted Chitlow's gun free, straightened up, and dropped the gun on the desk. His left ear felt as if a church bell were ringing in it.

He started to breath a sigh of relief when he saw a movement out of the corner of his eye. "Duck," he hollered, and he was surprised at how fast the sheriff hit the floor. Jim hit the floor too, drawing Skeeter's .44. A gun fired and then fired again. A bullet raised splinters in the floor close to Jim's face.

Jim didn't take aim, he just held the trigger back and fanned the hammer three times in rapid succession. The noise in the closeness of the room was painful to the ears.

Above it all a voice screamed, "I'm hit. Don't shoot."

The deputy was down, holding his right thigh with both hands and screaming with pain. The sheriff was picking himself up.

Then the sheriff yelled a warning, "Behind you."

Jim rolled over a split second before a bullet tore into the floor near him. He saw at a glance that Chitlow was on his knees, had another gun and was aiming it at him. Jim's gun arm was in an awkward position. He couldn't raise it quick enough.

Another gun boomed, and Chitlow's body jerked as if an electric shock were going through it. The marshal's eyes rolled up so only the whites showed, and he pitched forward onto his face and lay still.

Gunsmoke created a haze in the room. Four men were down. It was deathly quiet. Then two men slowly stood up. Another began moaning.

Jim suddenly felt drained of energy. His face was

expressionless and his eyes were blank as he looked over at Sheriff Umbaugh. His gun hand hung loosely at his side.

"You hurt, son?"

"No."

Umbaugh looked down at himself. "We're lucky."

"Yeah."

Faces appeared in the window, peering through the glass. Umbaugh walked slowly over to where Shorty lay groaning and picked up his gun, then turned to where Chitlow lay.

"Too bad. It's always bad when a lawman goes wrong. I'm sorry I had to shoot him."

Jim walked stiffly to the marshal's desk and carefully placed Skeeter's .44 on top of it.

"You sure you're all right, son?"

"Yeah, I'm all right." But for the second time that day, Jim felt a terrible need to get outdoors. He had to get out of there. "I, uh, I've got to go, Sheriff."

"You go ahead, son. I'll take care of this mess."

The cowboy stiff-legged it outside, out to the hitchrail. He was surprised to find his young horse still there after all the shooting and excitement. He unwrapped the reins from the hitchrail and crawled slowly into the saddle, ignoring questions from men on the boardwalk.

He did pause briefly to speak to someone special. "Day after tomorrow, Maria," he said, looking down at her from horseback. "Be ready."

"Yes, Jimmee."

He rode on out of town.

At first Jim didn't want to talk about it, and the Holcombs, even though they could tell by his manner that something terrible had happened, didn't press him. But he had to tell someone, and once he started talking he didn't stop until he had told them everything. They were surprised and sympathetic.

"That's terrible, Jim," Maggie Holcomb said. "I'm awfully sorry about your friend."

"It's a bad thing to happen," John Holcomb agreed. "But I'm sure surprised at everything. I would have sworn Jake Tooley was behind everything that happened."

"I would have too," Jim said.

"What made you suspect the marshal, Jim?"

Jim pondered the question and shrugged. "I don't know. I guess it was the marshal himself, the kind of man he was. He wanted to buy the Rafter H stud from me, said he was for sure goin' to buy a ranch, and I guessed he had his eye on this outfit.

"When I check Tooley's gun, I knew he didn't shoot Skeeter and that it had to be someone else."

Jim was rolling a cigarette as he talked. He put one end between his lips, held the other end over the kerosene lamp, and drew on it to light it.

"And when I saw that marshal lookin' out the window at us, I just knew he did it."

"Thank God you didn't kill anybody else," Maggie Holcomb said.

"Yeah. I fired off quite a few shots and hit two men, but I didn't kill 'em. I'm glad of that. I killed one man awhile back and I don't want to ever aim a gun at anybody again."

They talked until the boy, Chacho, fell asleep at the table. Jim carried him to the bunkhouse where the boy awakened long enough to undress himself and crawl into bed. Jim blew out the lamp and went to bed too, but he didn't sleep. He couldn't get Skeeter out of his mind.

Skeeter, the lively one. Skeeter, the prankster. Things were never dull when Skeeter was around. Jim had to grin when he remembered Skeeter's scheme for thinning out the men at the dance. It sure worked, he recalled. But the grin faded when he recalled Skeeter dying in the alley.

Jim didn't sleep that night.

The two Army officers were back at eight o'clock sharp next morning. Working grim-faced, Jim caught and rode all twenty-eight of the young horses. He didn't stop for lunch, and by midafternoon, the officers had paid one hundred and five dollars a head for all of them.

John Holcomb was pleasantly surprised at the price, and he was even more pleased when the officers told him they had bought twelve horses from Jake Tooley and paid only eighty-five dollars a head.

The voucher they gave Holcomb could be cashed at any national bank, they said. They said they would return in a few days for the horses, and rode out of the ranch yard just as Sheriff Walt Umbaugh drove his one-horse buggy into the yard.

"I bring good news, son," Umbaugh said to Jim. "There won't be a trial and you won't have to stick around. I got the judge to go to the doctor's house and hear what Shorty had to say. He told it all. It was just the way you figured."

Jim had not planned on staying around, law or no law, but he was relieved to hear that he could leave freely.

The sheriff chuckled and shook his head negatively. "You had it figured right except for one thing. I guessed wrong, too. You and I both thought Delmar Chitlow shot your friend. I put the screws to Shorty because I figured he was the weak one and would tell all to save himself. It surprised me to hear him confess to murder."

"Me too," Jim said, straight-faced. "How is Jake Tooley?"

"He's all right. Your bullet knocked a small chunk of flesh off his right shoulder, and he'll be stiff and sore for a long time, but he'll live. Shorty, too. He took a round in the muscle of his right thigh and it no doubt hurt like hell, but he'll live to go to prison."

"They ought to hang 'im," John Holcomb put in.

Again, the sheriff shook his head negatively. "That judge isn't a hanging judge, and he appreciated Shorty's confession and statement. He'll wait till Shorty is able to walk before he sentences him. And in the meantime, Shorty will be locked up in the county jail."

Jim had nothing to say about the matter.

It was Jim's last night at the Holcomb ranch, and Maggie Holcomb served an exceptionally good supper. She topped it off with peach cobbler and urged Jim to eat all he wanted of it. Next morning. Jim loaded his tarp-covered bedroll, saddle, and warbag in the spring wagon and they all went into San Lomah.

He was paid off at the bank, after leaving his belongings at the hotel stage-stop. He had hoped, briefly, that Holcomb would include a small bonus, but he was not disappointed when that didn't happen. He had long ago learned the nature of employers.

"Jim, if you're ever up this way again and I need help, you've got a job."

Maggie Holcomb was more generous. "I'll always set a place at the table for you, Jim."

Chacho was wide-eyed and somber when Jim turned to him. There were things the cowboy wanted to say to the boy, but he didn't know how to say them, and he was no speech-maker anyway, so he just patted the boy on the shoulder and said, "See you sometime, Chacho."

And then he walked away.

Jim looked up the street and saw the stage, pulled by a six-horse team, stop in front of the hotel. He didn't see Maria. His steps quickened and he became worried, afraid that Maria had changed her mind. A few people had gathered, either as passengers or merely to see the stage off, but he still didn't see Maria.

Among the gathering was a young woman, pretty and stylish, in a long dark dress with white lace. Men tipped their hats when they passed her. She was looking up and down the street, biting her lip, a worried frown on her face.

She saw Jim coming and smiled.

Jim was dumbfounded. He stopped and stared. He realized finally that this was the first time he had seen Maria when she was not wearing the cheap saloon dress and when she was not overloaded with makeup. He guessed that she was wearing the one good dress she owned and had carefully preserved. She was a very, pretty young woman.

"Jimmee. I was worried."

"Everything's all right, Maria." He went inside the hotel, paid their fares, and came out and loaded his belongings and Maria's two cardboard suitcases into the boot at the back of the coach.

The driver came out of the hotel, looked them over and said, "Reckon you're my only passengers this mornin'. Did I hear you say you want to catch the train in Durango?"

"Yep," said Jim.

"We'll make 'er." The driver climbed up to his seat and carefully gathered the lines when they were handed up to him by his helper. Jim and Maria got inside.

The teamster yelled at the six horses, a whip cracked, the Concord lurched forward, and they were off.

Both Jim and Maria were quiet. Jim was tense, his jaws clenched, and he looked straight ahead as the stage passed the bank. He didn't look back as they left San Lomah. Not until the stage was a mile out of town did he relax.

Maria sensed that his mind was heavy and she didn't disturb him with talk. Instead she hugged his arm and put her head on his shoulder to let him know she cared. The Concord swayed on its leather thorough braces. Trace chains and singletrees rattled.

Finally, Jim Kinslow freed his arm from Maria's grasp, put it around her shoulders, and pulled her close. He parked his feet on the seat opposite them and settled down comfortably. He smiled into Maria's upturned face.

"Yep, young lady. We're headed for some good times."

THE END

Be sure to check out the next novel in
Doyle Trent's Tales of the Old Wild West series:

TOMBSTONE LODE

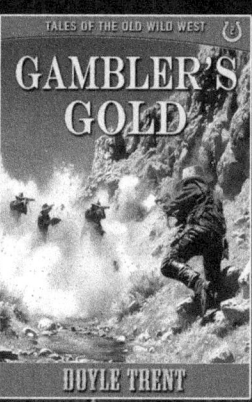

LOOKING FOR ACTION & ADVENTURE
AUTHOR ALAN CAILLOU
DELIVERS !

DON'T MISS ANY OF NEIL HUNTER'S NOVELS FROM CALIBER BOOKS

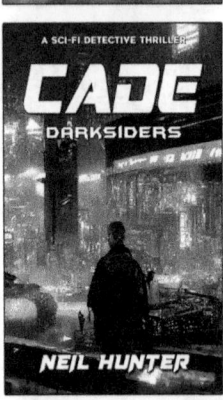

CALIBER COMICS GOES TO WAR!
HISTORICAL AND MILITARY THEMED GRAPHIC NOVELS

**WORLD WAR ONE:
MO MAN'S LAND**

ISBN: 9781635298123

*A look at World War 1 from
the French trenches as they
faced the Imperial German
Army.*

**CORTEZ AND THE FALL
OF THE AZTECS**

ISBN: 9781635299779

*Cortez battles the Aztecs
while in search of Inca
gold.*

**TROY:
AN EMPIRE UNDER SIEGE**

ISBN: 9781635298635

*Homer's famous The Iliad and
the Trojan War is given a
unique human perspective
rather than from the God's.*

WITNESS TO WAR

ISBN: 9781635299700

*WW2's Battle of the Bulge
is seen up close by an
embedded female war
reporter.*

THE LINCOLN BRIGADE

ISBN: 9781635298222

*American volunteers head
to Spain in the 1930s to
fight in their civil war
against the fascist regime.*

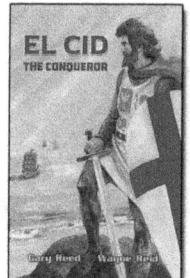

**EL CID:
THE CONQUEROR**

ISBN: 9780982654996

*Europe's greatest warrior
attempts to unify Spain
against invading foreign
and domestic armies.*

WINTER WAR

ISBN: 9780985749392

*At the outbreak of WW2
Finland fights against an
invading Soviet army.*

**ZULUNATION:
END OF EMPIRE**

ISBN: 9780941613415

*The global British Empire
and far-reaching influence
is threatened by a Zulu
uprising in southern Africa.*

AIR WARRIORS: WORLD WAR ONE #V1 - V4   *Take to the skys of WW1 as various fighter aces tell their harrowing stories.*
ISBN: 9781635297973 (V1), 9781635297980 (V2), 9781635297997 (V3), 9781635298000 (V4)

CALIBER COMICS GOES TO THE EDGE!
Science Fiction and Horror themed graphic novels

DEADWORLD
ISBN: 9781942351245

RENFIELD
ISBN: 9781942351825

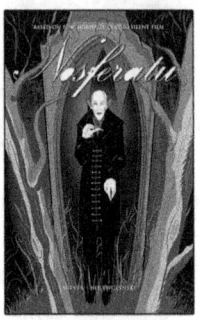

NOSFERATU
ISBN: 9781942351931

LOVECRAFT:
THE EARLY STORIES
ISBN: 9781942351634

THE WAR OF THE WORLDS:
INFESTATION
ISBN: 9781942351962

TIME GRUNTS
ISBN: 9781635299472

DRACULA
ISBN: 9780996030649

DRACULA:
THE SUICIDE CLUB
ISBN: 9781635299571

JACK THE RIPPER
ILLUSTRATED
ISBN: 9781942351917

THE SEARCHERS
ISBN: 9781942351979

A.A.I. WARS
ISBN: 9781635299168

AUTUMN: TERROR IN THE
LONDON UNDERGROUND
ISBN: 9781544624020

www.calibercomics.com

  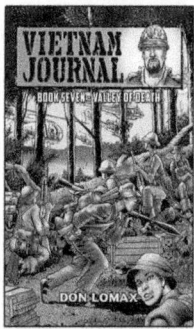